I0694721

NEON GRAY

Copyright 2023 by Brock C. Edwards

All rights reserved. No part of this book may be reproduced in any form or by any electronic or mechanical means, including information storage and retrieval systems, without permission in writing from the publisher, except by a reviewer who may quote brief passages in a review.

First Edition

The characters and events in this book are fictitious. Any similarity to real persons, living or dead, is coincidental and not intended by the author.

Published by:
Rustic Roads Publishing
www.BrockCEdwards.com
brock@brockcedwards.com

Artwork by Cassidy Fink.
Interior layout by TWA Solutions.

ISBN: 9798986068121 (paperback)
ISBN: 9798986068138 (ebook)

Printed in the United States

Follow Rustic Roads Publishing on Social Media.

the Phenomenal Walkerbright Saga
1

"The world is not black and white. More like black and gray."
-Graham Greene

"Life isn't black and white. It's a million gray areas, don't you find?"
-Ridley Scott

"The gray area, the place between black and white—that's the place where life happens."
-Justin Timberlake

"The color of truth is gray."
-Andre Gide

"The world, although well-lighted with fluorescents and incandescent bulbs and neon, is still full of odd dark corners and unsettling nooks and crannies."
-Stephen King

Howdy, folks!

I'd like to introduce myself to ya if that's alright. You can call me Amos. Most folks do these days. My family line has been here in the coastal plains regions of the Carolinas for hundreds of years now, even though we started out over in ol' Africa. We've seen all kinds of changes over time—some good and some bad—but hey, that's life for ya, ain't it?

Anyway, have I got a story for you! If you're interested, that is. I reckon you are, or you wouldn't be here, so I'll get on with it. It's a bit of a precautionary tale that takes place during a natural disaster with a love story or two sprinkled in. It also has plenty of action, drama, and intrigue, and I'm sure you'll even get a good hearty belly laugh or two out of it. Overall, it's a nice little adventure that has something most folks can appreciate. Ya see, here in the southeast of these big ol' United States, us residents are used to some storms, and boy oh we get 'em all the time. We get big ones, bad ones, and even full-blown hurricanes ain't no stranger 'round here. That big and salty Atlantic Ocean sure can churn out some tropical storms. It's like a dang ol' machine when it comes to that.

I'm certain this story I'm about to tell ya wouldn't be around if it wasn't for that fact. Down here in South Carolina, we are chock full of folklore, ghosts, and other countless legends. One of our most famous stories and most local folk's personal favorite is The Gray Man of Pawley's Island. If ya know anything about the South Carolina coast, then you've probably heard about this harbinger of ours, but just in case you haven't, then fear not! After hearing this story, you'll have a lot more knowledge and understanding about our most prominent phantom. Don't get it wrong, though. He ain't tethered to just that area. He's been seen all over neighboring Horry County, too. Don't laugh. I heard you giggle. Just so you know, you don't say the H in Horry, so you might as well get your mind out of the gutter.

Anyhow, the story starts with my new little pal, Walter. Let me tell ya, that little man is something special. I don't think I've ever met an individual as bright as him. He is staying at his grand folks' ol' vacation place with his big sister. He's about to have a life-changing event along with all the other folks you're fixin' to meet here, too. This story takes place in the fall of the year, so if you're reading it around then, I would get me a cup of something warm and get under my favorite blanket if I was you. If you happen to be reading it in the summertime, then I'd crawl up under a nice big umbrella on the beach and stick my toes in the sand while I ate on a big basket of some scrumptious sweet fruit. Either way, just get yourself good and comfortable and be sure to enjoy. Well, I reckon I've carried on long enough. I'd say it's time to get this story started now. I hope you're ready for it because here we go!

CHAPTER ONE

"Cereal" Killer

A high-spirited young boy screamed in frustration, "Ah! Take that, you stupid cartoon dog," as he shot the orange, plastic toy pistol connected to his grandfather's circa 1985 Nintendo home gaming system at the television, despite being out of bullets for the current round of play.

"Laugh at me, will ya? Just do your job and go pick up the ducks," he said with disgust, and hopped up from the old Lazy Boy recliner he'd been sitting in the past couple of hours and turned off the old eight-bit unit.

He patted his stomach. "Geez, I'm starving."

Without warning, he dropped and took cover from imaginary enemy fire behind the old, bulky coffee table littered with empty soda cans. "Copperhead to base. Do you copy? Copperhead to base. We're taking enemy fire and they have us pinned down!" he shouted into a pretend two-way radio. "Send us a chopper now! This whole platoon is going to be wiped out if you don't get your asses over here!" Pointing his index finger and cocking his thumb in a way that imitated a handgun, he shot back at the imaginary enemy.

Ducking and shooting several times, he threw a couple of imaginary grenades. "It's about damn time! Let's go, men! Get your asses to the chopper, now!" He laid down fire to cover his make-believe brothers-in-arms until he was out of bullets. "My M-16 is empty!" He tossed it down and pulled out an imaginary pistol from his waistband and fired. "Take that, you commie bastards!" Then he muttered, "Whatever that means."

Now running toward the kitchen, acting as if he were being hit in the back by the enemy combatant's bullets, he dropped to his knees right at the exit of the living room. He outstretched his arms and looked up as if he were watching the imaginary helicopter he had called in moments earlier leave him behind. "Guys, tell my wife that I love her!" he babbled out as he fell face-first to the white tile floor, pretending to die.

Seconds later, he was skipping through the cluttered kitchen. The sink was overflowing with dirty dishes and a few stacks of junk mail littered much of the counter space. After opening the squeaky door to the pantry and giving the area a thorough scan, he spotted a large box of chocolate cereal.

"Ah yes, come with me, Count." Attempting to sound ghoulish, he forcibly laughed out loud.

After pouring a huge amount of the crunchy goodness into a mixing bowl, he was now back in the recliner, watching a professional wrestling match on an Internet application. Just as he got settled in and had a tremendous mouthful of his flavorsome cereal, his phone rang. When he saw it was his mother calling, he pressed the accept button and shoved his shoulder up to the phone to hold it to his ear while he ate.

"Hey, Mom, what's happening?" He muttered between all the crunching.

"Hey, Walter, what are you doing, hon? Eating chips or something?" His mom's tone was nicer than usual as she hoped that he would get a hint and quiet down for a moment.

"Just watching The Priest while I eat. You know he's my favorite wrestler. Oh, guess what? I found that Count Chocula cereal I love so much!"

"You did? That's nice, dear. I couldn't tell from the sound of your chomping."

Walter was beyond oblivious to the hints his mother was dropping about his loud chewing. "You were right! You said they'd probably restock it around Halloween and they did!"

"That's great sweethe—"

"I got three boxes, so I'd be set for a while. Hey, I also wanted to tell you that I decided that I want to be The Priest for Halloween this year!" Walter clamored out before his mom could finish her sentence. Then the crunching resumed without wavering.

Fed up with the relentless eating in her ear, his mother sternly said, "For the love of God, Walter. Can you please stop eating for a second? Stop stuffing your mouth so full, and would it kill you to slow down a little?"

"Ah geez, Mom. My cereal will get soggy if I do that. It's not as good if that happens."

"Just put your phone on speaker then and get it away from your face!" She shook her head followed by an eye roll.

Walter put his phone on speaker and shoved another spoonful of cereal into his mouth. "How's that? Any better?"

"A little. At least it doesn't sound like I'm trying to talk to one of those wood chipper machines now."

Completely ignoring the snide comment, he asked, "How's Dad doing? Is he almost better yet? He'd love this match I'm watching. It's one of The Priest's classics; he ends up throwing a bunch of snakes in the ring at the end!"

She answered her youngest child in a somber voice. "He's about the same, unfortunately."

Walter stopped chewing for a second and stared off into the distance. "Ah, that's all right. He'll be better soon. Dad's the toughest man alive!"

Trying to avoid the subject, his mother got a tad aggressive. "Have you been doing all of your school work on a regular basis?"

"Of course, Mom, every day."

"I just don't want you falling behind. You worked so hard to get a grade ahead and I don't want you to lose that momentum."

"I won't, but what's the point of being home-schooled if I can't go at my own pace? Besides, I already got my algebra work done for the day. I did it as soon as I woke up. Is it a crime for me to have a little bit of fun in between subjects?"

"Of course not, Walter. I just don't want you playing video games and watching violence all day."

"So it is a crime for me to have some fun, then?"

After letting out a deep sigh, she shook her head. "I'm not saying that you can't have fun, Walter. I'm saying having fun isn't always about just doing those types of things."

"But that's what I like, Mom. What else am I supposed to do?"

"Hey wait, I know. Why don't you go out on the balcony and try to spot some dolphins? Your grandfather said he almost always saw a pod or two of them just about every day this time of year. Plus, it wouldn't hurt for you to get some sun. Just don't let your pale self get burned."

Walter stopped chewing for a second. "That's a great idea! I bet I could see them real good with his old telescope!"

"See? You don't always need video games to have fun. Please, just be careful with your grandparents' things. I know they are older and seem outdated, but they almost always bought the best items available back then."

"Don't worry, Mom, I will. I love all this old stuff."

"They'd be very pleased to hear you say that."

"Caroline's friend doesn't think much of it, though."

"Why? What did she say? Which friend was this? I've asked her not to have people over without telling me first."

"It was her friend Susan. She only stopped over for a few minutes after work one day. She's real nice. I just overheard her tell Sis nineteen ninety called and wants its decorations back."

"Does she live in a beach house?"

"No, she lives something like thirty minutes inland. Just outside of Conway, I think."

Aggravated by that information, Walter's mom said, "Well, until she has oceanfront property of her own, especially in Pawley's Island, she can keep her judgments to herself."

"Ah, don't sweat it, Mom, she's cool. I do agree with her opinion on the sofas, though. These faded pink flower prints all over the extra fluffy cushions really are kinda gaudy."

She rolled her eyes and let out a sigh. "I've got to get off of here. Your father's nurse needs me. Listen, just please make sure you keep helping Caroline out around the house. Okay?"

"Sure thing, Mom. I was going to load the dishwasher when I was done eating."

"Do you need anything? Have you got enough socks and undies?"

"I'm good on all that, but I do need a round pair of sunglasses like The Priest wears for my Halloween costume."

"You can probably find some at one of the beach stores. Just have Caroline stop by one next time you two are out. They have one every five hundred feet down there."

"Yeah, you're right. I didn't even think of that."

His mom let out a light chuckle. "I'm going to miss these days."

"What do you mean?"

"The days of my child telling me I'm right. In another year or so those words will be gone forever."

Walter was getting ready to annihilate his last bite of cereal when he said, "Ah, you're crazy."

"See, it's already starting."

"Geez, Mom."

"I've got to go. You be good. Okay?"

"Okay, I will. Love you."

"Love you, too. Bye."

Walter put his phone to the side and was now finished devouring his cereal. He spun his famous cartoon duck-shaped spoon through the chocolaty liquid. "Ah, the best part; getting to wash it all down with a bowl full of chocolate milk. Here we go, Count. Bottoms up!"

CHAPTER TWO

Taking Care of Business

In a sweltering hot county building at the furthest point north of what was considered the Myrtle Beach area, which sat just below the North Carolina border, an older man spoke with distinct authority in his voice. "I was really sorry to hear about your dad. Ken was one of a kind. He was a really good feller."

"Thank you, Mr. Davis." Nodding, the young businessman responded with noticeable respect. He was there to make a business pitch, but he was certainly not in control of the conversation.

"You in a hurry, Tommy?"

"No, sir. I left the entire day open. I wasn't sure how long we'd be, so I didn't want to inconvenience any customers." Overstated himself a bit, he was hoping to look super professional with that answer.

The older man belted out, "Hellfire, boy, we damn sure ain't gonna be here talking about this all day!"

Embarrassed by that response Tommy immediately tried to save face. "Well, I also wasn't sure what time we'd actually start talking…" He trailed off, as it felt like his words fell on deaf ears.

"Anyhow, I think it had to be in the early eighties, over at the old high school," the older man stated as he began telling an old story about the young man's father. "I was still teaching history and geography. Your dad was in my third-period class. He was in there with Jennifer Garland and boy, did he ever have a crush on her. Sad part was, she knew it and she had your dad eating out of her hand. He followed her around like a little puppy dog. It was unnatural seeing her drag him around. Especially since he was such a burly man to be so young. You know what I mean? He was tough, a real man's man, and it was hard seeing him be tamed so easy by a little spoiled brat. Hell of a man but his taste in women was horrible."

Nodding in agreement with a raised eyebrow, Tommy said, "Sadly, he never overcame that flaw."

"No, he didn't, did he? Like I was saying, little Miss Jen had your pop wrapped around her finger. This incident, I'm getting ready to tell you about, got started when Jen didn't have her homework one day and her flashing her puppy dog eyes didn't get her out of detention. After that happened, someone started stuffing small chunks of chalk into my blackboard erasers. I knew it was her. Up to that moment, I had never had to deal with that particular prank.

"Well, one time, as I was entering the room. I was pretty sure I saw her do it, but right before I went to call her out on it, the school had a surprise fire drill. By the time we got back in the classroom and settled down, I had forgotten about it until the next period. A couple of days later, I was having a real bad day. Headache, little sleep the night before, just a bad day all around and I was in a real bad mood. I went to erase the board and there were those damn little chunks, marking the board all up. Let me tell ya, I lost my temper something fierce. I threw that eraser to the back of the room and shouted, 'This stops today!'

"Even though I knew it was Jen, I still didn't have any real hard proof, so I thought I could put her on the spot by getting someone else in the class to rat her out. I had decided to threaten them all with a week's detention if they didn't give the culprit up. Of course, nobody said anything at first. I gave them a second warning and still nothing. On the third and final warning, two different students raised their hands, but before they could say anything, your dad stood straight up and said, 'It was me, Mr. Davis.'

"I looked him straight in his eyes and said, 'No. I don't believe that, Ken.'

"'Yes, sir, it was me,' he said with conviction in his voice this time.

"I said, 'I just don't believe you could be guilty of such a petty and childish act. Doing something that petty is beneath you.'

"'It was me, sir,' he said again, and he dropped his head this time. 'I'm willing to take my detention.'

"I looked over and saw Jen with this conniving grin on her face, and that infuriated me. Your dad was willing to take the heat for that rascal, and she didn't even have the slightest appreciation for that gesture. So since I was actually trying to get through to her, I told your dad, 'No, there's been a change of plans.' Detention was off the table now and besides, I couldn't justify sending him, since I knew for a fact he didn't do it. Son, let me tell ya, it wasn't just a different time back then. It was a different world completely. We could still paddle the students, if you can believe that!"

"Oh yes, sir," a young, bright-eyed Tommy concurred. "Granny lit my hide up on several occasions!"

"I bet she did! That's what I told your dad I was going to do to him. I really wanted to see him back off. I wanted her to own up to this. I wanted to bust her so bad, but he came to the front of the room and said, 'I'm ready, sir.' I didn't want to do it. Not at all, but I couldn't back down now. I'd lose those kids' respect and every class after that for the rest of my career if I'd let that slide. So instead of the paddle, I grabbed a yardstick. I don't know why I had one now that I think of it. Them damn things used to be everywhere. But anyway, I grabbed the yardstick and told him to bend over. Before I swung, I looked over at Jennifer and she still had that conniving grin just plastered on her face. I'll never forget it. It pissed me off so bad, but I didn't want to really hurt your dad, so I aimed for his billfold in his back pocket to cushion the blow. Boys used to have the fattest wallets back then. I don't know if it's because they used to carry condoms around in them, trying to be a big shot, or what. Do they still do that today?"

With wide eyes, Tommy shook his head. "I'm not sure, sir. I don't."

"Well, all I know is that mine never was that fat, but I was a schoolteacher for too damn long." He let out a small chuckle before continuing the story. "So then I had him lean over my desk and I swung for the fences. Fortunately for your pop, I hit smack on that fat wallet of his and that yardstick broke and the other piece slapped against the wall and made the loudest pop you could imagine. The entire class gasped except for you know who. I looked over at that spiteful wretch, and she was laughing. Not out loud, but she was covering her face and her body was shaking from keeping it in. It made me so mad. He took her punishment, and she didn't even care, laughed at him to top it off! But here's the real kicker: that evening after school, that very same day, my car broke down. Remember, I told you it was one of those days. So here I am on the side of the road, and who stops to help?"

"Dad?"

"Uh-huh. He knew it was me and he stopped anyway, even after breaking that yardstick on his rear end. He acted like it never happened. He even went and got one of your grandpa's trucks they used on their logging jobs and pulled my car to the mechanic's. I always thought that's why he was so manly, all that logging he used to do."

"Oh yeah, he'd told me plenty about his logging days with my pap."

"I'm sure, but I asked him, I said, 'Why do you let that little hussy do you like that? Son, I know that wasn't you.'

"He said, 'No, sir, but I'd missed out on our necking sessions between classes if she'd got detention.'

"I said, 'But son, I was going to give you detention at first.'

"He said, 'I know, sir, but you helped me out by breaking that stick over my ass instead. That's why I stopped to help. I figured I owed you one!'"

Thunderous laughter now filled the room as both men were cracked up from that comment.

Tommy nodded. "That was him in a nutshell!"

After the laughing settled down, Mr. Davis said, "I better shut my trap or I will have you here all day after all. I hope you didn't mind me telling you that. Some folks don't like to talk about loved ones after they are gone."

"Oh, no, sir. I absolutely love hearing old stories about Dad. I appreciate you telling me that."

Mr. Davis gave him a nod and he developed a serious look on his face. "Alright, let's talk business. So you're telling me that you think your cousin and you can handle an event this big? The Loris Bog-Off is a small-town festival, but it's the birthplace of chicken bog. Throw some chicken, rice, and sausage in a bowl and people go crazy. There's usually at least thirty thousand attendees every year and it's consistently getting bigger!" Story time had come to a definite end as the older gentleman watched for a response from the young and, presumed inexperienced, business owner through his thick-framed glasses.

"Yes, sir, Mr. Davis. Despite still being a small business, this is definitely in our wheelhouse. We can easily provide all the portable bathrooms you will need and we can match the competitor's price as well. I understand it seems risky to let a smaller operation take the reins on this, but why let a bigger company come in from

Wilmington and take that money out of the state? Josh and I always buy local and strive to take care of the county."

Mr. Davis leaned back in his chair and scratched the bald spot on top of his head. An old black and dust-ridden rotating fan blew his remaining white locks wildly around when the air from it hit directly on him. "Listen, Tommy, I don't doubt you at all. You're one of the finest fellers I've ever met."

"Thank you, sir, I appreciate that compliment very much," Tommy said from the old and well-worn generic chair he was sitting in. He had his average Caucasian frame dressed in his Sunday best and his medium brown hair had just enough styling gel in it to maintain its subtle right side part when the fan blew his way. He had high hopes of putting on a good impression for the head of the Chamber of Commerce. However, Mr. Davis's delayed reply currently had him worried, and he was preparing himself for a soul-crushing "But" that seemed inevitable at this point.

"I have no problems putting you in charge of this, Tommy, but to be honest with you, that cousin of yours worries me."

There it is, he thought, taking a deep breath. "I understand your concerns, but please keep in mind that Josh has been dealt some bad cards in life, sir." Tommy's heart rate increased and he was intently waiting for Mr. Davis to respond and hoping to appease any concerns he had.

"Yes, he has, and I know you have, too!" He pointed his right index finger at Tommy. "But it seems to me that you've learned to manage them pretty dang good. I'm proud of you for it!"

"Thank you, sir. I owe all to my grandmother. She was my rock in this stormy world."

Mr. Davis nodded in approval. "She sure was an amazing lady. The world needs more folks like her."

"That's a fact."

"From my point of view, it doesn't look like your cousin, Josh, has, though."

"There is truth in that statement, sir. I'm absolutely not denying that."

Mr. Davis gazed at the rotating fan for a few seconds, then he looked directly at Tommy. "Look, son, I can't tell you how to run your business; it's not my place to do so. But if you, and I mean you alone, can be the man in charge of this, then it would greatly improve your chances of getting the answer you're hoping for."

Tommy's eyebrows immediately rose, and he sat up even straighter. "Absolutely! Even though we co-own the company together, I always take the lead when it comes to actually taking care of business."

Mr. Davis gave Tommy a very long and mostly uncomfortable look. "I was hoping that's what you'd say. Tell ya what, as long as you can supply some handicapped stalls as well, then I'd say we got a deal."

Tommy hopped to his feet. "Yes, sir, that's no problem at all!" Then he reached out to Mr. Davis and performed a very enthusiastic handshake with the town official.

"I know you'll do us a fine job. Leave some of your business cards and I'll pass them out for ya!"

"Sure thing!" Tommy was full of joy as he pulled his chrome-plated card holder out of his pocket.

Minutes later, he was in the parking lot getting ready to enter his old pickup truck when his cell phone rang. After checking who was calling, he muttered, "Aw, come on! What do you want, you old hag?" Then he flung his head back in despair and closed his eyes. After a few rings, he finally answered bluntly. "Yeah?"

CHAPTER THREE

Sweet Caroline

A rather tall, slim young lady, appearing to be in her early twenties with dark red hair perfectly braided for her current working conditions, stood in the back of the commercial kitchen. "I swear to God if somebody else gives me crap about my Cowboys jersey today I'm going to lose it!"

After letting out a loud but short hissing sound behind her upward-pointed index finger, her petite coworker instructed, "Keep it down, Susan! The boss just got here!" She appeared to be about the same age as her rowdy work mate despite her more professional attitude.

"I don't give a crap. I'll tell Jamar off, too! I'm not afraid of him!"

"I know that you don't care if you get fired, but I'd really like to keep you around. I don't know why, but you are my friend, ya know!" She shook her head with disapproval as she adjusted her curly, dark brown ponytail.

"If that's true, then why don't we get our nails done after work today?" She flashed a sneaky grin. "On you."

"Ha, you wish!"

"Ah, come on, bestie. You always take home more than me!"

"That's just because I'm nice to the customers and, you know, actually do my job."

"Yeah, yeah. I try to be nice, but they can be so snobby and uppity. It always feels like they are looking down on me."

"That's because they are. We are servers in case you forgot."

"I know, they just irk me to death sometimes. Do they really have to be so rude and demanding?"

"My grandpa told me that sometimes the best way to get back at someone is to give them exactly what they want."

"So you just cower down and take the verbal abuse?"

"I wouldn't say that I necessarily cower down to them, but I acknowledge their requests and try to follow through with them the best I can."

"So you're saying you actually try to give them what they want?"

"That's one way to put it, but it could probably be best summed up by simply saying, I do my job."

"Touché. I guess that explains why you make more than me."

"Also, I try not to acknowledge the rude comments if I can. It really does help."

"I feel so worthless. I've been here at Loggerhead Dunes for almost two years and you just roll up in here and could take the place over just after two months!"

"Yeah right. You're the one that knows all the ins and outs of this place."

"What are you talking about?"

"I overheard Tony and Amero from the maintenance crew talking this morning as I walked in. He said you turned the cameras off so you guys wouldn't get caught having your after-hours rendezvous!"

"Jesus, Amero!" Susan exclaimed through clenched teeth. "He was supposed to keep his mouth shut! You better keep yours shut, too!"

"Don't worry. Who am I gonna tell? Besides my family, you are the only person I really talk to. I just don't understand why you didn't take him back to your place?"

"I would have loved to be able to take him back to my place, but my parents and the stupid little brothers are still there."

"Still?"

"Yep, and it'll be the end of the month before their new double-wide arrives."

"Oh wow! I thought they were already back home by now."

"Nope. They should have been, but there was some sort of holdup at the factory. Some crap about a material shortage or something to that effect. Either way, the delivery got delayed. I told Mom to sell that stupid chainsaw of his so that he doesn't cut a tree down on this one!"

"Wow, I'm very sorry to hear that. I got to get the check to one of my customers. I'll be back in a sec." She promptly left the bustling kitchen area utilizing her fast-paced style of walking that she normally reserved for work. As she approached the elegant tables that she was currently waiting on, she politely asked, "Anything else I can get for you, ma'am?"

"No, everything was delicious," an older lady said, as she slowly sat her glass of water down. "My friend suggested I come here for brunch and she was right. You guys serve terrific food!"

"Thank you. We try our best. Loggerhead Dunes has won the vote for best specialty omelets in Pawley's Island the past three years in a row!"

"I don't doubt that at all, but can you tell me why they call this place Loggerhead Dunes?"

"Um, I'm pretty sure it was named that because of all the sea turtles around here."

"Oh, that's odd. I thought all the sea turtles around here were called leatherbacks?"

"Uh, I think some of those come here, too, but I believe the most prevalent species in this area is the loggerhead."

"That most certainly explains the turtle on the sign!" She let out a laugh, and they both chuckled together for a moment. "I didn't realize there were a variety of sea turtles called that. Hey, I was wondering about something else, too. Why are all you workers wearing sports shirts? They are so colorful and bright but it seems a bit informal for such a place as this. Don't you think?"

The fair-skinned waitress smiled. "Oh, the head restaurant manager, Jamar, is a huge football fan. His father is the owner of the golf course and restaurant here and he talked him into letting all the workers wear our favorite team jerseys on Fridays during the NFL season."

"Well, that's neat. What's on yours? It sure is a pretty shade of purple."

"Oh, thank you. Mine is a replica of what the Baltimore Ravens wear."

"Shows what I know. I don't know anything about sports." The older lady half-grinned.

The waitress smiled. "I don't know a lot myself. Ravens' jerseys pretty much come as standard clothing back in Maryland."

"Oh, so you're from Maryland. I always had an appreciation for the Chesapeake area. I'm originally from Boston myself."

"I've been there before. It's a very unique city. Do you live down here now?" The waitress scanned her other tables, making sure everyone's cups were full enough.

"Yes, I live over in the Surfside area now."

"I like Surfside. One of my favorite shops is there."

"Really? What's it called?"

"Bounty Hunter's Emporium. It used to be called something else, but it got new owners a while back and that place is so awesome!"

"Ah, yes! I love that store. They literally have something for everyone. I go just about every week."

"I could easily spend my whole paycheck there! I just love all the collectibles, home furnishings, and local art they carry. Do you go back to visit Boston often?"

"Not too much. I do miss it sometimes, and there are plenty of beautiful beaches back up north. Cape Cod is very nice and almost everyone's favorite from up there. The locals just call it The Cape. I understand the appeal, but the beaches here in the Carolinas are my absolute favorite."

"I certainly agree with you. My family definitely thinks so as well. They liked this place so much that they named me after it."

"They did? What is your name? You told me earlier, but it has slipped my mind."

"Caroline. This is by far my parents' favorite place to visit and my grandparents actually bought beachfront property not far from here."

"How nice is that? Hey, maybe you could tell me, one of my grandsons is coming to stay with me for a few days. What should I do with him? What's a good place to take him? I rarely leave the seashore myself. The ocean and a good book are all I need, but I'm sure he'll want to do more than that."

Caroline's eyes shot toward the ceiling for a moment as she thought about how to reply. After a few seconds, she then answered the inquisitive customer with copious enthusiasm. "Well, there's always Barefoot Landing and Broadway at the Beach, of course, plenty to do at both of those locations and everybody loves Ripley's Aquarium. Uh, there's a newer place, called The Crazy Mason, that makes elaborate milkshakes. They make very outlandish desserts with a ton of toppings and, of course, they come in a glass jar, hence the name Crazy Mason. That place is always fun."

The customer's face lit up. "Wow, that sounds interesting! He'd definitely get a sugar rush there." Then she let out a low chuckle.

"Oh yeah, make sure you show up hungry. They give you a lot. Also, he might like the gator place up in North Myrtle, Alligator

Adventure. They have one of the largest crocodiles in the world there. That's my little brother's favorite place to visit. They have all kinds of other wildlife there, too."

"Oh, that would be perfect! He loves animals."

"If you decide to take him, go on a Sunday and hit up the Gospel Brunch at the House of Blues next door. Their food there is top notch, and they have a lot of historical items on display."

"Really, I thought that was just a music venue."

"Oh no, they have an amazing restaurant as well and their food is to die for! Be sure to ask for Cassidy, she is the lead server there and does a fantastic job. Have her show you the Gator Bar. It is a massive antique that was shipped down from Chicago, and it once belonged to Al Capone."

"The old gangster?"

"Yeah, it even has a handful of authentic bullet holes in it from back in the day! And there's lots of other awesome things in there as well."

"I'll be sure to do that with him!"

"Then, as I'm sure you certainly know, there are dozens and dozens of mini golf courses. You really can't go wrong. I'm positive that he will have a wonderful time regardless of where you take him."

"Oh yes, those are all fabulous suggestions. I can't wait for him to get here."

Caroline smiled as she collected the dirty dishes from the table. "I'll be right back." She headed to the kitchen. After passing through the double-swinging silver doors, a preteen boy bombarded her.

"Sis, sis, you're never going to believe this!" The panic-stricken young lad was her younger brother, whose shaggy, medium-length, chestnut-colored hair bounced around as he circled her. His face was paler than usual and his blue jean-covered legs were wobbly from verifiable fear.

CHAPTER FOUR

Stepmom From Hell

An older and well-versed-looking lady, dressed in a fuzzy purple housecoat along with matching purple slippers, stood by the screen door that led out to the side porch of her house. With a menthol cigarette in her left hand, smoke came out of her mouth as she said, "Hey, Tommy, are you there?" She glanced at the dated cordless phone she was holding with her right hand, as if looking at it could help strengthen the connection.

"Yeah, what do you want, Inez?" Tommy didn't sound too pleased. Just the sound of his stepmother's voice alone already made him regret answering her call.

"I was wondering if you could bring that yellow thing you've got for dead batteries. I don't remember what you called it."

"It's called a jump box."

"Yeah, that's it! Can you bring it over, please? And soon?"

Tommy let out a frustrating low growl. "Did you seriously let the Woody die again?"

"I'm sorry."

"Damn it, Inez! All you had to do was start it once a week, back it out of the shed, and let it run for thirty minutes or so."

"I know, I'm sorry. I keep forgetting about it. I wouldn't be bothering you if I didn't have a guy coming to look at it today."

"Who's coming to look at it? And why?"

"He's from an auction company out of Atlanta. I called them and told them all about the car. They're going to have him appraise it and possibly make me an offer on it on the spot!"

Tommy had a sick feeling arise in his stomach after hearing that unsettling information. Several seconds passed before he could finally ask, "So you're seriously going to sell it?"

"If the price is right, I will."

As if the upset stomach wasn't bad enough, Tommy could now feel his blood pressure beginning to rise at a rapid rate. He took a deep breath and masked his rage the best he could. "I'll be right there."

Before he could get into his truck, Mr. Davis shouted out from the entrance of the building he had just exited. "Hey, Tommy, I almost forgot. My neighbor needs you to empty her septic tank. I was just talking to her last week, and she had mentioned it. Do you think you could do it today?"

"Yes, sir. You still live off of Red Bluff, don't ya?"

"Yeah, Snapper Pond Drive. She's the brown house to the left of mine."

"It'll be this afternoon before I can get to it, but we can definitely get it done today."

"I'll let her know. Thanks, Tommy."

"Yes, sir, thank you!"

Right as Tommy attempted to enter his truck once more, a voice came from behind him. "Tommy, is that you, pal?"

Good grief, can I just get in my truck? Tommy thought, just before turning around to see a white gentleman wearing very dusty work clothes. He looked to be about his age as he approached him from behind. After a few more steps, he finally recognized his old friend and with noticeable excitement hollered out to him, "Greg! How the heck are ya? Aw man, it's been ages!"

"I thought that was you. Then when I saw the red and white Ranger, I knew it couldn't be anyone else!" The two gave each other a long, friendly handshake. "How the heck ya been?"

"Not bad, just trying to keep Uncle Floyd's business afloat."

"Well, if the way you have taken care of his old truck is any indication, you'll do just fine. You've had this thing since your junior year of high school, haven't ya?"

"Yeah, that's right. Since about halfway through my junior year."

"What year is it again?"

"1975. Uncle Floyd bought it brand new, the Ford F-250 Ranger XLT." Tommy wiped a smudge off of the mirror with the sleeve of his shirt. "It was my payment for all the work I would do for him in the summers."

"Yeah, that's right! I remember that. He just died a few months ago, didn't he?"

"Unfortunately. I lost him and my dad just within several months of each other. Uncle Floyd had really gone downhill a few years back. Josh and I had been basically running the wastewater removal business for him, but it's all ours now."

"Well, I'm sure you'll do great. I'm real sorry for your loss. I felt horrible about missing your dad's funeral. We were out of town that week."

"Ah, don't worry about it. That's no problem at all. What have you been up to, man? Still doing drywall work, it appears."

"Can't hide that, can I?" He laughed as he dusted himself off. I got an early start this morning, so I decided to take an early lunch break and get something to eat at the Sunshine House. You wanna go over with me? I'll pay."

"I'd love to, bro. Some of Ernie's world-famous gravy and biscuits would hit the spot, but I have a lot going on today."

"I know how that goes. Hey, what's your number? I'll send you an invitation to my fiancé's baby shower."

"Baby shower? That's great man, congratulations! Here's my card. It's a textable number, so send me the address and date and I'll be there."

"That's brave of ya, man. I definitely could use a wingman with all those women around!"

"I can imagine. Do you need anything in particular for the baby?"

"Gift cards for diapers would be best, but I'd be more than happy to just have you there."

"Well, unless something just prevents me from coming, I'll see you then!"

"Sounds great pal. See you then!"

A very short time later, Tommy was pulling up to his father's old house. To his surprise, the car that needed a jump-start was already out of the shed. He could feel his blood pressure rise once more, so he took a deep breath as he exited his trusty red and white Ford Ranger. Before he got to the car, Inez came walking up to him, still wearing her purple housecoat and slippers. "I thought it needed to be jumped off?" He tried concealing his disgust for her.

She lit another menthol-flavored cigarette. "The guy from the auction company got here earlier than I thought and he was able to get it started."

As Tommy walked up to the stunning classic, the unknown man popped out from under the hood. "Hello." He nodded. "Are you Tommy?"

"Yeah," he mumbled in an unfriendly manner. Tommy immediately felt bad for misplacing his anger on the stranger. The thoughts of someone else acquiring his father's car were nearly unbearable for him.

"Hell of a restoration. I believe this is the nicest Woody I've ever seen!"

Tommy ignored the older, gray-haired man and stared at the classic for a few seconds. "1948 Chevrolet Fleetmaster. The nicest damn Woody station wagon ever made. Period."

"I can't argue with that. Is that the original engine?"

"Yep, three-point-five straight six. My dad bought it off a man he'd known for a long time. Surprisingly, it was still in great shape considering the age, but even so, we still had to put a ton of work into it."

"I've heard there are less than a hundred of these left. That's a very low number, considering they made over ten thousand!"

"Yeah, I guess they just didn't hold up well. Dad kept saying this thing was something special."

After taking a quick drag off of her cigarette, Inez chimed in. "So what do ya think you could give me for it?"

The man scratched his neck. "Well, the pre-World War Two models can usually bring more money, but this thing is fabulous. What shade of teal is that?"

Tommy answered back in an almost robotic tone. "Tropical Turquoise. It's a GM code from the mid-fifties. The original color was Live Oak Green. It wasn't very appealing, so Dad decided on a beachy fun color that seemed more appropriate for such a beauty."

"I didn't think it was original. That could potentially hurt the price a bit." The man circled the pristine auto.

Inez let out a disappointing huff. "Damn it."

After shooting her a firm look of contempt, Tommy turned to the man. "He didn't care about the resale value. We were making a work of art. Besides, he never had any intentions of selling it." He shot her a nasty look once more.

"Well, it's certainly a work of art, that's for dang sure!" The man continued to gaze at the rarity. "I'd have probably picked that color myself if I'd been in your dad's shoes. It won't hurt the value too much; the industry's purist group will be the only ones to really care about that."

"So what do you think it could bring at auction?" Inez asked with her robe barely keeping her covered at this point. She took a long drag off of her cigarette while she waited for a response.

"I've got to talk to my boss, but I'd be shocked if it didn't bring at least six figures."

"Oh yeah! Cha-ching!" Inez waved her arms around and danced left to right.

Tommy bit his bottom lip and looked down, trying his best to contain the rage she was provoking within him.

The man from the auction company saw the distress in Tommy. "That's not a guarantee, that's just my opinion. You never know how any auction is going to go."

Inez immediately stopped her moronic celebration dance. "So you're not going to give me a check for that amount today?"

The man tried not to laugh. "No, ma'am. That's not how this works. There's never any guarantee of what something can bring, so we can't give you anything today unless you want to sell it outright."

"I'll sell it any way you want as long as I get a hundred grand out of it!"

"I'm not certain my boss will offer you that much."

"Well, send him the pictures! I want my money! Let's do this!"

"I have already sent them, ma'am. I'm waiting to hear back from him."

"You let me know what he says. I'm going inside to get changed. I had no idea that hunk of junk could be that valuable. This calls for a celebration!" She jolted inside, completely ignoring Tommy.

The man from the auction company could see just how upset Tommy had become. He hung his head. "I'm sorry, son. Are you going to be okay?"

His face was now beet red, and he appeared completely defeated. "Honestly, I've never been okay and from the looks of it, I never will be. That bitch has taken everything my dad ever had from me and sold it for alcohol and cigarette money. Besides, what do you care?"

"I do care, son. I had a father once, too, ya know. I understand the symbol of love and appreciation a car can offer from another person. The memories it can hold. They can be a time capsule of sorts, from better times."

Tommy stared off into the distance. He just wanted to be away from it all. Despite the anger he felt, he looked at the man. "Have a good one." He started walking to his truck.

"Wait. I'm real sorry this has gone this way, son. If I'd known the situation, I'd told my boss to pass on this one, but I had already sent him the pictures."

"Don't sweat it. It's not your fault." Tommy continued walking.

"Listen, for what it's worth, I can slow down this transaction. It might give you time to buy it from her yourself."

"How long can you hold it off?"

"A couple weeks at least. Probably 'til the first of November."

"Thanks for that, but I doubt it will do any good. I appreciate the gesture, though." Tommy entered his truck and got on his phone. As he pulled out of the driveway he said, "Hey Josh, meet me at the shop. We got a job this afternoon."

CHAPTER FIVE

Now You See Him

Shocked that her younger and only sibling had the audacity to interrupt her at work, especially by bursting into the kitchen among all her coworkers, after countless warnings against doing anything of the such, Caroline grabbed him by his arm while handling a stack of dirty dishes from the table. "What are you doing here, Walter?" She stared into his wide brown eyes. Her own set of almost identical colored eyes were immeasurably furious at this point as they impatiently waited for a satisfactory answer.

"I know you're pissed off at me, but you have to listen!" Despite the prominent visual warning radiating from his sister's face, he always cowered away from her when she displayed that level of anger. This time, though, he was undeniably fervent about being heard.

A prominent and very well-dressed Black man, appearing to be in his mid-thirties, approached the two. "Is there a problem here, Ms. Berger?" To Caroline's dismay, it was Jamar, the manager she was just talking about with the customer just minutes earlier.

Caroline's heart sank at the sound of her superior's intimidating voice. This was exactly what she didn't want to happen. "No, sir. My brother was just leaving." Her eyes bulged at Walter, and then she nodded toward the door, signaling for him to exit it immediately.

Instead, Walter looked directly at Jamar. "I'm very sorry, sir. Please don't be angry at my sister. It's not her fault that I'm here. There's an emergency or I wouldn't be here, I swear!"

"Please take this matter outside then and hurry back, Ms. Berger." Jamar stomped off to reprimand another employee that had dropped a tray of drinks just as Walter began his plea to him.

Setting the dishes down and, with her hand still affixed to his arm, Caroline led Walter to the back door. "This better be good, spazoid!" she said through clenched teeth. Her dark brown ponytail swung around wildly as they exited the large commercial kitchen.

With tremendous zeal, Walter belted out, "I'm sorry, sis, but I just had to tell you! It was the most incredible thing I've ever seen!"

Now outside, Caroline shielded her eyes from the bright yellow sun as her eyes adjusted from the dimness of the restaurant. She slowly scanned the well-manicured grounds of the top-notch golf course that surrounded the establishment as she waited for whatever ridiculous yarn Walter was going to spin for her.

Walter began his story with great enthusiasm. "So it all started when I was in my room, right? And I had just gotten Grandpa's old telescope out."

"What? You better be careful with Grandma and Grandpa's stuff! Mom will beat your butt if you tear anything up! We're beyond lucky that she's even letting us stay in their old vacation house to begin with!"

"Chill out! Gramps taught me how to use it years ago. Besides, it was Mom's idea! I was just trying to see some dolphins; she claims they are usually easier to spot this time of year."

"Yeah, right, you little perv! You were checking out all the girls in their bikinis on the beach!" Caroline snarled up her nose.

"So what if I like girls? But that's not all I was doing! Besides, there aren't that many people visiting the ocean right now. I really was looking for a pod of dolphins, I swear. Even though Mom said everyone's always saying that they are easy to spot during the fall, I just couldn't find any. So I brought the scope back to the shore, and that's when I caught sight of this strange-looking dude in gray clothes."

Caroline was unimpressed with his earlier account thus far. Then she slowly lowered her hands as her eyes adjusted to the bright green grass surrounding the area as she let out an impudent, "Yeah, so?"

"So?" he muttered in disapproval of the underwhelming response. "So it was weird!"

"If you have come all the way here to my work just to tell me you saw some a man with unusual clothes on, then I'm going to beat your butt myself!"

"Wait! That's not all!" He stretched his arms out in front of him defensively, as if he was ready to beg for mercy at any second. "This man looked just like he could have come out of a movie set or something. It's almost ninety degrees out here and he had this long gray coat on. All of his clothes were gray. He really looked like he was an old soldier back in the old days, kinda like the guys on Gramp's Civil War DVDs."

"Maybe he's one of those old battle reenactors or something. We are in the South, you know. I swear, Walter, I can't believe you risked getting me fired over this!"

"Let me finish!" He pointed his finger in her face.

"Fine, then finish!" She gave his finger a threatening look.

"Well, I still can't believe it, but even his face was gray. Not as gray as his clothes, but still a weird color for skin, and no, it wasn't some sort of paint, I could tell. It's almost like he wasn't even real, but he definitely was." Walter became pale once more and clammed up in befuddlement of what he was about to say.

Noticing how upset her little brother truly was, Caroline couldn't help but show him a small amount of compassion, so she took a step toward him and placed her hand on his shoulder. "It's okay, Walter. Tell me what you saw."

Walter looked at her with widened eyes. "He, um, he disappeared."

"What do you mean?"

"The man looked right at me. Not above me, not below me, or just in my surrounding area. It was just as if he knew I was watching him and it felt like he looked straight into my soul or something."

"That's absurd, Walter. Nobody could have seen you from that distance unless you were out on the porch watching. Maybe then—"

Walter briskly shook his head. "No, I wasn't outside. I was in my room. He looked right at me, then he turned to the right and vanished! I swear it! I know it sounds crazy, but that's just what he did. No one else seemed to notice him at all. It freaked me out so bad that I didn't know what else to do, so I hopped on my bike and rode it over here as fast as I could. Now that I think of it, I'm not sure that I even locked the door."

Caroline cut her eyes in disbelief at her distraught sibling. "Are you sure that's what you saw?"

"Yes! I swear it! I hadn't been drinking any energy drinks, and I didn't stay up all night playing video games. The weird gray dude looked right at me and then he just disappeared without a trace! He literally faded away into thin air!" Indubitably baffled and feeling nutty after verbalizing the account, Walter dropped his head, but he was positively certain of what he saw on the sandy stretch of land. He eventually looked back up at his big sister. "Am I cursed now or something?"

"You're not cursed, boy, but that fellow you saw on the beach sure is!" The deep, intimidating voice boomed out from behind the siblings, startling them both.

CHAPTER SIX

Just Some Good Ol' Boys

"Welcome back to the show, folks!" the vivacious voice of an enthusiastic male radio personality eagerly announced to the listeners of the popular morning broadcast. The sound of the local celebrity's shtick echoed from a very dated and dusty old radio throughout the dark workshop where Tommy told his cousin Josh to meet him. "We're here, live on air, talking about the latest sultry love triangle to hit the Grand Strand area. And to make it even more scandalous, it's in the geriatric community! So before the commercial break, we found out that while Linda was out of the state, visiting some family members, apparently her fiancé, Jim, had the audacity to cheat on her with her best friend, of all people, Rose! I guess it's true what they say, when the cats away the mice will play!"

In an evenly matched tone of fervor, a perky female voice cosigned her colleague. "What makes it even worse—now listen up because this is where it gets good—is the rumor that Linda apparently took care of Rose when her plastic surgery wounds got severely infected. Can you believe that they were that close, that good of friends, and Rose had the nerve to stab Linda in the back like that?"

Tommy was now entering the old metal building. He had changed clothes, and it was noticeable that he had a distinctly established outdoor worker's tan. He was now wearing dark blue work pants and a black tee shirt with their bright-colored business logo on it. As he approached his cousin, he shouted out, "Hey, Josh, turn that crap off! I've got good news!"

"Crap? Man, this is quality entertainment, Tommy." Josh, with his arms held out to his sides, had a similar-looking skin tone along with the same type of tan, but his hair was black and almost shoulder length. Also, like Tommy, he was wearing the same tee shirt. He had found a bag of Tommy's potato chips on his desk and was munching on them.

"Sorry, cuz, but that's just more ammo for those who hold a poor image of the South. They already think that we're all a bunch of backwoods hicks that are out of touch with modern society. So much so that they think we all believe it's acceptable to marry our own relatives," Tommy clamored out with more than noticeable sarcasm, especially while using air quotes with his fingers when he said "modern society."

"Piss on 'em!" Josh belted out, without missing a beat as he continued shoveling the salty chips into his mouth.

"Yeah, that's the spirit," Tommy mumbled, with an ample amount of sarcasm once more. "Anyway, like I was originally saying, we got the spot at the Loris Chicken Bog Cook Off. We'll be supplying the portable bathrooms!"

"Woohoo!" Josh yelled out in a fake, yet melodramatic, and disappointed tone. "More shit work for us to do!"

"Hey, that's going to be a very good payday. We got to keep expanding. At this rate, we'll be the biggest waste water removal business in all of Horry County!"

Without warning, Josh jumped to his feet, flailing his arms, just barely holding onto his yellow chip bag while pleading, "Tommy, man, how long are we going to do this? This is horrible! We're better than this!"

"Hey, Uncle Floyd made a real good living with this business and we're damn lucky he left it to us! Yeah sure, this isn't a dream job, by no means, but considering how hard life has hit us, it's been a real blessing!"

"Man, this eternal optimism bit you constantly spew is beyond annoying."

"What do you want me to say, Josh? Life sucks, I get it!" Tommy flung his arms out toward Josh and then turned his side to him.

"But life doesn't have to suck, Tommy. Not anymore. I have an idea."

Tommy faced Josh. "You always have ideas. What makes this any different, or good for that matter?"

Josh set down his bag of chips and started talking in a low and serious tone. "Tommy, bro, you don't understand. I actually have a way out. Now, listen close, cuz. You know Sabrina at the Loggerhead Dunes Golf Club?"

"I think so. Are you talking about my old friend from school, Greg Hoilman's mom? It's weird you mention her because I literally just saw Greg. She's kind of an older lady now, I would think."

"Yeah, that's her!"

"What about her, Josh?" Tommy had a noticeable concern growing on his face. "She's a full-blown cougar. Scratch that, she's a straight up skank. She's almost as bad as that bitch stepmom of mine, Inez!"

"Well, let's just say that I had an adult encounter with ol' Ms. Hoilman."

"Yeah right."

Josh raised his right hand in a waggish way. "Scout's honor."

Tommy grabbed the sides of his head in disbelief. "What? That's gross, Josh! She's literally old enough to be your mother! Heck, she might be old enough to be your grandmother!"

"Nah, she's not that old, but I'd definitely I'll call her Mommy anytime!" Josh said in a mischievous tone, then he followed the disturbing comment with a low chuckle.

"You're disgusting, man! There's all kinds of shameless tales on her. They say she'll even sell you tickets to the train, if you catch my drift. Now that I think of it, that's probably the reason Greg and I got along so well back in the day. We both had horrible mother figures as kids."

"Why don't you get off your high horse and stop judging me!" Josh barked with more than noticeable anger. "That crap gets old. If you'd drop your preconceived notions of what you think love is supposed to be, you might not be a twenty-five-year-old virgin."

"Preconceived? Kiss my ass! You go ahead and do whoever you want, but don't you tell me I'm wrong for believing that a relationship is about more than just getting some nooky! I could have had countless one-night stands, but in the end, they would have been useless encounters. Like the old saying, just because you can doesn't mean you should!"

Josh stood silent for a moment. "Who the hell says nooky these days?"

"Screw you, man!"

"Easy, easy. I'm just jerking your chain. You're right, dude, you do you. I'm sorry, bro. You're wrong about this encounter, though. It wasn't just another useless one-night stand."

Tommy gave Josh a hard look. "What the heck, man? Why are you telling me about all this?"

"I'm telling you this because Ms. Hoilman didn't realize that she gave us a first-class ticket to easy street!"

"What do you mean?"

"During the downtime of our lovely encounter, I found the safe combination on her desk."

"Dude, you had your encounter with her at the golf course?" Tommy was now confounded as well as appalled.

"Hey, when the magic hits, it hits. Besides, you're missing the point here, Tommy."

"What's the point? To make me sick?"

"No, dumbass, didn't you hear what I just said?"

Tommy shuddered. "Sadly, yes."

"Damn it, man, I found the combination to the safe at the golf course!"

"So? Why are you so excited about that? Especially considering how you had to find it."

"Let me tell ya, cuz, that safe has a fortune in it!"

Tommy's face turned serious, then he plopped down on an old brown sofa they kept in the shop. "I don't know what you're getting at, so why don't you just stop? Just drop it. We have a big event to plan for and, on top of that, we have to empty a septic tank today. You need to focus on the jobs at hand and the last time I checked, we ain't thieves."

"You're exactly right, we're not thieves, we're opportunists! Just like you captured the opportunity to get us in the bog off, I've managed to get us an opportunity at landing a real payday."

"Payday insinuates work. You're talking about straight up theft. Besides, there can't be enough cash in there to even justify attempting to take it. I'd bet there ain't even twenty grand in it."

"You see, I thought the same thing at first, but after a few too many drinks at Drunken Jack's, ol' Ms. Hoilman starts getting chatty and starts really opening up and, man, she opened up a lot!"

"Gross!" Tommy mumbled, before cringing and turning his head. His medium brown hair fell just a bit from where it was parted as he did so.

"She started talking about one of the managers. Jamal or Jamar, I can't remember which, but anyway he's the owner's son and somehow, he's involved with illegal sports betting or something of the sorts. Now get this—this is where it gets good—

ol' Ms. Hoilman said that he's currently laundering the money from his winnings through the golf course."

Tommy sat perfectly still, showing no emotion, until he finally proclaimed, "Oh, that sounds great."

Angered by Tommy's sarcasm, Josh hollered, "It is great! Frosted Flakes tiger great because that safe has over three hundred thousand dollars in it!"

"I don't care if it has over three million in it! There's no need to talk about this any further." Tommy thrust himself off of the old couch.

"Wait just a second! Just hear me out, please!"

Tommy stood across from Josh completely silent while giving him a cold stare.

"It's dirty money!" Josh declared with a loud shout. "Nobody can report it missing! The owner of the golf course doesn't even know about it! And his son can't just waltz up to the police station and say that the money that he obtained illegally is now missing!"

"So, let's recap this situation right quick." Tommy held out his hands in front of his chest in a reasoning fashion. "You've got the combination to a safe."

"Yes."

"A safe full of money that no one has legal rights to."

"Yes."

"A safe that just happens to sit inside one of the biggest golf clubs on Pawley's Island. Is that correct?"

"Yes," Josh confirmed yet again with great confidence.

"So the assumption comes in at that you want to waltz into a very well know, very well secured, and extremely busy golf course and remove the illegal money from its safe. The safe that just so happens is the one that you have the combination to. Is this assumption correct?"

"Yes!"

"You're crazy!" Tommy shouted with visible disdain after crossing his arms.

"Why do you say that? I already have a plan."

"I get the appeal of taking the money, especially with it being dirty, I do, but even if the money could be gotten out without being caught, there would still be huge consequences. People like that are going to come looking for the people that stole from them. This won't end well. Actual criminals play by a completely different set of rules."

"Listen, bro, I know this is a lot to take in, but I swear to you that I do have a solid plan. Once it's over, we can live the lives we want. "

"I know I already said it, but I don't think you heard me. You're crazy, man! This is what happens after only watching all those murder documentaries, heist movies, and crime shows. You've poisoned your mind. You think you can actually pull something like this off?"

"So it'd be better if I only watched stuff like Wally and the Beaver and used terms like nooky?"

"That's it, I'm going to knock the gee willikers straight outta your ass!"

"Wait!" Josh looked down and stayed silent for a moment. "Don't you want to get your dad's old Chevy Woody?"

With an ardent gaze Tommy pointed straight at Josh. "You know damn good and well that I want my dad's car! It's a miracle that bitch, Inez, has waited 'til now to sell it. I'm surprised she didn't drive it to the funeral with a for sale sign on the windshield!"

"Well, this is a chance to get it from her! I know it's scary, I know this is a lot to take in, but we can do this. Trust me; I have a plan, a real solid plan!"

"I can't take comfort in that. This is legit crazy, you know. How can you even think that any plan you can come up with will be remotely successful with that many people around?"

"Because there won't be that many people around during a hurricane." Josh held an assertive glare.

"Hurricane? What are you talking about? Last I heard, the closest storm to us was heading back out to sea."

Just then the radio switched from the morning personalities to the weather forecaster. "Bad news, folks. It appears that Hurricane Faye has made a drastic left turn and current projections show her making a direct hit into the Grand Strand area."

Josh looked at Tommy and gave him a huge, condescending smile and then took a bite out of a chip in an exceedingly bumptious style.

CHAPTER SEVEN

Certain Uncertainty

Caroline shouted, "Geez, mister, you about scared the stuffing out of me!"

"My apologies, Miss. I can promise you that I didn't mean to." The older Black man stood next to the young siblings, outfitted in faded denim overalls with a heavily worn and very thin white tee shirt.

Walter stood as still as a statue in astonishment at the strange fellow that had seemed to appear out of nowhere. He had a distinctive look of mostly salt, with some pepper-colored, tight curly hair, along with his neatly manicured goatee. It contrasted amazingly with his well-aged, antique, bronze-colored skin.

"I wasn't meaning to listen in on y'all's conversation. Please forgive me for intruding. I'm a new worker here. The ground's manager just hired me to help out the crew for a few weeks and I was around the corner having a smoke break when I heard you two talking about the Gray Man."

Walter was still staring at the newly hired grounds worker. He didn't see a cigarette or cigar, or smell smoke. "So you've seen him, too?"

He shook his head. "No, not me." He looked at some golfers passing by. "No, son, I've never seen the ghost of the Gray Man myself, but I've heard about him. I've probably heard everything there is to know about him, as a matter of fact."

"So my runt brother here isn't full of crap?" Caroline pointed at him in a listless style.

"No, missy, from what I understand, I'd say what he saw is very real."

"I'm Caroline and this is Walter. What's your name, mister?"

"Most folks just call me Amos."

"It's very nice to meet you, Amos." Caroline smiled. "I really want to stay and chat, but I must get back to work."

"You go ahead, darling. I'll keep an eye on your brother here for a spell."

"Thank you, sir." Caroline turned to Walter. "Can you get back home okay?"

Walter looked at her with sincere concern. "I don't want to! Can't I just hang out at your car 'til you get off work?"

"That's not really safe. Besides, if you did leave the door unlocked, you need to get back ASAP!"

"Please, I won't do anything stupid, I swear. I probably did lock it."

"Son, if you're scared to go home because of the Gray Man, I can promise you that he won't hurt you. I know it sounds crazy, but from what I understand, it's actually a good thing to see him."

"You hear that? You'll be fine," Caroline said to Walter, then she gave him an encouraging nudge on the arm.

Walter wasn't convinced though. He stood in silence and looked down.

"Tell you what; you talk to Mr. Amos here for a few minutes then head on home. I was supposed to stay over and help put up Halloween decorations, but I'll get Susan to cover for me. Instead of me doing that, we'll go out for pizza at that place you like later. Deal?"

Walter shrugged as he spoke just above a whisper. "I guess so."

"K, good. I really gotta get back inside. You go straight home, okay?"

"Fine," Walter said with very noticeable displeasure.

"Take care, Mr. Amos. I'm sure I'll be seeing you around later since you're working with the grounds crew." Caroline headed back in.

"Oh yeah, I'll be around. You can count on that." Amos gave a slow wave with his right hand.

Walter was disappointed with the outcome, but despite that fact, he was still in awe of the older man. "So how is seeing a ghost a good thing? Is he a ghost?"

"Son, I'm not exactly sure how this ol' world works. Most folks are fine with believing what the folks in charge tell 'em. Not me, though. It's very ignorant to think that we have life all figured out. Everything is based on what we can see and what we think we know, but there's a lot more going on in this crazy place than we could ever imagine. Not everything is as clear-cut as black and white, and that's one thing I do know." Amos looked out toward the tree line of the stunning golf course. "There's a whole lotta gray out there, just like that man you saw."

"So he was a man once?"

"I reckon so. At least that's what I've been told. I grew up in this area and I've always been proud to call it home. I've heard all kinds of legends, ghost stories, and tall tales of the sort. Of all those tales, though, the story of the Gray Man is probably the one that has had the most attention."

"Was he a Civil War soldier?"

"Well, that's where more of the gray area I was just telling you about comes in. They call him the Gray Man because of how he looks, but that name works just as well for his back story, too. It ain't completely clear on who he was, but it's narrowed down pretty good when you figure in how long the legend's been around."

"How long has he been around?" Walter asked, still not taking his eyes off Amos, not even for a second.

"Well, there's a few different trains of thought about who he could have been. Some folks say he was, in fact, a Civil War soldier. Others believe he was Percival Pawley, the man the island was named after. But one of the most popular beliefs is that he was a young man from the 1820s that was rushing home after being out at sea for several months. His ship had docked down in Charleston and was hell-bent on getting back to his fiancée here on Pawley's Island. The thing was, though, a bad storm was brewing, but he just couldn't wait to get back to his love. He refused to hunker down and wait it out. He thought he'd take some shortcuts through the marshes to stay in front of the incoming storm, but turns out that wasn't such a good idea. Not a good idea at all. Oh, and some say he had one of his family's servants with him and my grandpappy said that particular servant was our kinfolk."

"So you're related to someone who knew the Gray Man back then?"

"In my grandpappy's account of the story, yes."

Walter's eyes grew even wider in amazement. "So what happened next?"

"Well, according to some, the servant begged the Gray Man to stay out of the marshes. He warned him that there was no way anybody could get through there, especially on horseback. But whether or not the servant was there, the Gray Man threw all caution to the wind and took to the marshlands anyway, and unfortunately, that decision is what did him in."

"I don't understand. What made the marshes so dangerous?"

"Well, ya see, the marshlands ain't all solid land or all just water. Most of 'em are a deadly mix of both. That makes for a thick mud that hides under different kinds of grasses that you can get stuck in way too easy. The more you struggle to get out, the deeper you go."

"So it's kind of like quicksand?" Walter tilted his head as he processed the story.

"I'd say that's a pretty good comparison. I recon in his hurry, he was just plain reckless and took his horse straight in there with him, but he never made it out. Then they say his fiancée found out about her lover man's demise and it tore her up so bad that she just walked the beach every day hoping to see him again."

"Wow, that's so sad."

"Yep, that's for sure. They say she just paced on the sand, back and forth every day. I guess she was just trying to heal her broken heart. To everyone's surprise, though, she did finally get to see him again sometime later, right there on that very stretch of the beach. Some say that in her excitement she ran up to him and tried to hug him, but her arms just went straight through his body."

"So he had turned into a ghost at that point?"

Amos shrugged. "Seems to be the case. It wasn't a joyous reunion for the love birds though, not by any means. The Gray Man was there to tell her that not only was a bad storm coming in, but a full-blown hurricane was on the way. He ordered her to take her family and livestock and leave the house immediately. Fortunately, she listened to his warning and when her family came back, everything around was absolutely destroyed except for her family's house. It was perfectly intact."

"How? Did he protect it or something?"

"Yes, sir. Nothing was even out of place while the rest of the area looked like a war zone."

"Geez, that's amazing. And no one knows what his name was?"

"Not in that account. Now, in one of the other stories, some folks claim he is a fellow by the name of Plowden Weston. I reckon Mr. Weston loved Pawley's Island so much that he even protects it after death. His old house was turned into The Pelican Inn."

"Really? The Pelican Inn? My grandparents' vacation house is pretty close to that place!"

"Oh yeah? It became known by that name sometime in the early nineteen hundreds. Old Mr. Weston really loved this place. He did a lot to keep it protected during the Battle Between the States. It makes a lot of sense that he could possibly be the Gray Man."

"Battle Between the States? Do you mean the Civil War?"

Amos nodded. "Yeah, that's it. Also known as the War of Northern Aggression. It's got different names depending on who you ask, but ol' Mr. Weston did what he could to protect this area, but he died from tuberculosis before the war ended."

"It sounds like it really could be him. When I saw him, it did look like he was wearing Civil War-style clothes. Is there anyone else you think it could have been?"

"Well, there's no telling for sure, but the last one that makes some folks' lists is that ol' scallywag pirate himself, Blackbeard."

"Blackbeard? No way!"

"Yep. They say he's cursed to protect the coast due to his savage way of life. It's his punishment for all the bloodshed and suffering he caused."

"Wow, that's interesting! Who do you think the Gray Man is?"

"Son, I don't really know. In some ways, I reckon it don't much matter to the living folks who he was. I'd say the lesson to be learned from the Gray Man is far more important."

"What lesson, Mr. Amos?" Walter eagerly awaited the answer.

"Even though we ain't sure who the Gray Man was back then, we do know for sure what he is now. At first glance, he's not much more than a harbinger. Just a warning that bad weather is coming. But when you use your ol' noggin, you can see that he's a prime example of why it's dangerous to let things consume you, whether it's love or anything else; a body has to stay levelheaded. He's an example of why you can't cause suffering, either. It just ain't right to go around hurting folks for your own personal gain or any other reason, for that matter. And last, I believe he's proof that if you take care of the things you love, especially people, they will be okay. A danged ol' hurricane can't even hurt 'em." Amos looked at Walter for a moment. "Does all my gibberish make any sense to ya, boy?"

Without any wavering, Walter answered, "Yes, sir!"

"Good. Now you'd better do like your big sister told ya and get yourself back home. Okay?"

Walter nodded and started walking toward his bike.

Amos took a few steps with him while patting his back. "Now don't you worry any. This ol' world can be scary at times and we don't always like what happens to us, but despite how bad things might seem, as long as you do the right thing, everything will be alright in the end."

Walter got on his bike and began buckling his helmet on. "How do I know if I'm doing the right thing?"

"Just listen to that voice in your head. It won't steer you wrong."

Walter nodded and began peddling his bike. After riding several feet, he looked back to give Amos a goodbye wave but his new friend was already gone.

CHAPTER EIGHT

Don't Cross the Boss

Jamar's tall, athletic body, along with his intimidating presence, kept his workers on edge, especially when they knew he was angry. After giving the unfortunate worker that dropped the dishes earlier a severe reprimanding, it was obvious that he was indeed very angry, so everyone made sure to stay out of his way at all costs. He cast a large intimidating shadow as he walked down the dimly lit hallway that led to his immaculate sports-themed office. Once inside, he called for his primary assistant to meet with him. Moments later, she was casually standing before his desk. "What can I do for you, sir?"

"Have a seat, Ms. Hoilman." He waved his left hand. "We've got some things to talk about."

"I don't understand. Is something wrong?" Anxiety was building in her chest. She always felt like she had to walk on eggshells around him, but it was so much worse when he was already visibly upset.

"It certainly isn't all right, that's for damn sure," he responded with growing aggression. He crossed his arms and leaned back in his chair. "Do you like working here?"

She placed her hand on her chest and slightly leaned forward. "I just don't understand what's going on here. Why are you asking me this?"

"Just answer the question, please. Do you like working here for me?"

Her mind raced wildly, and her face became flush. She knew she was in trouble from the tone of voice Jamar was using, along with the questions, but she wasn't sure of her offense. "I mean, if I had my choice, I'd be sitting by a pool in a fancy resort with a margarita in my hand, but since I'm not independently wealthy, I make do. I don't hate it here, if that's what you're asking." She pushed her heavily heighted blond hair behind her shoulders.

Jamar sat up and placed his elbows on his expensive wooden desk and stared at her for a few seconds, though it felt like an eternity. "You don't hate it here?"

Ms. Hoilman dropped her head then and raised her eyes to Jamar. "I didn't mean anything bad by that comment."

He continued to stare her down with his piercing light brown colored eyes. "You don't hate it here?"

She realized from past altercations that cowering down to him didn't always help when these hostile situations occurred. So she sat up tall in her chair and looked directly at him. "No, sir. I don't hate it here. I feel like I do my job with appropriate effort and I accomplish every task you send my way."

"But you don't hate it here." His tone was flat.

"I don't understand what I've done wrong. Can you just tell me so I'll be sure not to do it again?"

"It's not that you've necessarily done anything wrong, Sabrina."

"I'm certainly glad to hear that. What seems to be the problem, then?"

"I decided to check the cameras last night."

Ms. Hoilman's heart rate instantly rose. She knew she had been caught bringing Josh into her office. "What did you see?"

"I saw you bring a strange man into your office after hours."

You've gotta be freaking kidding me, she thought. *The one time I'm here after dark and that's when you finally decide to check the cameras!* Knowing that there was no denying that fact, she decided her best defense was to go on the offensive with him. "Why is that a problem, sir? I thought we had an agreement that as long as did my work for you, I pretty much had free rein around here."

"Yes, we do have that agreement, and I'm sure you're not foolish enough to let our private working arrangement out or discuss it with anyone. Are you?"

"Of course not. I'm not going to bite the hand that feeds. My entire career as a CPA was a complete waste until you brought me in on your little side endeavor. There's no need to worry, sir."

"It's not the man you brought in here that I'm necessarily worried about."

"Well, that's good. I can assure you there's nothing to be worried about with him."

"I didn't think so, but what does worry me is that not long after you entered the building with him, the camera feed went dead."

"Went dead, sir?"

"It was offline until about forty minutes before opening this morning."

"I don't understand why."

"I don't either. I was really hoping you would know something since you were here."

"No. I'm sorry about that. We were only in my office for about fifteen minutes or so then we left. Do you think the Wi-Fi could have gone out or something? It couldn't have been a power outage if they stopped working before we left."

"It's probably nothing to worry about. I did a sweep of the entire building and nothing was out of sorts, but I did have to ask you about it. I'm sure you understand, don't you?"

Ms. Hoilman gave the biggest fake smile she could muster up. "Of course. I'm sorry I wasn't any help."

"That's fine, Ms. Hoilman," he stated with warm reassurance before turning cold. "I have to be honest with you, that response of 'I don't hate it here.' That's what really worries me."

She had relaxed until that statement. She sat up and tried to explain herself. "Oh, please, Jamar, I didn't mean anyth—"

Jamar held his hands out in a rude fashion. "Save it. People's first response is always their most genuine. I find it very disturbing that I go out on a major limb for you and make you a very important part of my side business, and you don't even seem to care. You don't seem grateful for it at all."

"Sir, I assure you, that's not the case!"

Jamar completely ignored her response. "I have paid you a premium price for your skills for a couple of years now and I have no issues at all with doing that. You are very good at what you do. What I do have an issue with is your enthusiasm. You should consider yourself very fortunate to be in this position."

"I absolutely do! This is the most money I've made in my entire life! I'm very thankful for my job!"

"If you're so thankful for your handpicked position, then please act like it. If anyone asks if you like working here, I expect a little more than a sour comment of 'I don't hate it here.' I expect some freakin' loyalty!"

Anyone else would have been in complete shock from Jamar's sudden outburst but for Ms. Hoilman this was normal. She had found herself on the wrong side of his bad moods on a regular basis. Without any hesitation she clamored out, "Absolutely, sir!"

"I'm glad you understand. We've got one of the best golf courses in the entire state as well as one of the most successful restaurants in the area. We have to hold ourselves to a higher standard and need to be sure to give off the vibes that portray that we are indeed the best. My job here isn't just about my side gig. I'm fully committed to making this a world-renowned location and I expect everyone that works for me to have the same vision, especially the very one that I have let into my private business."

"You don't have anything to worry about, I assure you. I'm completely on board and I very clearly understand what is expected of me."

"I'm glad to hear it. You may go now."

Wasting no time, she got out of his chair and made a beeline for the door.

"Oh, if you don't mind, please keep your ear to the ground so we can figure out why the cameras were off."

"Yes, sir!" She entered the hallway. As she power-walked to her office, she immediately thought, *I'll keep your ear to the ground, you piece of crap. I'll put it in the ground with it still attached to your head! How dare you use your manipulating brainwashing tactics on me! I invented most of them myself!* She slammed the door to her office. "You're going to get yours, jackass, and soon!" After a couple of deep breaths and regaining her composure, she sat down in her chair and slowly leaned back into it. After getting comfortable, she whispered, "Freakin' soon."

CHAPTER NINE

Master Plan From a Bachelor's Mind

"Good Lord, that thing was full!" Tommy climbed into the passenger seat of the used but well-taken-care-of business vacuum truck. Josh hopped in behind the steering wheel of the mighty beast, slammed the door, and quickly jerked his seat belt on without saying a word. After firing up the medium blue colored machine, he put on his black, expensive-looking sunglasses and cranked the radio up so loud that it hurt Tommy's ears. Tommy shook his head in disgust. He wanted to call out Josh and tell him he was acting like a spoiled brat that didn't get what he wanted at Christmas, but he knew that would only make things worse.

After a few miles down the road, Tommy had had enough of the noise and the attitude, so he turned the radio down. "That's uncalled for. I know you're pissed, but ruining our hearing ain't gonna help anything."

"It don't hurt my ears. I guess you're too old," Josh remarked without any show of emotion.

Annoyed by the nugatory comment, Tommy rolled his eyes. "We'll if you weren't almost four years older than me, you might have a point."

"I might be older, but you're the one that acts like a damn old man."

"You think I act like an old man because I try to be professional?"

Josh ignored that statement and kept staring out the window as he drove.

"Look, man, I know you hate this job, but you mean to tell me there isn't the smallest part of you that feels good for helping that poor sweet ol' lady out? She was so appreciative of what we did that she even gave us a freshly baked peach cobbler. When's the last time you've had a cobbler? I know I haven't had one since Granny died."

Josh still sat quietly, ignoring every word from his cousin.

Tommy was becoming exceedingly frustrated and shouted, "Answer me, damn it!"

"No! I don't give a single rat's ass about that old bat," Josh screamed out, then he tugged at the seatbelt, trying to get it off his neck.

Tommy shook his head. He detested the impertinent reply. "I'm sorry you hate this job that bad. So bad you can't even take a little joy in helping someone out."

They both sat in silence for a few awkward moments

Tommy heavily sighed. "Look, I'd buy your part of the business out from you if I could. I don't like that you hate this, but there's nothing I can do."

"Yes, there is!" The passion was back in Josh's voice.

Tommy flung his head back against the seat's headrest and groaned. "Geez, man, please don't start this crap again."

"Three-hundred-K! If you help me get it from the golf course, I'll walk away."

Tommy leaned toward his cousin. "What do you mean you'll walk away?"

"If you help me get the money out of that safe, I'll take two hundred thousand of it and walk away. That's how you can buy me out. You'll have a hundred-K to buy your dad's car from that bitch stepmom that you, unfortunately, got stuck with and the world famous Porter Potties and Waste Water Management business will be all yours. Free and clear!"

Tommy had to be honest with himself. He desperately wanted his father's car and the thought of being the sole owner of the business was certainly more than just appealing to him. He cared for his cousin despite his ill-disposed disposition on life, but had grown beyond tired of his constant complaints and negative attitude. After a long look out the window, he broke the silence. "What would you do?"

"Me? I'd take my money and go to Vegas. Hands down."

Tommy shook his head in disapproval, then theorized a grim possibility of that scenario out loud. "You still want to go out there? You'd just lose all your money in those crooked casinos and come crawling back and guilt trip me into giving you your old job, and all that money would be long gone."

"Nope. You're wrong on that one, dude. I'd start a new life out there and a new business."

"Just what kind of business would you start? And why all the way out there?"

"I'm not sure yet. Maybe a private investigator, repo man, get my Uber certification, not exactly sure of those details, but something along those lines. As long as I'm self-employed, I'll be set."

Tommy flung his arms out. "Dude, you're self-employed now!"

"Yeah, but my new job won't be handling somebody else's fecal matter. Besides, I've had enough of this boring place. For this to be such a big vacation destination, it sure is dull. I want to be where the action is."

"There ain't nothing wrong with this place. It's a fine area to live in and even raise a family."

"That's just it, Tommy. I don't want a family. I don't want to be stuck taking care of a bunch of crumb busters and playing daddy. I love being a bachelor and I will always be one."

"Considering how this family has been, I can understand you being cautious about having a family of your own, but you don't even want a wife someday?"

"Hell no! Nobody to answer to but me, that's how it's always going to be."

Tommy reflected on his cousin's words. He was sad for Josh as well as disturbed by his selfishness.

"So whattaya say? You gonna help me? It's a win-win for both of us."

"I don't know, man. You kept saying you had a plan." With noticeable hesitation, Tommy asked anyway. "What is it?"

Josh pushed his sunglasses up on top of his head so that he could make solid eye contact with his cousin. "We'll wait 'til the hurricane's starting to make landfall. That's when we make our move. Most everyone will have evacuated by then so they'll be less people around to see us, if any at all."

Tommy slowly nodded in approval. "Okay, that makes sense, but what about the police? I'm sure there'll be still patrolling the streets, at least 'til the weather gets too bad. And what if they close the roads and what about security cameras? Some of them still work even if the power's out."

Josh chuckled. "This is where my genius plan really starts to shine. You know Old Man Hardee with the junkyard up on Tobacco Drive?"

"Yeah, what about him?"

"He's got an old, decommissioned ambulance and it's still in great shape. I figured that I'd buy it off him and we'll fix it up like it's an official medical hauler again. Nobody's ever gonna question an ambulance driving around. As for the cameras, I've ordered some signal blockers. If there are any cameras recording within a hundred feet, the signal will be jammed."

"Those don't sound legal."

"Don't worry, *Mom*, they are. I got three already." Josh pulled one out from under his seat. "I figured we'd leave one in the ambulance and we'd both keep one on us the whole time. They block out audio as well. We'll be completely undetected. Just like ghosts."

"That, uh, that's actually pretty badass." Tommy was in awe. He figured Josh's plan would be full of holes, but so far, he was genuinely impressed. "I got to admit, that sounds really damn clever, but what if Old Man Hardee doesn't sell you the ambulance? I've always heard that he can be hard to deal with. They say he's a real ball buster."

"Ah, I ain't worried about him. He'll sell it."

Just then, Tommy noticed Josh was about to miss the road up ahead. "Hey, you're going to miss the turn to the draining fields."

Josh shook his head. "No, I'm not; we're not emptying the truck just yet."

"Why not?"

"Chill. It's part of the plan."

Tommy shot Josh a look of confusion.

"Don't worry, it'll make sense soon."

"If you say so. Where the heck are we headed, then?"

"We're going to Salty's Pool and Pizza Plaza. I'm gonna find some naïve, out-of-town suckers and hustle them for the ambulance money. Well, some of it at least. Tourists always make the best marks."

Dissatisfied with Josh's pool scheme idea, Tommy let out a disapproving chuckle and shook his head. "I guess I could go for some good pizza. I ain't agreed to this plan of yours just yet, though."

"Sure ya have."

Tommy's eyebrows rose, and he shot his shady cousin a dirty look. "Oh yeah? Just how in the world do ya figure that?"

Josh pulled his sunglasses back down over his eyes. "Because you didn't call me crazy this time!"

CHAPTER TEN

Hit by Cupid's Probe

"Yes! We're finally here!" Walter exuded overbearing joy. "I've been looking forward to this ever since you said you'd bring me!"

"Yeah, yeah, settle down, nerd." Caroline pulled into a parking spot in front of Salty's Pool and Pizza Plaza, next to a blue vacuum truck.

"Sis, look out!"

Walter's attempt to warn his sister was futile, as a loud bang rang out from the hood of Caroline's car.

"Oh, my God! I didn't see him!" She put the car in park and jumped out to check on the hapless victim.

Josh rushed around the truck. "Tommy! You okay, man?"

Tommy was laying on the hood of the bright pink car in complete bewilderment. "What the heck just happened?"

Completely distraught, Caroline was now beside Tommy. "Are you okay? I'm so sorry! I didn't see you! The sun was blocking my vision. I had no idea you were standing there!"

"I believe that it's blinding me now!" Tommy tried to block the sun with his right arm as he slid off of the left fender of the older coup.

"Are you okay?" Caroline grabbed him by the shoulders, trying to assess his well-being as she looked him over. She couldn't help but notice her immediate attraction to him, despite her despair.

Still very confused by the impromptu and unforeseen incident, Tommy regained his footing and his eyes adjusted from the blinding sun to what he now perceived as a dark-haired angel standing before him. "Oh, hello." He felt his heart rate spike. Then his phone dropped to the pavement without warning. "Oh, looks like my cell phone holder broke."

"Oh, I'm so sorry. I'll buy you a new one. I promise."

Josh had noticed some guys playing on the billiard tables right before Caroline struck Tommy, and he could tell from the smile on his face that he wasn't injured at all. The cousins had hurt each other far worse, playing in the yard as kids. "If you're good, Tommy, I'm gonna head on in. I see some fruit ripe for the picking." Josh impatiently waited for an answer.

Tommy couldn't peel his eyes off Caroline. "Yeah, I'm good. Go pluck your fruit."

"K. Be more careful next time, miss," Josh said in a rude tone. "Fortunately, this ended up not being a big deal, but you could have really hurt my cousin there."

Still gazing into the brown eyes of his accidental offender, Tommy said, "Chill out, Josh. She didn't mean to, and I'm completely fine."

Seemingly angered by Tommy's defense of Caroline, Josh stormed inside without saying another word.

Still in shock from the accident and seeing Josh walking away in anger significantly concerned Walter for Caroline's sake. "Please don't call the cops on my sister, mister!"

Finally breaking the gaze with the lovely young lady, Tommy looked over at Walter for a second on the other side of the car and smiled. "Don't worry, kid, she didn't hurt me. No need for the cops to get involved." Then he looked at Caroline with a big smile.

"Are you sure?" Caroline got close to his face and purposely gazed deeply into Tommy's greenish-hazel-colored eyes, trying to assure that his health was fully intact.

Tommy responded with a light chuckle, trying to ease Caroline's worries. "I'm good, I swear!"

Finally convinced that she hadn't seriously injured Tommy, she slowly relinquished her hold on his shoulders, even though she didn't really want to. "I can't apologize enough." Then she picked up his phone and carefully handed it to him.

"It's absolutely fine, I promise." Tommy attempted to calm Caroline, then looked down at the noticeable dent he left in the hood. "Besides, you might have to call the cops on me. I've destroyed your poor hood."

"You can't hurt this old thing. It was my grandma's old car. Her and my grandpa had several. They used this one to leave parked at airports and loan out to family and friends. And other stuff like that."

"Is it a Ford Taurus?"

"Close, it's a ninety-seven Probe. Grandpa had it custom-painted Grandma's favorite color."

"Ah, yes, a Probe. At least it ain't brown. I'd hate to tell anyone I got hit by a brown Probe."

Caroline just looked at Tommy, a bit confused by that statement.

"Oh, there's an old joke about a proctologist that drives a brown Probe around. Sorry."

"Oh, no, that's fine. My nerves are just still shot from hitting you." Caroline took in a deep breath.

Tommy smiled, trying to reassure her. "I'm good. My belt clip cell phone holder took the brunt of the hit." He chuckled.

"Actually, I think I know where I can get you a new one... wait, I do." She looked at her brother. "Go on in and get us a table, Walter."

"Wait, what?" Walter was happy that his sister would not be in trouble for hitting Tommy, but he was ready to fully process his story from seeing the Gray Man earlier. Now it felt like he was being blown off even though he had talked about the elusive encounter nonstop on the drive up to Myrtle Beach.

"Go ahead and get a table and order the pizzas. And get me a Cheerwine, please."

Astounded by her drink choice, Tommy looked at Caroline. "Hey, Cheerwine is my favorite drink!"

"Really? Mine, too!" Caroline looked surprised. "It's got the richest cherry flavor of any cherry soda I've ever had. It has been my favorite ever since my grandparents brought me some back from here when I was a kid."

"That's so cool! And I love that bite it has on the way down, it's so refreshing!" Then he looked at Walter and said, "You better listen to your sister, kid. She hit a stranger with a car, no telling what she might do to you if you don't obey." Tommy chuckled and grinned.

Walter wasn't amused, though. "I can't believe this! I've waited all day to be here and now you're blowing me off!"

"We're just going down here to the Gay Dolphin right quick so I can buy—Tommy, is it?"

"Yes, I'm Tommy. I didn't catch your name."

"I'm Caroline and this is my brother, Walter." She looked at her sibling. "I'm going to buy Tommy a new phone holder. I'll be right back."

"That's not necessary. It's fine. That thing was ancient."

"No, I insist. I'm almost certain I've seen them in there before. That place has everything." Caroline looked back at Walter. "We'll probably be back before the pizza even comes out."

Tommy felt bad for Walter, but he wasn't disappointed with her plan. He was immediately smitten with her and was quite excited about taking a walk with his lovely new acquaintance. In an attempt to make everyone happy, he said, "Tell ya what, kid. Do what your sister asked and I'll play you a few rounds of air hockey, completely on me. What do ya say? I gotta warn ya, though, I'm really good and I always play for keeps."

Walter shook his head in disapproval. "Fine. I'm not waiting on you, though. When the food comes out, I'm eating without you. I'm starving!"

"That's fine. Oh, and don't forget the Cheerwine!" She and Tommy headed down the sidewalk.

"This really isn't necessary." Tommy slid his hands into his pockets and began slowly walking.

"Yes, I insist." Caroline looked back to ensure that Walter had walked into Salty's. "I still can't believe I hit you with my car. I'm always being super careful and just plowed right over you."

"The time of year has a lot to do with it. In the fall the sun's on the move, casting dark shadows in some places then blinding the heck out of you in others."

"That makes sense, I guess. So are you from around here?"

"Yeah, I grew up about forty minutes inland. You're from Maryland, I take it?"

Caroline looked down at her jersey. "Yeah. I spend a great deal of time in South Carolina, though. My family always spends our vacations here, a lot of holidays, too. I'm currently living in my grandparents' old summer home on Pawley's Island. My mom sent my brother down to stay with me while she tries to nurse my father back to health. It's starting to seem like a lost cause, though, unfortunately."

"Sorry to hear that. What's going on with your dad?" Tommy's concern was genuine.

"Well, a couple of things actually, but most recently, he had a stroke. He isn't doing well at all. Mom didn't want Walter to see him in that shape. He can't talk at all and needs constant care. I'm bracing myself for the call to come in at any moment that he's passed on."

"Gah, that's awful. I'm so sorry. Does Walter realize how bad he is? Is he taking this okay?"

"No, I don't think he realizes how bad dad is, but he likes it here at least. I wish he had some friends that lived close by, but he's a loner. He's always been homeschooled, which he loves, and he keeps to himself."

"Sounds like me as a kid. I hated school with a passion. I lost my dad a little bit ago." Tommy shook his head in disbelief when it dawned on him how long ago he had died. "Geez, I can't believe it's been almost two years already!"

"Oh, I'm sorry." Caroline gave Tommy's arm a light touch.

"It's fine. We didn't have that great of a relationship. His bitch wife made sure of that."

Caroline shot him a surprised look.

"Sorry, that's not very nice of me."

"No, you're fine. I'm sorry to hear that you got stuck with a bad step-parent. I can't imagine having to deal with that."

"Wait a minute." Tommy stopped in his tracks and gazed ahead.

"What's wrong?"

"Speak of the devil and she'll appear, I guess."

CHAPTER ELEVEN

Pool Shark Sighting

"Excuse me, Miss," Walter was being very timid as he spoke to a young waitress. "I'd like to place an order."

"Where's your parents, champ?"

Caught off guard by that question, Walter answered back in a flat tone, "Back in Maryland."

The waitress was rude as she replied, "You can't place an order here without an adult present."

"My big sister will be here in a few minutes and she wanted me to go ahead and put an order in for us."

"Oh, no you don't! You kids aren't pulling that trick around here anymore!"

"I don't understand. We just want to order a pizza. There's no trick."

"All sorts of kids about your age have been coming in here and placing orders, then playing the games and after they are done, they've been slipping out without paying for the food. My boss gave me explicit orders to not take food orders from kids anymore. If your sister wants food, then she will have to order it herself."

"Geez, okay." Walter walked over to the arcade area. It was a grand spectacle with all kinds of amazing machines, bright lights, and endless sounds. Over in the back corner, he saw Josh playing pool with some younger guys. Just then he sank the eight ball. Walter got positioned to where he could watch without being noticed.

"Wow, I can't believe I just made that! Sorry, man, I guess that was a lucky shot." Josh flashed a disingenuous grin.

"My ass. You're a stone-cold hustler, and you know it." One of the younger guys squawked out.

"Well then, let's cut the crap and play for some serious cash. If you've got the nerves to, that is," Josh said with a menacing look. "Five hundred per game. Or do you want to go back up north and tell the rest of your friends you chickened out to a stupid southern boy?"

"I ain't got that kind of money. I'm out. Why don't you take him on, Aiden?"

"I don't know, homie, that's some serious cash."

Josh chimed in, "Yes, it is serious cash. Why mess around with chump change? It ain't any fun if the stakes ain't high."

Another guy from the group stepped forward. "I'm not afraid. I live for high stakes. Go ahead and rack 'em, bitch."

"Uh no. I don't know how y'all do it back in New England, but the loser racks 'em here." Josh smirked as he carefully chalked his cue.

His first opponent begrudgingly placed all the balls back on the table and got them all into the plastic triangle. They were now ready for the next game to begin. "Well, where I'm from, the loser also breaks the next round. I know I've not lost to you yet, but since my friend had to rack the balls, I think I should break."

"That's fine. Be my guest."

The next young opponent was noticeably livid from the way Josh was subtly talking down to them and he was determined to beat Josh. He turned his dark blue navy Yankees hat backward and began grinding the cue tip of the stick into the small square chalk with great force. "I'm warmed up now. You better watch out!"

Josh was amused at his intimidation tactics. He had to hold back laughter as he thought, *Just by the way you chalk your cue shows what little you actually know. There's chalk all over the ferrule and everywhere else, for that matter."*

His opponent aimed and struck the cue ball as hard as he could, but to his dismay, very few of them even moved. He let out some explicit phrases as he walked to the table that held his drink. Josh carefully examined the pool table as he now circled it like a vulture eyeing up his prey. He was taking his sweet time, and this appeared to agitate his opponent and his friends even more. One bystander finally said, "Hurry it up already!"

Josh completely ignored the comment as he continued to study the table. After a few more seconds, he finally aimed when his opponent demanded, "Shoot now!"

"Look, that was technically an illegal break. I have the option of re-racking if I want. I'm trying to be a good sport, though, and play on through this mess you made."

"Illegal break? What are you talking about, homes?"

"If the breaker doesn't pocket a ball and fails to drive at least four balls to one or more rails, then it is considered an illegal break. In that case, I have the option to re-rack and trust me, you don't want that."

"That's a load of crap!" cried out one bystander.

Josh shot him a nasty look. "Are you calling me a liar?" Then he approached him with frightening speed. The bystander's face grew pale, and he became as quiet as a church mouse as Josh got in his face. "So now you don't have anything to say? I don't know what kind of billiards you ball bangers are used to playing, but we play by the official rules around here!"

The bystander dropped his head and looked down while slowly turning away from Josh. He mumbled, "My bad."

"That's what I thought." Josh went back to the table and wasted no time taking his shot. He sank the solid blue number two ball, but the eight ball fell in the opposite corner. "Damn it!"

"That's all right, homes. We're here to play," his opponent said with a snarky grin. "Let's go again…after you rack 'em, that is."

Josh was holding back a smile of his own as he thought, *That's right, boys, let that confidence flow. Y'all are making this way too easy! It's gonna be like buttering a biscuit with half-melted butter.* Two games later, Josh was up two games to his opponent's one. After intentionally throwing the first game, Josh narrowly won the next two with some supposed lucky shots. "Sorry, boys. I consider myself to be a damn good pool player but I'm even shocked that I pulled that off. I can't blame you for being mad."

"Well then, let's go again. Double or nothing," his opponent exclaimed. "Let's just see when that luck of yours runs out."

Josh put on an air of coyness. "Nah, don't even bother with me. I'm not worth your time. I could tell after the second game that you are actually a better player than me. I'm just going to quit while I'm ahead!"

"Nah, it ain't gonna be like that. You're gonna prove how good you are at least one more time."

"Are you threatening me?" Josh gazed at his opponent and all of his entourage.

"You can call it whatever you want, but we're playing again!"

Josh took a few steps toward his foe. "You look here. You and your boys ain't ever really had a bad day until you've crossed paths with me! If you really want to play a game, then we'll play! We're going to play for three grand!"

In that instant, his opponent's rage left his body, replaced with shock. "No, homes, I ain't okay with that. Three Gs on a game of pool? No way!"

"You're gonna throw down the gauntlet and call me out only to back out when I add in my stipulations? You big city fellas just don't know nothing, do ya?"

"Just what is it that you think we don't know?"

"Well, you obviously don't know how calling someone out works. If you make a declaration against somebody, then you have to be ready for everything that goes along with it! If you can't abide by them rules, then that makes you lower than a dog."

"The only dog I see is the bitch standing in front of me!"

"I'll tell ya what. If you can beat me, then I'll say that. Right to you and all your boy's faces, I'll say I'm a bitch!"

"Is that a fact?"

"Yep. As long as you're playing for three grand." The two gave each other a long stare. "Come on, man, let's do this! Let's make it interesting. So what if ya lose? You can always hang your hat off the fact that you didn't back down. Look at it this way; even if you were to lose, you still actually win. Imagine the respect you'll get when you get back home and your pals here tell everybody how they watched you play a game of pool in Myrtle Beach with three grand on the line. That's how legends are made."

His opponent stood silent for several seconds, as if in deep thought. "Fine, I'm in on three grand, but I'll have a few conditions of my own."

"Okay, let's hear them."

"With three grand on the line, you best be for sure calling yourself a bitch when you lose and you are racking the balls."

Josh gave him a slight smile along with a head nod. "You got it chief!"

CHAPTER TWELVE

Beware of the Evil Succubus

"Tommy, is that you?" A woman wearing minimal clothing, of middle age, inquired as she walked across the street. She awkwardly stumbled up in absurd high heels with a very spurious smile. Caroline was taken aback by her caked-on makeup, overly bleached hair, and revealing tank top with cutoff blue jeans.

She's way too old to be dressed like that! Caroline thought. *Then again, I'm not sure anyone should ever dress like that.*

Tommy wanted to just berate her with insults, but he kept his composure in front of Caroline. "Hello, Inez. How many times am I going to have to see you today?" he said in a low voice, with obvious insincerity.

"Who's your girlfriend here? She's a cutie. You all look good together." Inez was trying to be cool in front of Caroline, but it wasn't coming off that way.

"She's not my—this is my new friend Caroline," Tommy said with hesitation, not wanting to rule out the idea of her possibly becoming his girlfriend.

"Hello, Caroline. That's a pretty name. I'm Inez. I'm Tommy's stepmom." She reached out to shake her hand.

"Not anymore," Tommy cracked out before he even realized he said it.

"Now don't be like that, Tommy. Your father would have wanted us to get along."

"My father would have also wanted me to have his car. He wouldn't have wanted it sold off to some stranger just so your lazy rear end wouldn't have to work."

"Now don't start this again, Tommy. Your father left behind some hefty bills. He made it clear that he wanted me taken care of and—"

"I'd seen him tell you myself that if something were to happen to him, I was to get the Woody. I know that doesn't mean anything now because you've made it damn clear that you didn't give a crap about his wishes."

"I know he said that the one time, but later on he changed his mind. He felt bad for all the debt he had accrued and told me to do what I had to. I feel horrible about all this but there's nothing I can do now. I was on the hook for a lot of that debt. I held off on selling his car as long as I could."

"How much would you sell it to me for?"

Inez looked down and slowly shook her head. "I know it's a lot, but I can't take less than one hundred thousand for it. You were there when the man from that car auction place was. You heard what he had to say."

"He said that was a possibility, not a guarantee! Even if it did bring a hundred thousand at auction, you'd only be getting a percentage of that. There're all kinds of fees and taxes and countless other charges. You wouldn't be getting nowhere near that much after all that is taken out."

"That's where you're wrong. The auction guy's boss called back after you left and said he'd be glad to buy it for that much. He said he wanted it for his own personal collection."

Tommy flung his head back and took a deep breath. He was really trying not to have a meltdown in front of Caroline. "When is he coming to get it?"

"The guy that was there working for him said that he couldn't come and pick it up until the first of November. Something about some prior arrangements his boss already had and he couldn't come before then."

"If I bring you the money before he does, you better not raise the price or back out!"

"Where are you going to get that much money, Tommy?"

"Don't you worry about it. I'll see you soon." He walked across the street.

"Nice to meet you, Caroline." Inez watched her follow Tommy.

"You, too." She gave a very subtle and awkward wave.

Now safely across the street, Tommy looked at Caroline. "Sorry you had to see that. I thought Halloween was still a few weeks away."

Caroline let out a slight chuckle but immediately caught herself. "It's no problem."

"Yeah, it is. It's embarrassing. I'm ashamed to even know someone like that, much less formally be related by marriage."

"That's not your fault, Tommy. You can vent about her with me. I'm a good listener."

"Careful what you ask for!" Tommy said with a charming smirk.

"I can handle it, I swear!"

"Okay then, here goes nothing." He smiled. "That sorry bitch took my dad from me and now she's gonna profit off his car that he wanted me to have. I helped him build the most amazing Chevy Woody in the entire country. I know that probably sounds arrogant, but it is the truth. Some of the best days I ever had were with Dad in that car right here on Ocean Boulevard. That all ended once she came into the picture."

"Not to be nosy, but how did she manage to end that?"

"She didn't like sharing my dad with me, so she kept manipulating the situation until he sent me to live with my grandma. She didn't stop until she got what she wanted."

"What? That's crazy. How did she manage to make that happen?"

"Straight-up lies. She'd do stuff like steal money out of his wallet or make sure things went missing and I always got the blame, of course."

"I just don't get it. Why didn't she want you around?"

"Because I could see that she was an evil bitch. She's one of those lady demon things. Ah shoot, I can't remember the word."

"Succubus?"

"Yeah, that's it! She's a succubus, and she knew that I knew that she was one, so that meant that I had to go."

"Wow, I'm really sorry. You should do whatever it takes to get your dad's car."

"Do you really think so?"

"Absolutely! That's not right for her to do you that way. It's disgusting for her to sell it out from under you like that. Wow, that bitch really is heartless. Where's your real mom, if you don't mind me asking, that is?"

"Your guess is as good as mine. She took off before I got to know her. It was just me and Dad for a long time and we had a blast 'til Inez showed up. Curse the day that wicked witch of the south stuck her meat hooks in my dad. I guess it's somewhat of a blessing in disguise. I got close to my great-uncle Floyd. He was a fantastic human being. He lived with Granny as well and ended up leaving his business to Josh and me when he passed. I don't know where I'd be or what I'd be doing right now if it wasn't for ol' Uncle Floyd."

"Oh, that's so sad, but so sweet of your uncle to do that. Is that the business on your shirt? Does that say Porter Potties?"

"Yeah, he named it that after his dad, Porter. He had died a real long time ago. I never got to meet him. But now I get to wear his name on my shirt. I'm sure he would have been beyond flattered to have a wastewater company named after him." Tommy chuckled.

"Not to pry or anything, but what's up with your cousin Josh? He's not cool like you. He seems a little uptight."

"Wait, did you just say I'm cool?" Tommy asked with a sneaky grin.

"Well, so far so good, I guess." She looked at him out of the corner of her eye.

He was pleased with her response. "Oh man, I don't even know where to start with Josh. That dude is a long, complicated story that we definitely don't have time to get into right now." Tommy then pulled open the door to the Gay Dolphin and gestured for Caroline to go in with his left arm. "Here we are."

Time felt as if it stood still for the two as they spent the next fifteen minutes or so looking at all the countless items the tremendously stocked store had to offer. They tried on funny hats with outlandish hair; sword fought with some pirate toys and talked about which high-end pieces of art and other furnishings they thought would look best in a dream beach house. They eventually found the cell phone holder and after purchasing it, they began walking back to Salty's. They had almost reached the halfway point and Tommy was seconds away from asking Caroline out on a date when Walter unexpectedly came running up to them.

"What's going on, Walter? Why aren't you with the pizzas?" Caroline looked confused.

"They wouldn't let me order," Walter belted out between breaths.

"What?"

"That's not why I'm here." He gasped, then he looked at Tommy. "That dude you're here with is in a fight!"

"What!" Tommy tremendously tensed up.

"He's in a fight with several guys."

"Just great!" Tommy mumbled as they all ran toward Salty's.

CHAPTER THIRTEEN

Unfair Advantage

"I swear to goodness, that idiot is going to be the death of me!" Tommy uttered out between breaths as he and his new friends ran as fast as they could.

"He was actually kicking their asses pretty good, especially considering he was way outnumbered, and then I heard one of them tell another one to go get Ty and the gang. That's when I figured he was going to need some help," Walter explained as best he could while taking in quick breaths.

Just as the trio almost reached the front door, they saw Josh pulling a younger guy out of the main entrance forcibly by his ear. Before they fully realized what was happening, he was slamming his opponent onto the sidewalk just in front of Caroline's neon pink Probe. "Where's my money?" The guy tried to get up off the ground. Then Josh punched him in the face, almost knocking him out. He reached into the guy's back pocket and grabbed his wallet. After pulling the cash out of it, he dropped the now empty piece of leather into the poor chump's face. "You don't make a bet you can't back up!" He placed two hard kicks to the guy's stomach.

"That's enough, Josh! It's time to get the hell outta here!" Tommy instructed, as they came to a stop right in front of the fight. Just then screeching tires rang out as a car full of young guys was quickly approaching the Probe.

Josh was calmly walking to the back of the vacuum truck as he yelled to Tommy, "Get the truck started!"

Tommy had a look of concern come across his face as he glanced at Caroline and Walter, then he shouted, "Get the hell outta here!"

"Wait, how can I contact you? Will I ever see you again?" Caroline asked as she was getting ready to open the car door.

"Porter Potties on Facebook! Message me there! Now get in your car and get ready to roll!" Tommy climbed in the truck and it fired to life as Caroline and Walter got into their car.

The small silver compact full of the pool player's friends had finally come to a complete stop just behind the Probe and everyone inside was now climbing out and running toward Josh. To their surprise, though, he had grabbed the vacuum hose and calmly pulled the lever back, which immediately caused it to spray out the contents of the septic tank they had just emptied earlier in the day. The raw sewage shot straight out of the hose onto the would-be combatants. Josh spread his legs, taking a wide stance, and screamed, "Say hello to my stinky friend!" Then he laughed uncontrollably in a sadistic manner as the guys screamed out in terror and instantly fled from the putrid human waste. Most of them just ran away as far as they could while the driver of the car made it back inside and fled. Josh continued to spray his car. It was now a disgusting shade of brown. Once it was out of range, he shut the hose off and dashed for the cab of the truck.

Walter yelled out, "That guy's nuts!" as Caroline and he watched the inconceivable skirmish from inside the Probe.

Tommy got the vacuum truck pulled out onto the road and fled the scene as he looked into the rearview mirror and saw Caroline and Walter driving off in the opposite direction, while Josh uncontrollably laughed from the passenger's seat. "What the hell was that?"

"Hilarious is what that was!" Josh continued to laugh like a madman.

"That was real smart, jackass! The cops will probably be waiting for us at the house!"

Josh's laughter finally waned. "No, they won't! I had the camera jammers going the entire time!"

"How do you know they worked?"

"Because I checked the security cameras at Salty's. You can see into the back room where they are on the way to the restrooms and they were showing nothing but pure static.

"I guess at least there's some good news. That whole stunt was still uncalled for, though!"

"That was a perfect test! Now we know that the camera jammers work for sure and I got over a thousand bucks to add toward the ambulance fund."

"Is that why we didn't go to the draining fields earlier? Just so you could violate some punk tourists?"

"No, that's a different part of the plan, but I sure am glad we didn't go to the draining fields yet. That shit sure came in handy, for once!" Then he continued with his maniacal laughter.

Tommy now sat in silence. He was thinking about Caroline and hoped that she didn't hate his guts for being related to a psychopath. He had enjoyed every second with her and was certainly going to ask her out until Josh's stunt cut the conversation short. *Man, I could be eating pizza and drinking Cheerwine with a beautiful girl right now if it wasn't for this idiot. I gotta get away from him!*

Back in the Probe, Walter was complaining about missing out on his favorite pizza. "I can't believe this. Why did we have to leave just because that crazy dude got in a fight?"

"Trust me, you didn't want to be there if the cops showed up. Besides, we couldn't hang around with those guys there. They saw us talking to Tommy. They might have come after us just for associating with them. I'm really sorry, squirt. I know this isn't fair.

I know I promised you your favorite pizza. We'll get it another time. I absolutely promise you that we will." Just then, her phone started ringing. "Great, it's Mom. If you don't tell her about any of this, we'll go straight to McDonald's and you can get anything you want. Deal?"

"Fine," Walter responded with a head shake of disapproval. "Hello, Mom?"

"Hey. Are you driving? Yes, but don't worry, it's on speaker. Walt is with me and we are headed out to grab a bite."

"I just saw on the news that the hurricane is expected to hit there in a few days. We need to figure out what to do."

"I'd really like to see Dad," Walter said. "Maybe we can come home for a few days while the hurricane's here?"

"I don't think that's a good idea."

"Why not, Mom?"

"Because your father isn't doing well at all."

"I don't care! I want to see him!" Walter shouted to his mother.

"I'm sorry, sweetheart, but he wouldn't want you to see him like he is in his current condition."

"Is he ever going to be better? I'm tired of this!"

"We all are, sweetheart. Listen, I want you two to stay as long as you're able to safely be there. Enjoy yourselves while you can," she said in a noticeably ominous tone.

Without hesitation, Caroline asked, "While we can? What do you mean, Mom?"

"Oh, I hate talking about this! You see, ever since your father's stroke, we have kept falling further and further behind on bills, so much so that the insurance has lapsed on the beach house."

"What? Why didn't you tell me? I could have been making payments towards it!"

"You've barely been able to keep gas in the car and your cell phone bill paid."

"Wow, thanks, Mom."

"That's not an insult, Caroline. You've done so well and I'm so proud of you! You're an excellent daughter and you've been a terrific big sister to Walter! I just want you two to enjoy yourselves. Life hasn't been very nice to us lately and I'm very sorry for that. We need a plan for the hurricane, though, and you need to know that if the house gets tore up, I'm not so sure we'll be able to fix it."

"No, I won't let that happen. We'll figure something out," Caroline declared with great passion.

Their mom let out a small laugh. "I love that fighting spirit of yours. Do you have some friends you can hunker down with, somewhere to ride the storm out? It's certainly not safe enough to stay in the house with it being right there on the beach. We'll definitely bring you home if we absolutely need to, but I promise you both, you're not missing anything here."

"Don't worry, Mom. I've got some ideas. We'll be fine."

The trio talked for a few more minutes until they got to the drive-thru.

Now that their mother wasn't on the phone, Walter looked over at Caroline. "What are we going to do? What are your ideas about riding out this storm that's coming in?"

Caroline glanced back at Walter and shrugged. "I only said that to pacify Mom. I have no clue."

Back at Tommy and Josh's place, the vacuum truck's brakes let out a slight squeak as Tommy brought it to a halt.

"Don't turn it off yet?"

Tommy shot him a look. "Why? What are you going to do?"

"I'm actively working on our plan to be financially free. Why don't you go call your new girlfriend?"

"I'd happily do that if I'd been able to get her number!" Tommy said in an exasperated tone as he climbed out of the truck.

"Just look her up on Facebook!" Josh slid into the driver's seat. "And don't wait up!"

"Don't worry, jackass," Tommy mumbled as he walked to the front door of the house.

CHAPTER FOURTEEN

Storm's a Brewing

Tommy looked at his alarm clock and saw that it was 3:22 a.m. He grabbed his phone to see if he had any notifications. He deeply wanted to hear from Caroline, but to his dismay, he had zero. Taking a deep breath, he tried to push away the sense of disappointment as he stumbled out of the bed and moved toward the bathroom. He noticed the faded yellow glow of the kitchen light shining out in the corner of his eye. *What's up with that?* He entered the overly dated scullery of his grandmother's old place. Josh stayed up late but it was rare for him to leave his room after midnight when he was actually home. When his vision adapted, he noticed from his side view that the lid of the bin was on incorrectly. Finding that odd, he picked it up and discovered Josh's clothes from the previous day were stuffed inside. *That's weird. What the hell did that dumbass do now?* He put the lid back on in its proper position. *Why would he throw out his clothes? It was nothing short of a miracle that he didn't get any waste on him while violating those pool punks.* He shook his head in confusion. "Whatever." He closed the door and headed back to back to the bathroom before returning to his bed.

Not long after sunrise, a somewhat familiar but very odd face shook Tommy awake. Once he came to enough, he let out a quick shout and flinched.

"Relax, dingleberry, it's just me!"

"What did—did you seriously shave your head?" Tommy looked at him with genuine puzzlement.

"Yep, and you're next, buttercup!"

"The hell I am. Why on earth did you cut all your hair off? What the heck is wrong with you?"

"We're getting ready to pull off a major heist and we need every little advantage we can get!"

Tommy's face wrinkled up. "How in the world is having a shaved head going to give us an advantage? Don't tell me it helps with aerodynamics."

Completely ignoring his cousin's wisecrack, Josh exclaimed, "It adds to our disguises, Einstein! We need to stay unrecognizable at all costs just in case things go south or we were to end up in a picture or video."

"Wait a minute. I thought you said this was a foolproof plan. Isn't this like planning for failure?"

"First off, I never said it was foolproof. Second, any great plan requires contingencies for any possible situation. Trust me; I have this thing covered from every aspect. Now get your lazy butt up. We got to do yours before we start on the ambulance."

"Ambulance? You got it already?" Tommy threw the sheets back and sat up on the edge of his bed.

"Already? We should have been done with it before now! The hurricane should be here in about four days and we have a ton of crap to get done before then. Now come on, let's shave your head, princess."

"You are not shaving my head! Besides, wouldn't it look suspicious if we were both bald, and what about our faces?"

After a few seconds of awkward silence Josh explained in an unconvincing manner, "Uh, I wasn't actually going to shave yours all the way off. I was just going to give you a buzz cut, so it's at least different than what you have now."

Tommy felt as if Josh had changed his plan when he pointed out the flaws in them both being bald. Then his mind went to Caroline. He wasn't sure if he'd ever see her again, but he wasn't going to let Josh ruin his hair just in case. He wanted to look his best for her if their paths were to cross. "I see where you're coming from, but you are not cutting my hair and you're for damn sure not shaving it. What if we use something like one of those Halloween spray colors? Something I can wash out later, at least."

Josh shrugged. "I guess that would work. We can pick something up when we go for supplies. We need to get a lot of things; as for our faces, we'll be wearing medical masks."

"Why would we be wearing them? What's the reason?"

"Don't worry, man, I got it figured out! Now come on, we've got to get busy!"

Tommy rolled his eyes and felt his neck tense up. *Man, I hope this ain't a mistake.*

A good while later, the duo returned from their supply run. Josh went to the bathroom while Tommy went to check out the ambulance securely tucked away in the shop they used for their business. To Tommy's surprise, the smell of bleach overwhelmed him the second he opened the door and he could see that Josh had thoroughly washed the big machine.

"Good gravy. How much bleach did he use?" he mumbled before opening the driver's door. Once he was inside, he started flipping the switches for the lights and sirens, but they didn't work because the engine was off. He looked at the ignition to check for the key, but it wasn't there. *I guess Josh has it.* He slipped into the back and was instantly amazed at how clean everything was. It was all still very damp as well from the apparent scrubbing it had received last night. After giving everything what he thought was a pretty good look over and the fact that he could no longer stand the near breathtaking smell of the strong disinfectant, he open the back door and hopped out. Josh was standing there in an odd manner. "Holy crap, man, you scared me to death. Why the heck are you just standing there like that?"

In a near-emotionless tone, Josh responded, "I was just letting you check this ol' beast out. Pretty sweet, ain't it?"

"Yeah, it's badass. Do you think you used enough bleach on it though? And why the hell did you do all this last night?"

"I couldn't sleep after picking it up, so I figured I'd make good use of my time."

"That makes sense, but why all the bleach?"

"Ah, that damned Old Man Hardee had been using this thing to transport butchered cows. It was full of blood in the back and stunk to high heaven."

"Really? That's nuts. Did he give you a hard time about selling it? What did you give for it?

Josh responded in an unemotional manner. He seemed irritated. "He didn't want to sell it at first, but when I showed him three thousand dollars in cash, he about took my arm off with it."

"Wow, you got this thing for only three grand? Considering how good of shape it's in, it looks like it's probably worth at least ten!"

"Yeah, I was surprised he went for that offer, too."

"For real! You just can't pick up a Chevy Express ambulance just anywhere. I can't believe he was using it to haul meat." Then Tommy cracked a grin. "Old Man Hardee was using a meat wagon to haul meat. Go figure!"

"Yeah, go figure," Josh said just above a whisper.

"You sure got it clean, considering that fact? All the bleach makes sense now. How many bottles did you use on it?"

"Uh, I don't really know for sure. It was enough, though. Come on, man, we can chat later. We still have a ton of work to do."

"Yeah, sure thing." Tommy was caught off guard by Josh's sudden aggravation. He was always moody, but Tommy could tell something was definitely off with his older cousin.

CHAPTER FIFTEEN

Batten Down the Hatches

Back at Caroline and Walter's grandparents' house, the two siblings were busy preparing the old holiday haven for the wicked incoming weather.

"After you get the patio chairs put away, I need you to go ahead and get the hurricane shutters closed, too," Caroline instructed Walter while she changed the batteries in their emergency flashlights.

"I'm not sure I can reach the upper ones. Even with the ladder, I think it's a little too short. We might have to ask someone for help."

"Just who would that be? There's no one around to help. We'll just have to figure something out on our own."

"What about that dude, Tommy? I bet he wouldn't mind coming over."

"I'm sure he's got better things to do."

"Maybe not. Did you ever try to message him? He said you could find him online."

"No, Walter. I'm not going to either."

He shot her a bewildered look. "Why not? He seemed like a really awesome guy."

"He did, but please, just let it go."

"I don't understand this at all. You really seemed to like him."

"I hit him with my car, Walter. I was just being nice to him so he wouldn't sue me."

He shot her another look of confusion. "If you didn't like him, then why did you talk on the phone to Susan about him for nearly an hour when we got home that night?"

"Just drop it, Walter!"

"Mom's right, you know. She said you need to work on your confidence. Tommy for sure liked you, too, or he wouldn't have been so cool about you hitting him with a car."

"Oh, so you two are physiological experts all of a sudden?" She responded with an easily detectable dissatisfaction with that comment. "Whatever. Let's just finish getting the house prepped."

"Why are we already doing this? The hurricane isn't supposed to hit for another three or four days."

"Please don't argue with me, Walter! We've got to protect this place the best we can. It doesn't have insurance anymore, so if something happens to it, we're screwed. They are already evacuating like crazy. Interstate 26 has traffic going out both ways, a state of emergency has been declared, and we don't have anywhere to go!"

"Why are you so worried? I saw the Gray Man, so everything is going to be okay."

"Do you seriously believe that?" Caroline asked with her arms outstretched to her sides and a doubting sneer plastered on her face.

"Of course! Amos told me that everything would be fine as long as we weren't here during the hurricane."

"Amos? Do you mean that kooky guy we saw at work?"

"He wasn't kooky, he was awesome! He was really nice to me."

"Yes, Walter, he was nice, but he was also a little weird. I haven't seen him around since. Besides, even if he's right, where are we supposed to stay?"

"Why can't we just go home?"

"That's not an option."

"But why?"

"We just can't."

"Tell me why!" Walter shouted. "I'm tired of not seeing Mom and Dad! I'm also tired of feeling like you guys are talking behind my back and keeping something from me!"

Caroline's head dropped. She stood quiet for a moment before walking over, face to face with Walter. "You're right. This whole scenario is so messed up. We have just been trying to protect you."

"Protect me from what?"

"We can't go home because Dad doesn't want us there."

"Don't you mean Mom? I thought she wanted us out of the way while Dad got better."

Caroline slowly and slightly shook her head. "That's not entirely true. Mom did want us to give Dad space, but Dad is the real reason we can't go back."

"Dad? Why doesn't he want us there? I'd think he'd be okay with us staying there through this storm. Wouldn't he?"

"He would, but we're not going to go."

Walter flung his arms out in protest. "But why?"

Caroline closed in and grabbed Walter's shoulders, took a deep breath, and finally muttered out, "Dad's dying."

"What?"

"Dad has a rare bone cancer."

Walter broke loose of Caroline's grip. "No!" He was now frantic as he started wildly looking around. "I gotta go!"

"Go where?" Caroline inched towards him. It was obvious that he was having trouble processing such horrible news, and she wanted to be there to comfort him.

"I gotta go see Dad!" He continued to franticly look around, unsure of what to do.

"Walter, I'm sorry. I know this is awful."

"If you're telling the truth, then why can't we at least go tell him bye?"

"First off, why would I lie about something like this? Second, Dad was in the process of telling us bye when he had that massive stroke."

"What do you mean?"

"Remember when we were doing something really fun nearly every day? It started with the Orioles game and then that day we spent at the Inner Harbor and all the other things in that time frame, too. It lasted about a week or so before he had the stroke."

Walter stood in absolute silence, processing the information. "So that's why we were doing all that? Hershey Park, Kings Dominion, the Inner Harbor, all those things were because he's dying."

"That was Dad's way of telling us bye. He wanted to go out with a blast. He was going to do all he could before being bedridden. It was supposed to last a little longer, but the stupid stroke he had cut it short."

"I still don't understand why he doesn't want us there! I thought everyone wanted their loved ones around when they were passing."

"Most people do, but Mom said that Dad didn't want us to see him waste away. He wanted us to have good memories of him. Not ones of him being sick and helpless. I don't like being away from him either, but I do understand his logic. He's sacrificing his comfort for our sake. That's how much he loves us."

Walter gave his sister a blank stare, then slowly walked over to the back door and looked out at the ocean. "I just—" He broke down crying.

Caroline rushed to his side and put her arm around him and cried, too.

"This sucks!"

"I know, little brother, I know." She rubbed his back.

"I want to go home so bad! The way everyone's been acting makes sense to me now. I hate it, but I get it."

"This is awful. You don't deserve this. None of us do."

After a few more moments of crying and continuing to process the grim information, Walter finally said, "So, where are we going to ride the storm out?"

"I don't know, little brother. I don't know."

CHAPTER SIXTEEN

One For the Money

A few days later, the skies were now dark as charred ash from a well-used fireplace as Josh and Tommy finished packing up their proverbial steed for battle. Of course, the steed was the newly acquired ambulance, and the battle was surviving a full-blown hurricane while avoiding the police and any other authority figures. The expected spoils of victory were coming home with three hundred thousand dollars in cash that couldn't be reported to the authorities when discovered missing.

"Did you get the backup chain for the chainsaw?" Josh asked Tommy as he loaded a case of tools into the back.

"Yeah, I got it. Why are we bringing so much gas, though? The ambulance uses diesel and if we have to cut up so many downed trees that we need that much gas, we're screwed. Besides, it doesn't seem safe hauling that much fuel around."

"Relax, I'm putting it in one of the outer compartments. It will be fine there."

"Good. At least the containers won't be trying to slide all over the back while we drive."

Minutes later, the fully prepared cousins pulled out of the dusty gravel driveway that led to their wastewater removal business. Josh was full of confidence as he piloted the newly labeled ambulance. He was more than satisfied with the fake Carolina Palms Ambulance Company name and logo he came up with. The dark blue letters complemented the plain white paint perfectly and the iconic palmetto tree from the South Carolina state flag had the caduceus medical symbol cleverly placed inside. The attention to detail truly made them look like they belonged to a fleet from a genuine medical transportation company. He looked over at his cousin and said, "Well, this is it. No turning back now."

Tommy, full of worry and concern, watched the massive clouds churning in the sky. It was reminiscent of salt water taffy being made on a pulling machine only this wasn't a sweet treat. The time was only a little past seven a.m., but the immense cloud cover produced a look that was easily comparable to early twilight. He readjusted his body in the seat to get a better look. "Man, just look at that. This storm's going to be a bad one. My stomach is in knots. Are you sure we can pull this off?"

"Of course, man! Look at how good the decals turned out. This thing looks like it did in its glory days, a hundred percent legit."

"Yeah, the ambulance looks great. That's not what I'm worried about, though. I just hope we don't get busted." Tommy put on his fake EMT cap that matched the rest of their false uniforms. Although the clothes weren't genuine, they still looked like actual professionals with the authentic-looking knockoff replacements Josh had found for them.

"You need to chill, bro. We won't get busted; this is going to be easier than scoring with a drunk chick on prom night." Josh gave Tommy a hard look. "You look like a damn old man with that gray spray crap in your hair."

Tommy quickly inspected his hair that was sticking out from underneath his cap in the rearview mirror. "This stuff is staying in better than I thought. I'm really glad I didn't let you talk me into shaving my head."

Josh shot him a nasty look. "Did you pack your pistol?"

Tommy shook his head. "I already told you, man, I ain't shooting somebody if this thing goes south."

"Are you freaking stupid? I told you—"

"And I told you I'm as pro 2A as they come, but we're the ones doing something illegal here and I'm not adding any kind of gun charge to the list if we get busted!"

Josh was quiet, eventually his shoulders shrugged in an melodramatic fashion and he pointed his right index finger toward Tommy's face. "Fine! It's your funeral if something happens."

"So it's every man for himself, then?"

Caught off guard by that question, Josh stuttered, "Well, uh no, but you might get in a spot that I can't help you with but your pistol could have."

"We're already taking a major chance here, so if that happens, I'll deal with it, I guess." Tommy gazed at him for a second, then went back to looking at the dark and amazing sky. "I was watching some videos online last night, and they said that hurricanes can release as much energy as ten thousand nuclear bombs."

"That's crazy. I wonder how the experts figured that out."

"Yeah, I don't know. I also saw most hurricanes that hit the U.S. come from a point off of the west coast of Africa where the dry and hot air from the Sahara desert collides with cool and moist air coming up from the south. It creates powerful winds called the African Easterly Jet."

It was obvious Josh didn't care about Tommy's hurricane fun facts, but he humored him, anyway. "That makes sense."

"Then they went on to say that the word hurricane comes from a Native American word meaning evil spirit of the wind."

"Well, we owe the evil spirit of the wind one. It's about to make us rich!"

A few moments later, the radio announcer began giving weather updates. "Hurricane Faye is almost here, folks! She's still a category four at the moment, but most experts are expecting her to downgrade to a three after making landfall in about two hours or so. That's the best-case scenario, though, because there's always the chance of The Brown Ocean Effect possibly adding fuel to the fire, causing the storm to worsen."

With a big grin and puffed-out chest, Josh was full of confidence as he boasted, "My timing is going to be spot on! We're only about thirty minutes away. According to my calculations, I figure it'll take us about forty-five minutes or so to get into the clubhouse, get the safe open, and then get the money loaded up. Then we should be halfway back to the shop as the brunt of the storm is actually hitting land. This is absolutely perfect!"

Tommy gave him a short, blank stare, then he went back to watching the skies.

The radio station had switched announcers and the current one had started talking about another subject. "The hunt for the missing seventy-three-year-old man will be put on hold—" Josh abruptly changed the station to Tommy's surprise and the radio now played an eerie classic rock song that perfectly fit the astonishing scene out of the windshield.

The duo sat in silence while the wind blew the mighty emergency vehicle to and fro. With substantial force, Josh kept it in the correct lane and out of the ditches while Tommy sat in amazement at the blustery sky and spooky vibe that the normally busy road was now radiating because of the lack of other drivers. After what felt like an eternity but a too-short-of-a-ride, the colluding cousins were just minutes from their destination.

Josh turned the radio off. "Put your mask on. The golf course isn't far."

As Tommy was doing so, he looked over and saw red hair hanging out from the bottom of Josh's mask, making it appear as if he had a long red goatee. "What the world is up with your mask?"

"It's a part of my disguise. I stopped by Benny's barbershop and picked up some hair. I told him I needed it to keep the deer out of my bean patch."

"Bean patch? That's hilarious. Like you'd ever grow one of those." After letting out a small snicker and getting a second look at the ridiculous mask, Tommy's face wrinkled up in disgust. "So you've got some stranger's nasty hair on your face right now?"

"Come on, man, I disinfected it. I also spread some of the hair all over the ambulance, so it wouldn't just be our DNA in here in case the cops ended up having a chance to check it for some reason." Josh turned the big machine to the right at a building they were now passing.

"Wow, that's actually pretty sma— Oh crap, cops!" Tommy shouted out with extreme fear and bulging eyes. Unfortunately, it was too late for them to take a different route as they had come directly into the police's line of sight after fully completing the wide right turn.

CHAPTER SEVENTEEN

A Big Sister's Gotta Do
What a Big Sister's Gotta Do

"Hello," Caroline unceremoniously said into her bright pink phone.

"What are you two still doing there?" Her mom demanded to know with a tremendously stressed tone of voice.

Caroline was now flustered. "Do you seriously still have that stupid tracking app on our phones?"

"Of course I do. When you're a mother, you will be the same way. Now tell me why you're still there. I thought you were going to your friend Susan's house?"

Caroline rolled her eyes and flung her head back, displaying her frustration to Walter. She was extra quiet to ensure that she wouldn't expose her dissatisfaction with her mother, which would have just made matters much worse. "We were just leaving." She responded in a fake upbeat tone, hoping that she would appease her perceived overly cautious parent.

To her dismay, it didn't work. Her mother responded to the casual comment with great haste, "You should have already been there! The hurricane isn't far from land!"

"I know, Mom. I just hate to impose on someone. Susan already has a full house."

"That's understandable, but you most certainly cannot stay there!" The frustration her mom was emitting was now transforming into a panic.

"We were never going to stay here. We just had to pack some things and we're literally leaving now. I'll call you as soon as we get there, as long as I have a service that is."

"You'd better call me! I love you two. Please be careful!"

"Relax, Mom, we will. We love you, too." She pressed the end call button and stared at Walter.

"What the hell are we supposed to do now?" Walter asked with a solid look of consternation.

"Watch your mouth, turd face. I guess we'll drop our phones off at Susan's. Mom still has that stupid tracking app on our phones. That will at least get her off our case."

"That's just great; we have to leave all our stuff behind here at the house and drop off our phones, too! What the heck are we supposed to do to entertain ourselves? Gah, this is going to be so boring!"

"I told you to pack things that could be done without power. Even if we could keep our phones, the power would be out at some point and they would eventually die. Why don't you pack your school books? You might as well be productive."

"That was the first thing I packed. Mom was already on my case about it. She's right, though, we definitely can't stay here. Why is it that we can't just stay at Susan's again?"

"Because she's got a house full of family already hunkering down there, remember?"

"Oh yeah, I guess we're screwed then." Walter declared before hanging his head. "Wait, why can't we just head west and stay at a hotel or something?"

"Do you actually think I didn't look into that already? All of them are either fully booked or shut down because they evacuated."

"Oh. Sorry, I had just thought of that." There was a loud knock on the door. "Who the heck is that?"

Caroline shot him a concerned look before inching toward the door. Before she could get there and try to get a peek at who was knocking, the person on the other side of the door performed another really loud knock. "Hello? Anyone in there? This is the police department."

Walter whispered, "Why the heck is the police here?"

Caroline's eyes widened, and she hurried to the door and immediately opened it to see the middle-aged public servant. He was a big man, but Caroline was slightly amused at his yellow rain gear as it seemed like something Walter would wear.

"Hello. I'm from the police department and we are encouraging everyone to evacuate. We feel that you are in grave danger staying here and must insist that you leave."

"We are. We were just finishing up packing supplies before heading out."

"That's excellent news. Trust me, you don't want to ride the storm out here on the shore. It is beyond dangerous. You are literally risking your life if you do so."

"Of course, we never had any intentions of staying. We're just running behind."

"If I may, I suggest that you go ahead and turn your power off on your way out. The flickers and surges can potentially cause damage and if the house gets torn up real bad, exposed and damaged wires can cause fires once the power returns."

"That makes a lot of sense, we'll be sure to do that."

"Okay good. And remember; if you come up on any standing water on the roads while you're traveling, never try to cross through it. Like the old saying goes, turn around, don't drown. Be sure to always go by that rhyme if you come upon water on a road."

"That's great advice, sir. I'm definitely not brave enough to try something like that in the first place."

"That's good to know. It only takes a foot of water to make a car float and two feet of rushing water can carry a car away like it's nothing!"

"Oh wow, that's scary. Thanks for stopping by." She began to close the door.

He reached and prevented the door from closing. "One more thing!" He nervously smiled. "I almost forgot. We've got a missing man in his seventies. We've been looking for him for a couple of days now, but this hurricane has halted the search party. If you were to run across an elderly Caucasian man in that age range, be sure to let the authorities know ASAP."

"Absolutely!"

"He may be or seem confused. We're not sure if Alzheimer's has played a factor or not."

"Okay, we'll be sure to call if we see him."

"Thank you, be safe."

After closing the door, Walter said, "Wow, I didn't expect it to be a police officer."

"Yeah, neither did I. I didn't think he was ever going to leave."

"Back to square one. We can't stay here and we don't have anywhere to go." Walter sat down at the small breakfast table that was currently holding their makeshift bugout bags.

Caroline was feeling beyond defeated. After a few moments of looking at Walter, she realized she had no other choice. It was her very last resort, and she was being forced to take it.

"Come on, let's go! This will probably get us in trouble, but we don't have another option."

CHAPTER EIGHTEEN

Like a Charm

"Just keep your mouth shut! I got this!" Josh whispered in a hushed tone.

Tommy's heart felt as if it was going to burst out of his chest right there on the spot as the overweight city cop approached the ambulance. Josh rolled the window down and the cab immediately filled with rushing air. "Hey!"

"What the hell you guys doing out here?" he yelled over the wind.

"I was about to ask you the same thing!"

"What? I can't hear you with that damn mask on! Why do you even have it on right now?"

"We were exposed to a contagious patient earlier!"

The police officer backed up at least three feet instantly.

Josh couldn't help but grin a bit. His mask plan was working, and he was stoked about it. He was also glad the mask hid his satisfied smile.

"What are you doing out here, then? Shouldn't you be in quarantine or something?"

"Ya, I wish! Short-staffed, but I'm sure you know how that goes. We got orders to pick up a rare medicine for a client."

"Well, what the hell's he got to justify sending you guys into a full-blown hurricane?"

"Not sure, but the crew that picked him up forgot to grab his medicine, and they asked us to pick it up as we came through. We were already in the area. Lucky us!"

"What was the medicine? The hospital couldn't just prescribe more?"

Josh shot Tommy a worried look with wide eyes. Tommy's face went pale and his eyes widened as well. Then Josh smiled and gave him a wink before turning back to the officer. "It's a really expensive medicine called Actimmune."

"Oh, yeah, that explains why they sent you out. The price of that stuff is outrageous!"

"Yes, it is." Josh nodded his head in agreement.

"I can move the barricade to let you guys through, but you'll have to let yourselves out. I was just getting ready to get my fat derriere outta here!"

"I was actually surprised to see you out here. Did you piss somebody off to get stuck out here on guard duty?"

The officer let out a chuckle. "Something like that! You guys better not waste any time. Flooding will just keep getting worse at this point, especially once the rain really starts falling. Remember, turn around, don't drown!"

"Of course! You stay safe, pal! Josh yelled out in what Tommy noticed as an insincere tone.

The police officer trotted over to the wooden barricade adorned with the Road Closed sign. He hoisted it up as far as he could and scooted it along the pavement, giving Josh and Tommy enough room to get by.

"Yes! Don't you ever doubt me!" Josh spoke with unfeigned delight as he pointed at Tommy.

The police officer motioned them to drive through and as they passed, suddenly the officer, without warning, raised his arms and shouted out, instructing them to stop.

Josh's confidence suddenly waned as he rolled the window down. "Something wrong?"

"Hey, do you guys need help getting in the patient's place? I can probably help you out if I need to."

"No, thanks, though. We got it under control. They told us where a hideaway key is at."

"Okay. Oh hey, be sure to put the barricade back when you guys leave."

"Will do, thanks!" Josh resumed driving while rolling the window back up.

"Good Lord, man! I think I'm having a heart attack!" Tommy held his chest in a droll-like manner.

Josh replied with a snarky attitude, "Why are you so tore up? I figured we'd see at least one cop on the way in. I told you, man, I got this figured out! We're golden!"

Tommy was feeling immense relief. "Holy crap, that was—"

A loud beep came from the ambulance's dashboard and the mighty vehicle suddenly slowed down, causing Josh to yell, "Oh great! The engine has kicked into low-power mode!"

Tommy's stress returned that instance and was even worse now with the new development. "Thought we were golden?"

"Damn it! It felt like the accelerator was acting up driving in, but I thought it was just from all the wind blowing us around."

"The particulate filter is probably clogged. No telling how long it's been since it was cleaned out." Tommy buried his head in his hands.

"I brought plenty of tools; I'll just bypass the damn thing!"

"Uh, no you won't. I'm no diesel expert, but I do know you have to manipulate the ECU or it will just stay in low-power mode. I'd say a max speed of thirty-five miles an hour is definitely a kink in your plan!"

The scowl plastered on Josh's face more than expressed his current emotions. "Let's just get to the golf course! I'll check it out when we get there!"

The ride was now excruciatingly slow as the ambulance barely crept along, pegged out at thirty-five miles per hour despite Josh holding the acceleration pedal to the floor. After what seemed like an eternity, the duo finally arrived at the golf course. They sat in silence as they scanned the area. It was tucked in the back of the road, which gave the upscale gathering place a sense of isolation.

"I know when we left the shop you said there was no turning back, but I think this is where that statement actually applies," Tommy said barely above a whisper. "Considering the condition of the ambulance, I think we should really reconsider following through with this."

Josh sat quietly and stared at the clubhouse that contained the cash-filled safe. Bright green grass surrounded the entire area along with trees dancing in the hurricane with great ferocity. "Let's get the safe open and while you're packing the cash into the body bag on the stretcher, I'll see if I can figure out what's wrong with this thing."

"That's all fine and dandy, but what if the ambulance can't be fixed here? Are we supposed to drive all the way back to the house doing only thirty-five miles an hour in the absolute middle of a hurricane? And what if this thing conks out altogether, and we get stranded, in the middle of a literal hurricane?"

"Okay, smart-ass, you've made some good points, but either way, we are already here. So should we attempt to drive home with the cash or without the cash? If we're chancing breaking down in a hurricane, I'd rather do it with the money."

Now Tommy sat quite processing Josh's view on the situation. He wished he'd never agreed to this, but to his regret, it was too late now. "You've made your point. I guess if we are risking our lives either way, then I reckon we might as well do it with the money."

"Atta boy, now let's do this!"

CHAPTER NINETEEN

Safety Hazard

"Just where the hell is the safe?" Tommy pulled the heavy metal framed stretcher from the ambulance through the window opening. Josh had just broken the glass of what appeared to be an employee break room with an emergency tool.

After handing Tommy their backpacks full of gear for just about any situation they might face, Josh carefully slid through the sharp shard-ridden opening and pulled a decent-sized broken tree branch in behind him. After a few seconds of studying the immediate area, he dropped the branch among the broken glass. "That oughta do it. Looks like the hurricane made this mess."

Tommy held his mask out a few inches with his glove-covered hands to be heard easier as he asked, "How do we know that we didn't trigger a silent alarm?"

"Jammers we got should be doing their jobs. Let's hurry and get out of this room." Josh helped Tommy wheel the stretcher into a hallway and closed the break room door. "Holy crap, I didn't realize how loud the wind really is 'til we got out of it."

"Yeah, for real." Tommy agreed before scanning the dark and quiet clubhouse. There wasn't a sound to be heard except for the relentless wind coming from outside. Despite the power still currently being on, which caused some security lights to subtly shine, keeping the darkness slightly at bay, the ritzy joint gave him an uneasy feeling. The high-end spooky Halloween decorations didn't help how he felt either.

Josh pointed to the left side of the building. "The office with the safe is back this way. Just leave the stretcher here 'til we get it open. Then, as you pack the money into the body bag, I'll see if I can fix the ambulance."

Before Tommy could reply, he noticed a shadow-like movement out of the corner of his eye. "What the hell was that?"

With concern growing in his eyes, Josh asked, "What are you talking about?"

"I just saw something move!"

"No way. There couldn't be anybody here."

"You'd think, but I saw something, man! I know I did!"

In a flash, Josh pulled out a Taser from his side cargo pants pocket and started down the hallway. "Follow me. We gotta check this place out."

"Don't do anything stupid with that thing," Tommy instructed with a quick finger point.

"I'll do what I have to. Now let's go sweep this place."

The two cousins used immense caution as they exited the dark hallway and entered the dining room of the restaurant. They visually scanned the area as Josh snuck over to the left and Tommy quietly treaded to the right side, heading toward the bar. After a few steps, Tommy screamed out in fear as he saw a bat flying at his head. Startled by the winged mammal, Tommy ducked into a squatting position.

Once Josh saw that the ferocious bat connected to a thin clear line, he let out a thunderous laugh. "Look at you, scared to death by a lame decoration!"

As Josh indulged in the humor Tommy was inadvertently supplying, he lost his balance and stumbled back, causing a life-sized zombie statue to activate. Its eyes lit up red and a raspy voice recording called out, "Brains!"

Now startled, and frozen stiff from freight for a few seconds, Josh turned and punched the obnoxious ornament in the face. "Get off me!"

"Ha! Ain't so funny now, is it?" Tommy said with a hardy chuckle. "That was instant karma!"

"Come on! We got work to do!" Josh barked and then stomped down the hallway. After finding a luxurious office decorated with expensive-looking sports memorabilia, Josh said, "This is it! The safe is in here."

Tommy gazed at the impressive collection of autograph balls and jerseys from several different major sports. He also noticed all the framed pictures Jamar had of himself with dozens of famous athletes. "Dude's got connections! Look at all this!"

Josh snickered. "If we can't get the safe open, then we'll steal this crap and sell it."

"Taking his ill-gained money is one thing, but you don't mess with a man's collection, especially one like this!"

"How do you think he got it, nimrod? He used his dirty money. No honor among thieves." Josh opened a set of bi-fold doors, revealing the loot-filled strongbox.

"That's just it, I'm not a thief," Tommy mumbled just before standing in awe of the massive safe. It was almost big enough to walk into. "Holy crap, get it open!"

"Says the one claiming not to be a thief." Josh chuckled while turning the knob.

"I'm not; I just can't believe it's real. It's actually right here in person!"

"Of course, it's real, idiot! I wouldn't have gone through all this if it wasn't. Did you really think I was lying?"

"It's not that I doubted you. It just seemed too good to be true."

Josh started spinning the dial to the black behemoth, and every click caused his heart to beat faster. Finally, on the third try, the safe let out a loud clunk and swung open. The duo stood in complete shock at the massive stacks of cash. From the best that they could tell, the money was separated into five-thousand-dollar stacks held together with wide rubber bands.

"Oh my…"

Tommy's mumble was interrupted by Josh exclaiming, "Yes!" followed by several fist-pumping actions, then he sang out the first few lines of the classic song "Viva Las Vegas" with a poor attempt at sounding like Elvis.

Unfortunately, that's not what happened. It was the scenario Tommy had imagined right as Josh first began spinning the dial to the safe. It was what Tommy desperately wanted to see, but sadly, the two cousins were panicking after several failed attempts at getting the door open. Josh was now frantic as he kept dialing the numbers and pulling the handle, only to hear a sickening clank instead of a joyous thud which would have signified the opening of the safe, revealing the heavily desired bounty.

"Damn it!" Josh unloaded three quick punches with his gloved hand onto the safe.

Tommy held out his hands. "Easy man! Take a breath and calm yourself. Turn it to the left a few times and start over, slowly. You said the combination was twenty-four, forty-eight, sixty-six. Right?"

"Yes." Josh flopped his head back in disgust. He pulled his mask away from his face to get some fresh air as he tried to compose himself. After a few seconds, he grabbed the dial again. "Okay, we got this." He slowly turned the knob to each number of the combination with exact precision. After finally landing on the last one, he looked at Tommy and pulled the handle. "Goddamn it to hell!"

Access was yet again denied by the cold, intimidating safety box. The stomach-churning clank sound made by the unwavering handle caused Tommy to drop to his knees. The key to everything they wanted was just on the other side of the door, the black soulless door that would not open. "Are you sure that was the combination to this safe that you saw?"

Josh rolled his eyes and rested his back against the safe. "Am I one thousand percent sure? No. But the way the conversation went that night made it seem like this was it. I know that sounds crazy, but if you had been there, you would understand."

Tommy wanted to crack a joke about being glad he wasn't there, but this wasn't the time. "Is there a safe in Ms. Hoilman's office?"

"There's a small one under her desk."

"Let's go try it. Maybe the combination to this safe is hidden in that one. I know it's a long shot, but at this point, what do we have to lose?"

Josh was visibly perplexed and definitely frustrated. "You go ahead and give it a shot. I need to start on the ambulance. I wouldn't mind risking my hide by driving home in a hurricane for three hundred Gs but if we are going to have to leave from here empty-handed then we need to get our asses away from here as fast as possible!"

Moments later Josh unlocked the front door and ran straight to their getaway vehicle, hoping to get it fixed in a timely fashion. Meanwhile, Tommy glanced outside to get a peep of the frightening sky before heading toward the safe in Ms. Hoilman's office. Right before he entered the hallway, a voice from behind the bar stopped him in his tracks.

"Tommy? Is that you?"

CHAPTER TWENTY

Fancy Meeting You Here

Tommy tried to flee the shadow-filled bar area where a soft yet disturbing voice eerily called out his name, but the spine-chilling incident scared him so badly that he physically couldn't move. His legs would just not work, even though that's all he wanted at the moment. He was literally paralyzed from fear and after a few agonizing seconds, he was finally able to gather the courage to speak up and he eventually stammered out, "Who, who's there?"

A dark figure slowly emerged from behind the bar, triggering the flying bat that had scared him senseless earlier. This caused Tommy to break free from his immobilized state and he immediately ran back to the foyer area where there was more light. With his back up against the fancy wood and glass entry door. "Who are you? How do you know my name?"

"It's okay, Tommy. It's me, Caroline. The girl that accidentally hit you with my bright pink car at Salty's a few days ago."

"Caroline?" Tommy was in complete shock that someone was there as a hurricane was barreling down on the area, but that it was Caroline, left him beyond stupefied. "What on Earth are you doing here?" He inched his way toward the bar to get a closer look. "You scared the absolute crap outta me!"

"What am I doing here? I could ask you the very same thing!" She surprisingly snapped back with growing confidence in her tone of voice. "You guys scared the crap out of us, too, when you broke in. And what's with the gray hair?"

"I let myself get talked into a bad idea and a real bad one at that."

"Well, at least you didn't shave your head or something crazy like that, but I'm not sure that color is very becoming on you."

Her mentioning a shaved head shocked Tommy, and he wanted to tell her it was what his cousin wanted to do, but it was obviously not the time for that conversation. He was also now curious as to what color she thought his hair should be. "Oh, you think I should have gone for young Eminem blonde? Or maybe Billie Eilish green?"

"I don't know, but your original color was pretty much perfect."

That statement flattered Tommy and he held back a blushing grin. "Well, at least it will wash out easily. I hope!"

"It'd be hilarious if it didn't and you had to wear that color while it grew out!" Then she let out a hardy laugh before adding, "That'd serve you right!"

Tommy's blushing grin left him as he felt he was getting mixed signals. He shifted the conversation off his hair. "What about you? What's the story?"

"Well, unfortunately, Walter and I didn't have anywhere else to go to ride the storm out, so we decided to just hunker down here."

Just then, Walter playfully poked his head out from behind his sister. "Hi. Why are you wearing a mask?"

"So that any potential cameras around wouldn't capture my face."

"Why don't you want your face seen by cameras?" Caroline asked with a raised eyebrow, indicating her confusion. Besides, I already disabled them earlier, so there's nothing to worry about."

"How did you disable them?"

"My work bestie knew I didn't have anywhere else to go, so she told me how to turn them off."

"That was nice of her, but why didn't you just stay with your friend?"

"She physically didn't have any room for us. Her family members are staying over."

Now sitting on a bar stool, Walter asked, "So what are you guys doing here? You're lucky we didn't have our phones with us or the police would probably already be here. We were so scared that you were robbers or something."

Tommy dropped his head, ashamed of the fact that they were indeed robbers. "It's a long story, kid. I know I shouldn't be here. So you guys would have called the cops on us?"

After carefully processing that question, Caroline responded, "We didn't know it was you guys at first. I was a lot less worried once I realized who it was."

"Well, I can't say that I blame you for wanting to call them, but thanks for holding off. There's definitely nothing to worry about. At least with us. This massive hurricane moving in on us is another story. Is there a reason that you two don't have your phones?"

Caroline let out a short sigh. "That's a long story, too." Then she looked over at Walter. "Why don't you go hang out in Jamar's office? You can chill on his couch, but like I told you earlier, don't touch anything! Just look." Walter walked down the hallway and stood in the doorway to the office so he could eavesdrop on his sister and Tommy for a moment.

"I'm really sorry you two didn't have anywhere to go."

"It's not your fault. Just one of those things, I guess." She shrugged. "You can take that mask off. I swear the cameras aren't on."

Tommy was hesitant at first, but he eventually pulled the protective medical cover off. "Geez, that thing is so hot. It's nice to get some fresh air." Then he gazed at Caroline. "I just gotta know, how on Earth did you know it was me?"

She shot him a subtle smile. "I could pick up that accent of yours anywhere. Walter and I almost lost it when that bat scared you earlier!" Then she belted out a tremendous laugh while Tommy looked down with an embarrassing grin.

"What can I say? I thought I was got. The dim light in here with all the Halloween decorations and constant wind really sets the tone. It feels like a horror movie set in here."

"That's true; it is a little spooky. But just so you know, the real monsters are only here during business hours."

"Are you referring to the boss or the customers?"

"Both, now that you mention it."

Tommy let out a hardy laugh. "That sounds terrifying!"

"It could be worse. I didn't figure a big strong man like you would be afraid of anything, though."

Tommy gave her a side look. "Big strong man, huh?"

Walter was still listening in on the conversation at this point. "Gross. Get a room, you two." Then he went into Jamar's workspace.

"Well, you're certainly not a runt." Caroline smiled.

"Is that a good thing?"

"It's not a bad thing, that's for sure."

Tommy blushed. "That's good to know."

Caroline's tone turned a little rigid. "Seriously though, Tommy, what is going on? Why are you here?"

"Oh boy, I don't even know where to st—"

Before Tommy could even explain the bizarre situation he found himself in, the ambulance sirens wailed. Tommy and Caroline gave each other a puzzled look before dashing over to the window.

"Oh, my God! Caroline gasped. "It's Jamar!" Then she locked the front door before backing up to not be seen.

"Holy shit, the owner?"

"Yes! We are all so screwed!"

CHAPTER TWENTY-ONE

Who's In Charge Here?

"You can't park that here!" Jamar held his phone to his chest as he shouted toward Josh in vain because of the deafening and unrelenting wind coming from the hurricane. Josh had glimpsed Jamar once he pulled up to the clubhouse in his car, but he pretended not to notice him and continued to diagnose the problem with the ambulance. "Hey! Hey, you can't be here with that!" Josh faintly heard Jamar's screams, but once again, he ignored the demands of the overbearing property manager. Jamar was now furious and told the person on the phone to hold on as he walked toward the offending trespasser. Josh could see him approaching, so he reached into the cab and turned the siren on to warn Tommy about his unexpected appearance. Jamar tried to protect his ears with his hands and wasted no time in demanding that Josh turn the extremely loud noise off. To his dismay, Josh continued to ignore his presence until Jamar grabbed him by the shoulder. "Hey, turn that crap off!"

Finally, Josh had to acknowledge him. He reached in and turned off the siren. He looked directly at Jamar from behind his mask. "What's the problem?"

Jamar looked at Josh as if he'd lost his mind. "What's the problem? The problem is that you're on private property in the middle of a hurricane without permission. You're going to have to leave now!"

"Is this your property?"

"It's my father's."

"Do you think your pop would approve of you running off someone that was in trouble? Especially in these conditions?"

"He's not here, so what he would think is irrelevant."

"Do you even have the authority to make me leave?"

"Yes, I do! I'm the manager here and I'm in charge of everything!"

"I'm sure your father is so proud."

"What was that? Why don't you take that mask off, Mumbles?" Jamar was condescending as he closed in on Josh, trying to intimidate him.

Josh puffed out his chest and took a few steps closer to show he wasn't afraid of Jamar. "Why don't you go ahead and try to take it off for me?"

"There won't be no try. If I want to take it off, I will!"

"I doubt that, big boy. If you want to be exposed to a nasty contagion, go ahead and try."

"Contagion? What are you talking about?"

"I'm not wearing this mask for fun, jackass. I was possibly exposed to a nasty communicable disease from a patient transport earlier and now on top of the wonderful day I'm having, I have to wear this stupid thing on my face."

Jamar's willingness to fight noticeably diminished, and he slowly took a few steps back. "Look, man, I really don't have time for all this. Just go ahead and get packed up and leave. I can't be liable for you."

Josh chuckled. "Boy, that's gratitude for ya, ain't it! People like me are out here busting our asses to help keep rich assholes like you safe, and this is the thanks we get!"

Jamar took offense to him calling him a rich asshole, and he pointed his finger in Josh's face. "You better watch yourself! Nobody takes that tone with me!"

"Those are some big words coming from somebody that doesn't have to risk their life for a living!"

Josh's comment greatly infuriated Jamar, but the fear of being exposed to the nasty contagion kept him from attacking the unwanted guest. "You don't know me. You best give me some respect!"

Josh could see he had almost pushed his impromptu foe too far, so he shifted the conversation. "Do you know how short-staffed we are and how many hours I've already put in this week? All I'm trying to do is make a living out here and my under-serviced and overdriven rig is acting up. Do you think I actually want to be here in your stupid parking lot trying to fix it in the middle of weather like this? Trust me; I'd a whole lot rather be in a cabin over in the Smoky Mountains riding this storm out than being out in this crap. It is foolishness to be doing this, but somebody's gotta do the dirty work. What the hell kinda place is this? You'd actually run off a working paramedic while the entire state is in the middle of an emergency? I guess it's a good thing there's no old lady trying to pass through here right now. I'm sure a heartless bastard like yourself has a couple of hellhounds chained up in a dungeon to sic on innocent victims at will. Say, what's your name? I want to make sure I get it right when I take this story to the *Post and Courier*. If you didn't know, that's one of the biggest newspapers in the state, so I'm sure this would be great material for their hurricane coverage. I'm also sure the big wigs that run Pawley's Island would love the negative backlash for the area from such a disgusting story."

Jamar wasn't falling for Josh's working man shtick, but he absolutely didn't want any negative publicity to befall the golf course. "See here, homie, like I said, I don't have time for this. I'm sorry for the predicament you've found yourself in, but I can't help you. You can't be here out in the open during this storm."

"I'm sorry for having to be here, but this bitch kicked into low-power mode and headquarters said there were no tow trucks willing to come out since the storm is actively making landfall. I'm literally stuck here until I get this thing fixed, if I can, that is."

Jamar looked off in disgust. "Damn it!"

"Believe me; I understand that this is a huge inconvenience. I only came into your parking lot, so I'd be off the road while I tried to fix this hunk of junk. I'm truly sorry."

"Do you think you can fix it yourself?"

"It will take a while, but yes. I really think I can get it straightened out."

Jamar hung his head for a moment, then looked at his phone before getting back on it. "Hey, you still there? Give me just another minute while I take care of this." Then he held his phone to his side as he started telling Josh, "There's one thing I can do."

"Yeah, what's that?"

Jamar pointed to the other side of the parking lot. "Do you see that building over there?"

"Yeah. What about it?"

"That's where we keep the mowers and landscaping equipment."

"Really? That's a damn nice building for it to just be a storage shed."

"We're a five-star golf course. We always have the best of everything here."

"I can tell."

"There should be enough room for you to park in there until you get finished fixing the problem."

"Wait, are you telling me I can park the ambulance in there?"

"If you can promise me that you'll be out of here just as soon as you get it fixed and not sue me for any reason, then yes."

"Oh man, I'm sorry I misjudged you! I just wanted to be able to stay here in the parking lot 'til I got this thing running right, but now I can do it even faster being out of this wind."

"If you're going to have to be here, I'd rather have you inside than out. It will definitely be safer."

"Wow, I can't thank you enough!"

"The code to get in is pound sign, zero, nine, two, one."

"I'm so grateful! Thank you!" Josh said as sincerely as possible, even though he didn't mean it.

"You're welcome. Just make sure to hurry it up!"

With an enthusiastic response, he shouted, "You got it, pal!" Then he hopped into the ambulance and began backing it up. After getting it repositioned, he drove toward the shed and mumbled, "That's how it's done, Tommy. You think you're the only one that can talk to people. You ain't no better than me."

CHAPTER TWENTY-TWO

Ready or Not, Here He Comes...

Caroline looked around the sitting area of the restaurant in a panicked state. "How bad are we screwed, you asked? This is basically the worst-case scenario, especially if we get caught! Josh is screwed for sure! Will he tell on you being in here?"

Tommy shook his head. "No, he's got contingency plans, and he's a damn good liar on top of that but we still need to find a good place to hide though!"

"We've definitely got to hide! I can't lose this job!" She franticly looked around for an appropriate space that would conceal their unlawful presence in the building.

Tommy looked around as well and noticed that the stretcher was beyond conspicuous and sure to get them caught. "Crap! What are we going to do with that thing?" He pointed to the movable gurney in despair.

"Don't worry, I'll take care of that. I have an idea. You go find Walter and tell him to hide!"

Tommy did just that, but Walter was nowhere to be found. He began shouting out for him in a low tone of voice and checking the surrounding rooms that were close to Jamar's office, but he still had no luck locating him. "Walter! Where are you, kid! Come on, we got to hide! Your sister's boss just showed up!" He continued his search to the back of the building, where he eventually found Walter in a supply closet. He was franticly working on a trophy from Jamar's office. "What the heck are you doing, kid?

"Please don't tell Caroline, she'll kill me!" Walter put glue on the bottom of the clear football that had broken off of its base. He then placed the two very expensive-looking crystal pieces back together. "There, I think that should work."

"How did this even happen? Your sister told you not to touch anything!"

"It was an accident! I bumped into it and it just fell right over and the football broke loose! I swear I wasn't doing anything stupid; it was seriously an accident! Please don't tell Caroline!"

Tommy looked at the ceiling in despair as he processed Walter's information. He felt bad for him, but there wasn't any time for this. "Jamar could enter the building at any time! Just stay put, kid!" Tommy closed the door and ran down the hall in a flash.

"Wait!" Walter yelled out, but it was too soft for Tommy to hear. "This was on his desk! I have to put it back or he will probably notice it missing!" He turned his head sideways and looked at the trophy. To his satisfaction, it seemed like the glue was going to work so he quickly tried to wipe his fingerprints off of the expensive glass with the bottom of his jacket sleeve and then he carefully slipped out of the supply closet and started creeping back down the hallway with the extravagant object in hand.

Tommy had met back up with Caroline at the front of the building. "Where's Walter? Is he hidden well enough?"

"He should be good. What's going on out there with those two?" Then he used great caution as he peeked out the window.

"Last time I checked, they were just talking."

"Good! Maybe Jamar won't come in."

"I wouldn't bet on that. If he bothered to drive all the way out here in this mess, then I'm sure he must have a good reason for doing so. Be ready to hide under the bar if he does, though."

"You got it!" Tommy noticed Walter sneaking down the dark hallway. *Damn it, kid!* He started back in his direction to check on him.

"What are you doing? Where are you going?"

Tommy didn't want to alarm Caroline that her younger brother was no longer hiding where he left him. "I'll be right back! Just keep an eye out. I want to make sure your boss's office is in order."

A few seconds later, Tommy was coming up behind Walter in Jamar's office. "What are you doing in here, bro? I told you to stay in the closet! Please don't get us caught!"

He yelped from being startled. "I'm trying to get this stupid thing back in its place!" Walter wasn't expecting Tommy to come in on him as he placed the trophy back on the desk.

"That's good, ya got it! It's perfect! Now get out of here!" As Walter backed up from the desk, he seemed pleased with his lightning-quick efforts of getting the trophy fixed until he unknowingly backed into a football helmet that was on display, causing it to fall to the floor with a loud thud. The two gave each other panic-stricken looks and before either could say anything, they suddenly heard the backup alarm going off from the ambulance. The extra loud warning beeps terrified Tommy way worse than the sound the helmet made when it hit the floor. With extra wide eyes, he looked directly at Walter's face. "Put the helmet back up there and then get your hide back to that closest, now!"

Walter stammered around for a second, not knowing which way to go first. He finally got his wits about him. "Okay! I got it!"

Tommy was now on his way back to the front of the clubhouse when he saw the ambulance pulling into what he assumed to be a utility shed that appeared to house the maintenance equipment. *That's odd. What the heck is going on?"*

Caroline saw Tommy coming back. "Hurry, Tommy! We've got to get behind the bar!"

"Oh crap, here comes your boss!"

They crawled into an opening under the solid wooden structure. It was just big enough for them to fit, sitting with their crossed legs without being too uncomfortable.

"Hey, are you there?" Jamar said into his phone as he entered the building. "I'm inside now. I can talk. Some idiot ambulance driver was out front in the parking lot with engine trouble. He was out in the wide open, in the middle of this stupid hurricane, trying to fix it. I gave him the code to the ground keeper shed so he wouldn't get killed out there. Last thing I need is a damn lawsuit or some crap like that." Then he proceeded to walk to his office. Before he got to the hallway, the zombie decoration that scared Josh earlier cried out "Brains!" Jolted by the sound, he suddenly turned and saw the elaborate mannequin laying on the stretcher the cousins had just brought in for the heist earlier. "Stupid Halloween junk. This crap's getting out of hand." Then he headed down the hall with a disgusted look now on his face.

"Why the hell is he even here?" Tommy asked, with the lightest whisper possible. "I'd think a guy like him would be a million miles away at the moment."

Caroline shrugged. "I really don't know. It doesn't make any sense for him to be here, that's for sure. Where's Walter? Is he still hiding?"

"He's good. He's in a supply closet in the back." *I hope.*

At the end of the long, dark hallway Jamar casually opened the door to his immaculate office. He stopped in his tracks when he noticed the bi-fold doors to the closet that housed his safe and that he always kept closed were strangely standing wide open. He held the phone away from his face as he mumbled, "Wait, that's not right."

CHAPTER TWENTY-THREE

Have a Drink on Me

With ample anxiety Tommy looked around while he and Caroline hid beneath the bar, hoping not to be noticed by her employer. The two occasionally locked eyes and both would give each other an awkward smile before quickly looking away. He eventually whispered, "I'm really wondering what would be so important that he'd come out here in this weather. It doesn't make any sense."

Caroline shook her head. "No, it doesn't make sense. If I'd thought for a second that he'd showed up, I never would have come here."

"You guys would have been more than welcome to stay at my granny's old place."

"How was I supposed to know that?" Caroline shrugged.

"Well, I was hoping to hear from you on Facebook. I kinda thought we had something going. I really enjoyed the time we spent together. I guess my insane cousin scared you away."

Caroline's eyes locked directly onto Tommy's. "Yes, your cousin is scary, but that's not the reason I didn't reach out."

"Why didn't you then?"

"I don't know. I guess I was just so embarrassed that I hit you with my car. You were really nice about it and I guess I thought you were just playing along because you thought I was crazy or something. I didn't think you really wanted anything to do with me."

Tommy looked away from her lovely face and stared at her teal-colored sweatshirt that had Myrtle Beach written on it as he processed what she said. "I hate that you felt that way because it's not true. I do understand the feeling, though. I looked you up on Facebook and was afraid to message you because I thought you were outta my league."

"That's ridiculous!"

"Is it, though? You seriously would have gone out on a date with me?"

"I would like to have talked to you more and gotten to know you a little better before saying yes."

"So you would have made sure that I'm not like Josh?"

"It's more than obvious that you're not like him!"

Tommy dropped his head. "I hope so."

Meanwhile, down the hall, the boss stood in his office. "Hang on a second," Jamar said into his phone with a look of concern before lowering it to his side. He thoroughly scanned the room. Nothing else in his elaborate man cave seemed out of place to him, but before he could finish satisfying his uneasiness, the voice on the other end of the line started shouting out. He got back on the phone and a heated argument ensued. Within a few seconds, Jamar was shouting into his phone as he aggressively opened the safe.

Walter was full of concern, justifiably so considering he was hiding under Jamar's luxurious desk instead of the supply closet Tommy had told him to stay in. He regretted not getting out of the office in time, but there was nothing he could do about it now. The conversation Jamar was having on the phone had gotten even more explosive, causing Walter to wonder how much trouble he'd actually be in if he got caught. Despite his curiosity getting the best of him, he peeped around the edge of the desk right as the safe door opened, revealing several massive stacks of cash. Walter was completely flabbergasted as Jamar grabbed two big bundles from a pile and placed them into a black briefcase he grabbed from on top of the safe. Jamar began shouting with even more intensity and slammed the safe shut, pulled the closet doors closed, and stormed out of the office, slamming the door behind him. By the time he reached the bar, he was finishing up the call.

"You tell that lucky bottom sucker I got his damn money! I only had to come out in the middle of a hurricane to get it so it will be a few hours before I can get there!"

He slammed the briefcase down on top of the bar along with his phone and then he grabbed a liquor bottle. In his angered state, he accidentally shoved it into the surrounding bottles, causing several of them to crash to the floor right beside Caroline and Tommy. Shards of glass went flying wildly, and the contents splattered all over the two, drenching their clothes.

"Just great!" Jamar shouted, then he threw the bottle he had managed not to drop straight down in anger, scattering shards of glass. Several pieces managed to hit Tommy on the right side of his face, causing him to wince in pain. Caroline covered his mouth with her right hand to keep him from crying out so that they wouldn't get caught. She felt bad for the seemingly selfish move, so she began caressing the back of his head, hoping to help him cope with the pain.

"I don't need this crap!" Jamar shouted out loud then he grabbed the briefcase and exited the building, locking the door as he left.

"Oh God, Tommy! Are you okay?"

He grunted. "I hope so. It feels like there's a piece of glass in my eye."

"Come on, let's get to the office and I'll see if I can get it out."

"That sounds terrific, but we'd better wait a couple of minutes just to make sure he doesn't come back in."

"That's a good point. Can you watch for him out the window while I get changed out of these wet clothes and figure out how to clean this mess up? It smells like a distillery in here. I don't know about you, but if we're going to be stuck here, I'd rather not have to put up with this strong scent."

"I should be able to keep a lookout with my good eye," he joked as he carefully crawled out from under the bar and tiptoed through the glass pieces and spilled liquor.

"I'm sorry that happened to you, Tommy. We'll get you fixed up; at least I will try my best to." Then she ran off to her work locker and quickly changed into some spare clothes she had stashed there. Right before she closed the door to the locker, she spotted a four-pack of bottled Cheerwine she had left in there. Remembering that Tommy liked her favorite drink as much as she did, she trotted to the ice maker and grabbed a pail of ice and put the four bottles in it so that they could enjoy them in a chilled state later. On the way back, she grabbed some towels to throw on the mess Jamar made.

Tommy was keeping watch by the front door as he started taking off his alcohol-soaked jacket. Then Caroline returned and began placing the towels on the flammable liquid. He noticed the light blue shirt she was now wearing. "Cool! You like the Pelicans?"

"Well, it's not that I don't like them, but the only thing I know about them is that they are a baseball development team in Myrtle Beach. We hosted a party for them a while back and they gave all the workers some of these shirts."

"That's cool. Maybe we could go and see them play sometime." Tommy's insides cringed after he heard himself say that. He didn't mean to drop a pick-up line this soon and feared that he was coming on too strong.

To his surprise, though Caroline answered him with a smile as she said, "I'd like that." She finished putting the towels on all the liquid. "We'd better go check on Walter and see if we can fix your eye."

Tommy nodded. "Okay." Then he looked out the window once more before saying, "It doesn't look like your boss will be coming back, for now at least."

Just a few seconds later, as they went to enter Jamar's workspace from the dark hallway, they found Walter standing with his mouth and eyes wide open. He appeared to be in a state of shock.

"What's wrong?" Caroline asked her little brother as they walked on into the room and realized the safe was standing wide open, exposing the massive amounts of cash.

CHAPTER TWENTY-FOUR

Open Sesame

"How did you get it open, kid?" Tommy asked with enormous enthusiasm as he held his arms out to his sides, making a huge commotion in a celebratory fashion.

"I didn't. It looks like Jamar was so pissed that he must have left without making sure it was properly closed. I was just over there hiding under the desk when I heard the safe door bang against the closet doors after he stormed out."

Tommy grabbed his own cheeks in excitement. "Ha! I can't believe this! I've gotta get Josh in here!"

Caroline was trying to process the whole insane situation as she glanced at Tommy. "So this is why you're here, to rob my boss, Jamar?"

Tommy's head dropped, and his excitement disappeared. He felt utter shame as he tried to explain. "Yes, but it's not like we're actually taking hard-earned money from him. Josh found out that he's got some sort of illegal gambling operation going on. That means it's dirty money, so we are technically robbing from a crook." Caroline folded her arms and looked away without giving Tommy a verbal response. "You said I should do whatever it took to get my dad's car back, so that's what I'm doing. That's the only reason I'm here."

Walter surprised them both when he asked, "Could we have some of it?"

Tommy shrugged. "I don't see why you couldn't. Josh said he heard there was at least three hundred thousand in here. I only need—"

Caroline suddenly interrupted. "We can't take any of that, Walter."

"Why not? It could save the beach house!"

Tommy gave Caroline a look of concern and right as he started to ask her what Walter meant, there was a banging at the door. "I bet that's Josh. I'll let him in." A few seconds later Josh was now inside and before Tommy could even tell him that the safe was open, he was berating him for not wearing his mask. After several seconds of being scolded, Tommy exclaimed, "Dude, chill! It's all good! I've got awesome news!" Then he led him down the hallway to Jamar's office. "Oh, and thanks for firing up the siren to warn us about Jamar!"

Before Josh saw the open safe, his eyes widened when he made eye contact with Caroline and Walter. He spoke just above a whisper, "I guess that's why that neon pink Probe that hit you back at Salty's is in the mower shed."

Tommy chuckled. "It's open! Look at all this, man!"

Josh glanced at the cash, then back at the siblings. "Excuse us for a moment."

Moments later, the two cousins were just outside the front door. "What's wrong? We've got the cash now. You don't even seem to care." Tommy spoke extra loud to ensure he could be heard over the nonstop wind.

Josh shook his head in disapproval. "Not only is the ambulance still not fixed, but now we got witnesses!"

"Dude, take your mask off. I told you the cameras are shut down."

"I don't know that! The jammers should be working but in the event that they are not the masks protect us! Besides that, what makes you think we can trust them? We've got a big problem here! A huge one, as a matter of fact!"

"The only real problem we have here is the ambulance. Caroline and Walter are just here because they couldn't stay right on the beach during this hurricane."

"I wish that were true, but this is a loose end, Tommy! We can't leave any loose ends! What if they tried to blackmail us or something? We have to take care of them!"

Tommy stared at Josh with a stern look. "I'm not sure what you're getting at or what you mean by 'take care of them,' but I'm going back in here now to pack up the money. If you need help with the ambulance, be sure to let me know." He went inside, purposely slamming the door behind him. After grabbing the stretcher and carelessly throwing the zombie off to the side, in a flash, he was in front of the safe, packing up the money.

Caroline could see Tommy was upset. She walked over to him. "Is there anything we can do to help?"

Tommy gave her a serious gaze. "Who knows you're here? "

"Just my coworker Susan. We're pretty close. She's my best friend."

"Would she rat you out about being here?"

"No way."

"Even if she was offered a cash reward or something? Before I load all this up, I need to know that you won't get the blame for it being gone or be put in a situation where you have to rat Josh and me out."

"Well, first off, no one that works here likes Jamar. They'd be thrilled to know his money was gone. Second, nobody even knows about all this money. There're rumors always flying around about him dealing with the mob, but nobody knows anything for sure. And third and most importantly, I'd never tell on you, Tommy. I know you are just doing this to get your father's car. I don't like it at all, but I do understand why."

Tommy was lost in her deep, beautiful eyes for a second. "What about Ms. Hoilman? She knew about this." Then Tommy pointed to the cash. "She's how Josh found out it was here."

"That ol' hag never talks to anyone here. She'd most likely be the only person that would have to know about this since she's the accountant and that's only if he was laundering it or something."

"She went out and got drunk with Josh one night and told him that was exactly what Jamar was doing here. I'd say this loaded safe confirms that rumor, don't ya think?"

Caroline nodded in agreement. "Then that's the only real way you guys would get caught. They have to be the only ones that know. I'm telling you; if anyone else knew, then everyone that worked here would know." Then she found herself gazing into Tommy's eyes the same way he was gazing into hers earlier. "I swear to you, Tommy, we will never say anything."

"What about your car in the shed? Could that cause any problems?"

"I wouldn't think so. I got permission from Tony, the groundskeeper's head manager. I asked him if I could park it here before meeting up with Susan. He thinks I'm there with her. He knows that we live on the beach and that I couldn't leave it there."

Before Tommy could respond to Caroline, the power suddenly went out. The few security lights that were keeping the darkness at bay were now completely out of commission. Jamar's office, along with the rest of the clubhouse, was now very dim, with very little daylight protruding into the building since it was barely shining through the thick storm clouds. "That's great. I guess we're lucky it stayed on as long as it did." Then he pulled an LED-powered lantern out of his backpack. It was still daytime hours, but you'd hardly know it, considering how dark it had become. "Man, it's really getting bad out there. We couldn't drive away right now in this if we wanted to."

"Well, there's nothing else to do, so let's count the money as we pack it. I mean, if you want to. And if you want my help."

Tommy shot her a grin. "Let's get to it then!"

"Wait, how's your eye? We never got the glass out."

"Oh yeah, I was so excited about the money that I had almost forgotten. The adrenaline took away most of the pain; we'll deal with it later."

The two made short work of counting and packing the money while Walter relaxed on the sofa playing with his grandfather's antique portable gaming system.

About an hour after starting, Caroline said, "That's the last one." She placed the last stack of cash in the body bag. "If every single bundle has one thousand in it then there should be just over three hundred and fifty-eight thousand dollars!"

CHAPTER TWENTY-FIVE

Riding Out the Storm

Before Tommy could respond to Caroline's calculated assessment of the cash, the storm intensified severely, causing the three to huddle together in the center of the room. "It must be the eyewalls closing in!" Tommy said with noticeable concern in his voice. "We might as well just chill on the couch and hope for the best at this rate." Caroline shut the office door and then they all sat with Walter in the middle. He looked worried and was no longer playing his game. "You okay there, pal?"

He was sitting in the middle of the sofa, holding his backpack. He finally looked to his left at Tommy and answered him with a flat tone of voice. "Yeah, I guess."

Tommy could tell that Walter was concerned about the hurricane, and rightfully so. The raging wind alone was exceedingly troubling and now the power outage only added to the uneasiness in the air. He tried to cheer him up. "Who's that on your shirt?"

"Oh that, that's The Priest. He's a wrestler on TV." Walter slightly perked up.

"I thought that's who that was. It was hard to tell with the low lighting in here. I know about him very well, actually. Did you ever see that match he had where he was throwing live snakes in the ring?"

"I did! That was so awesome! Hey, guess what? I'm dressing up as The Priest for Halloween!"

Caroline snickered and shot Tommy a look. He smiled at her, then turned to Walter. "That'll be super cool! I hope I get to see your costume. Hey, you hungry, pal?"

Walter held his hands out. "Now that you mention it, I could use a snack."

Tommy dug into his backpack and pulled out a chocolate-flavored protein bar. "Here ya go, dude."

Walter took the treat and then inspected it with the light from his video game. "Oh wow, this looks tasty! Thanks!" Then he shot Caroline an inquisitive look. "Can I go to the kitchen and get a bottle of water, sis?"

"I guess so. Be careful, though!" Caroline instructed as Tommy gave him an extra flashlight. "Don't stand in front of the windows and watch out for all the broken glass at the bar!"

In the blink of an eye, he was halfway down the hall. Tommy gave Caroline a slight smile. "He seems like a real good kid. A smart one, too!"

"He is. He drives me nuts, though."

"I imagine that's what little brothers do."

"Yes." She chuckled. "I don't know what I'd do if something were to happen to him." They both sat quietly for a few seconds. "Oh! Your eye! Do you have any tweezers so I can get that glass out?"

"Yeah, just a sec. Let me get my other flashlight out first."

"Wow, you really came prepared."

"That's all thanks to Josh. He made sure we had just about two of everything that could be useful for any possible situation we could find ourselves in. I sure wish I had packed a second jacket, though. I didn't plan on getting alcohol spilled all over me." A moment later, he had Caroline equipped with the items needed to remove the glass shard from his eye.

"Here, lie down and pry your eye open for me." Tommy did just that. Caroline laid her bosom on Tommy's upper chest and she leaned her head in close to his so she could see. Then she shined the flashlight straight into his eye, causing him to wince. "Sorry."

"It's okay. It feels like it's in the bottom right area." Tommy held his eye open with his thumb and index finger.

"Ooh, I think I see it! Hold still, I'm going in."

Tommy didn't move an inch. He'd lay there all day if she told him to. He was very comfortable, considering he had a piece of glass in his eye. Some of her dark brown hair was hanging down, and it occasionally rubbed up against his face. It tickled him, but he remained still and enjoyed the fruity smell it gave off.

Without warning, Caroline suddenly shouted, "Got it!"

"Wow! You got it already?" Tommy tried to mask his disappointment. He was hoping to stay in that position for longer than a few dozen seconds.

"Yep, the light hit it just right, and I went for it while I had the chance. Does it hurt?"

Tommy sat up and blinked his eyes a few times and rolled them around. "That's a relief. It still stings a little, but at least it doesn't feel like there's a pine cone in there now."

"That's good. I'm really glad it didn't get in your pupil."

"Yeah, that could have been bad." Tommy scooted over and patted the couch. "Have a seat, doc. You seem to have real steady hands. You ever consider being a surgeon?"

"It's funny you say that. That's what my grandpa was." Just then Walter came in with a whole, two-layer, round chocolate cake. "What are you doing? Why do you have that?"

Walter smiled. "I found this in the cooler. I figured, why let it go to waste?"

"You're not eating that all by yourself!" Caroline said with a stern look.

"I didn't plan on it." He set the cake down and opened a plastic bag with plates, napkins, forks, and plastic water bottles.

"I thought we'd all have some." Then he pulled out the protein bar Tommy gave him and held it out to him. "Thanks, but I think I'll pass. I do appreciate it, though."

Tommy laughed. "Keep it for later. But for now, let's eat cake!"

"Give me that flashlight, runt. I've got a surprise of my own!" He did as she asked, then she hopped up and shot out the door.

Tommy shot Walter a puzzled look. "What's all that about?"

Walter gave him a blank stare. "I have no idea."

Tommy shrugged. "I guess we'll find out." Then he hopped up himself. "We're definitely going to be here a while, so let's make ourselves comfortable." Then he rearranged the furniture.

Just as Caroline reentered the room, Tommy was finishing up. "What's all this?" She sat the ice container down next to the couch. "It kinda looks like a campfire set up."

Tommy had pulled Jamar's desk chair across from the sofa and had placed a low-sitting coffee table between the two with the lantern in the middle. "I told your brother that we might as well make ourselves comfortable. We won't be going anywhere anytime soon. Where did you run off to?"

She reached down and grabbed the cherry-flavored sodas. "I thought we'd wash down the cake with something good."

Tommy glanced at the bucket. "Is that glass bottled Cheerwine?"

Walter chimed in. "No way, sis! Awesome score! All I could find was stupid water."

"Nice!" Tommy grinned. "Where did you find these?"

"I have my sources. They should be pretty cold by now."

Tommy grabbed the bucket from her and sat it down on the table next to the cake and lantern. He pulled out two bottles and handed them off to the siblings, then reached for his own. "Before we pop these bad boys open, I'd like to propose a toast."

"Toast? What for?" Walter asked with a wrinkled-up face.

Tommy looked at Caroline and smiled with noticeable excitement before turning to Walter. "Let's make a toast to my first official hurricane party."

Caroline stared at him with a confused look. "Wait, I thought you always lived here. Surely this isn't your first hurricane?"

Tommy smiled. "Oh, this definitely ain't my first hurricane, but it's my first hurricane party, though. We usually just slept through them at Granny's house then went straight to work cleaning up afterward."

Walter immediately held his hands out in front of him. "So you're telling me this is what a hurricane party is?"

"Yeah, what did you think a hurricane party was?" Caroline answered with an unsatisfactory snarl. "It's just a bunch of people hanging out while the storm passes."

A look of understanding washed over Walter's face. "Oh, I thought it had something to do with the Hurricane drink, like a party that only had Hurricanes or something."

Caroline scoffed at her naïve brother.

"So this is y'all's first hurricane party as well?"

They both nodded, causing Tommy to be even more excited as began his toast. "Well then, to our first hurricane party. May it be short, sweet, and most agreeable."

CHAPTER TWENTY-SIX

Scary Story Showdown

The thunder rumbled out at an almost constant rate and the wind howling was relentless as the three new friends sat in a satisfiable state of contentment in Jamar's elaborate office. Tommy sat on one end of the sofa and Caroline sat on the other side while Walter had taken over Jamar's desk chair across from them.

"Man, this is some good cake!" Tommy exclaimed just before taking a drink of his soda.

Walter mumbled in agreement with a full mouth. "Yes!"

"It's alright." Caroline turned up her face. "It's too sweet."

Tommy gave her a slight head nod in agreement. "It is definitely rich, but man, it's so good!"

Walter washed down a big bite with the last of his drink. "Reach me another Cheerwine, will ya Sis?"

"I will not!" Caroline bluntly stated with a mean look in her eyes.

Walter's face now displayed disconsolation. "And why not? Come on and hand it here. This cake is really choking me."

"Then get a drink of water," Caroline instructed with a stern look and powerful finger pointing to the bag that held the water bottles.

"But the Cheerwine washes it down so good. It's the best! Can I just please have it?"

"No, they're mine!"

"No, they're not! You just happened to find them!"

"Yeah, in my locker."

"What were they doing in there?"

"Because I bought them and put them in there. Like I said, they're mine!"

"No way, you're just lying so you can have the last Cheerwine to yourself!" Walter shouted. Then he looked over at Tommy. "Come on, man, back me up. This thing is still in play. Don't let her just take it from us!"

Tommy glanced at Caroline, then smiled at her before looking over at Walter. "Well, to be fair, even if she didn't buy them, she did find them. She brought them in here to share with us when she could have kept them for herself. I think we should be thankful that we got what we did."

Caroline pointed at her brother. "Ha! Told you they were mine, either way!"

Walter flung back in the desk chair in disgust. "This sucks! This is total crap!"

Caroline felt complete joy as she laughed out loud at Walter's reaction.

"Hold on, hold on. Now we have stated that they are indeed Caroline's drinks but as two-thirds of this illustrious hurricane party we would like to issue you a challenge, nay, request that you offer us a sporting chance to claim that sweet, sweet juice for ourselves."

Caroline sat up as she jokingly grew serious. "Request heard but further information is required before a decision can be made."

"I assure you that we are more than willing to supply you with the answers you seek."

Walter's nose curled up. "Why are you guys talking like that?"

"It's all in good spirit to the party, my chap," Tommy said with a grin and a head twist.

"Whatever," Walter mumbled as he repositioned in his chair.

Caroline then asked, "Why should the proper owner of these fabulous sodas be willing to lose one? I guess what I really mean to say is what do I have to gain by answering yes to this request?"

"My dear uh, co-partier, you could gain the respect of your fellow hurricane party members."

Caroline chuckled. "What would I want with that?"

Tommy looked at Walter, then slowly talked in his regular tone. "Come on, ya gotta give us something. Let's play a game or do some challenge for it. We've got nothing but time to kill. Let's make it interesting, at least."

Caroline held her head to the side as she considered the offer for a few seconds. Then to the boys' delight, she said, "Okay. That does sound like fun. What to do, though?"

Tommy looked at Walter. "You got any games or cards with ya, pal?"

"I got my most rare Pokémon cards with me."

"I have no idea how to play those. Do you have regular playing cards by chance?"

"No, I don't really have anything like that on me." Then he had an enlightened look come across his face. "What about we tell campfire stories? Caroline did say it looked like a camping setup in here. That spooky wind sound from the outside makes for the perfect background noise."

"I don't think so, Walter. I still haven't got you to shut up about seeing the Gray Man yet. I don't need you going on about something else for the rest of the month!"

Tommy looked at Walter. "You saw the Gray Man?"

Walter looked down for a moment. "Yeah. Have you ever seen him?"

"I haven't."

"It's probably just me. I'm just crazy or something."

"No, you're not. I know of plenty of people that have seen the Gray Man."

"For real?" Walter asked with a surprised look.

"For real! My uncle Floyd had an encounter with the Lizard Man."

"The Lizard Man? Who's that?"

"He's another one of the local legends around here."

"Can you tell us about him?"

Tommy looked at Caroline. "Well, I'd love to, but if we had a story competition, it would make it a lot more interesting. You know, in the spirit of the party and all."

Walter's face lit up. "Yeah, that's it! The scariest story wins the last Cheerwine!"

"I don't know, Walter," Caroline said with a long face.

"Come on, I can handle it! It will be fine!"

"Fine, birdbrain, but don't come crying to me if you have nightmares or something!"

Walter clenched his fists. "Yes! I'm going first, though. I have the perfect story!"

CHAPTER TWENTY-SEVEN

Walter's Spooky Space Story

Walter cleared his throat, as he began telling his story. *Imagine our world as we know it, but on a different timeline than ours. A timeline where the Space Age came into being before the Wild West was completely settled. Instead of cars being mass-produced the efforts by the rich and mighty men in the late eighteen hundreds, they skipped straight to conquering space. Almost as if they were trying to escape Earth and fast.*

"This better not be something stupid, you little twerp!" Caroline rudely interjected. "You watch all that old junk Pop liked and some of that stuff is just outdated crap, plain and simple, and you'd better not waste our time with a dumb story that ends up making no sense!"

Defensively, Walter belted, "It's not going to be dumb! The old stuff Pop liked is called the classics for a reason. Besides, this is my story that I've thought up a while ago. I might even write a book about it some day!"

"Well, just from that opening, you've got my attention," Tommy said. "You do seem to be very good with words, considering how young you are."

"He should be. All he does is read comics and watch TV and movies. He lives for stuff like this."

Tommy nodded. "Then this should be real good. Please continue, good sir."

Walter cleared his throat in an overly exaggerated manner then shot Caroline a nasty look before continuing. *The scientific discoveries and inventions made in the nineteen hundreds in this reality made ours look like a kindergarten class full of paste eaters. The advances in flight alone were mind-boggling. They had a man on the moon by 1911 and had figured out how to travel outside their galaxy by 1922. Meanwhile, on the streets, the amount of horses still outweighed cars even in the year 2000 when this story takes place. It was comparable to the Jetsons and the Flintstones living amongst each other at the same time.*

"Come on, Walter, how does that make any sense? How would the Jetsons and Flintstones live among each other? The Flintstones would turn into the Jetsons almost immediately if they had access to the same technology."

Walter shot her another nasty look. "Because things are different here. Technology advanced so fast that everyday people did things as simple as possible while the extremely wealthy and the scientist were working on actually advancing the human race instead of just trying to profit off of them like here in our reality."

"Well, if the elite were really so concerned with helping the human race, then why didn't they make sure everybody could have reliable transportation?"

"Because it wasn't necessary. The people in this reality lived in smaller, tight communities and because of this they could have simpler laid back lives. The rat race, I believe that's what it's called, didn't exist there."

"That's just not believable, Walter. All this space travel is supposed to be happening, yet everybody is living in the Wild West using horses?"

Tommy carefully spoke up. "Well, to be fair to Walt, we do have people that live like that right now."

Caroline squinted at him. "Where?"

"I think they are mostly in Pennsylvania and parts of Ohio and a few other places. They call them the Amish."

Caroline's face went blank.

"Ha!" Walter shouted. "We have a similar situation going on now in this world, so please stop judging my story until it's done!"

Tommy felt horrible for getting involved in the siblings' banter, but he felt Caroline was being a little too harsh on her brother. This was just supposed to be a fun activity to kill some time while the hurricane passed. But in Caroline's defense, Walter could be silly and nonsensical at times and perhaps she was being extra critical so he wouldn't waste everyone's time with useless rubbish. He decided he would just be the peacemaker and would defend any harsh judgments Walter may have of Caroline's story when it was her turn. He looked over at her and half-grinned before looking down.

Caroline sat back on the sofa. "Go ahead, Walter. I'm sorry that I was being rude. I just didn't fully understand. It makes more sense now that we've discussed it."

Walter gave her a slight head nod, then he continued. *It's the year 2000 in this alternate universe and the best space marshal in the Earth's Galaxy is Milton Mayberry, also known as The Neptune Kid. Despite being the youngest of the eighty-eight specially handpicked space patrollers that helped to protect our universe, he was considered by his peers to be the best. Being a descendant of Wild Bill Hickok himself had a big reason for that. Because of that fact, though, he was put in charge of Sector Seventeen. Sector Seventeen was by far the most dangerous of all the eighty-eight sectors. It was often referred to as Mako Sica or MS17. Mako Sica was a Native American term that meant badlands. MS17 was chocked full of the worst intergalactic law breakers imaginable.*

The marshal and his posse of twelve specially trained rangers that assisted him rode aboard the Thunderbird—GC. It was a fast ship designed especially for the pursuit of outlaws and smugglers that were frequently in that sector. It was shaped similar to a large bird with outstretched wings and it was colored mainly teal with white trim and tons of chrome. So far, it was very quiet for it to be a Halloween night as the marshal invited the captain to join him in the mess hall to get some real food in them before the Halloween party started.

Even though Caroline had just been put in her place, she couldn't help but question her brother once more. "Wait! They're in space, right?"

"Yeah. Why?"

"Then what does it matter that it's Halloween? It's just a little stereotypical to tell a scary story on Halloween. Don't you think?"

Walter just shrugged. "That's when my story takes place. Even though they are in space, the crew and all the workers still celebrate everything they do on Earth."

Caroline could see he didn't really get what she meant or care to get it at least, so she simply replied, "Okay."

Tommy sat up. "I just got a quick question. Is the marshal not also the captain of the ship?"

Walter had a slight smile. "No. They learned early on that it was best to have a ship with a captain and full crew that only focused on running the ship while the marshals and their posse worried about actually catching the bad guys and enforcing the law. Doing both jobs was just too much for one person, especially in Sector 17."

"Gotcha! That makes a lot of sense." Tommy cut another piece of cake.

Walter nodded. "Let's see, where was I?"

"The captain and the marshal were in the mess hall, I think."

"Oh, yeah!" He cleared his throat. *The marshal was getting ready to spoon out some chili when the captain walked up. "Hey, Skip!" the marshal said with a big smile. That was his nickname for his coworker. "Have some chili with me?"*

The captain ran his hand through his mostly black hair and took a breath. He was twelve years older than the marshal but he never acted like he was his superior. He always treated him as an equal and gave him the respect he deserved. "I'd love to, Marshal, but I just got word that a stray cargo container was spotted just up ahead."

"Probably nothing, but I'll check it out when it's safe to enter the loading deck. We are bringing it on board, ain't we Skip?" the marshal asked with a sideways look.

The captain looked at the floor for a moment then finally said, "As long as the eagle eye doesn't detect any explosions. That's what the book says to do."

The marshal thought that comment was odd coming from such an experienced captain. He had only been serving with him for just over a year, but Rex Dollar had been a range patrol captain for nearly two decades. A short time later, the marshal and three of his men were armed to the teeth with weapons, censors, and scanners as the door to the mysterious container swung open.

One of the marshal's men stood aghast as he mumbled, "What in tarnation?"

CHAPTER TWENTY-EIGHT

Walter's Spooky Space Story, Part 2

"You getting anything on the scanners, Lucky?" the marshal asked as the group of men stared into an empty container.

"Nothing, Marshal," Lucky answered with noticeable confusion. "Who would leave an empty container just floating in space? It seems to be in excellent condition. I imagine it would have to be worth several dozen greenbacks."

"There's no telling, Lucky," the marshal answered. "Let's get back to the mess hall before they start the party." Then the men headed toward the elevator.

"I'll be along later, if that's all right, Marshal. I want to see if I can find any markings or numbers that might tell us something about this thing."

"Have at it, Lucky, but don't be upset if the chili is all gone when you come up."

Lucky let out a laugh as the elevator door shut. "No, sir," he said, then he turned and walked into the container. He was all alone on the loading deck, but he suddenly felt like someone was watching him. He slowly took step after step as he looked for anything that could possibly give any clue whatsoever about why this container was left there and where it could have come from. His effort was to no avail, though, so after he had had enough of searching the big metal box, he started walking out. Right as he got to the entrance of the receptacle, to his horror, the doors shut closed without the slightest warning.

A few hours later, the party was in full swing in the mess hall. All the different workers of the crew had been filtering in and out between their shifts, meanwhile the marshal and the captain had planted themselves in a corner. They were downing plenty of apple cider as they watched the partygoers dancing and enjoying all the food and treats that were on hand.

"It's awfully quiet tonight, Skip."

"Don't you jinx us, Marshal! You don't ever say that when you're on a Galactic Cruiser."

"I didn't take you for the superstitious type."

"Call me what you want, but between what my gut feels and the crap I've seen doing this job, you have to be ready for anything at any time. Besides, haven't you done this job long enough to figure that out for yourself?"

The captain had just barely gotten those words out as Lucky came busting into the mess hall and started firing his rifle wildly about.

The marshal jumped to his feet and drew his pistol. "Lucky! What are you doing?"

Lucky turned to look at the marshal and, as he did, he pointed his rifle at his boss, but before he could pull the trigger, the marshal regrettably unloaded his pistol into one of his best men.

"What the hell is going on, Marshal?" the captain screamed out before calling for assistance on his radio.

The marshal stood in silence over Lucky. He was appalled at what he just had to do to one of his closest friends. "What happened, pal?" He mumbled as he squatted down to get a better look at his fallen comrade. Lucky's eyes had turned black and had blood running out of them.

"Don't touch him, Milton!" The captain screamed out. "He may be contagious!"

It was rare for the captain to call the marshal by his first name. He immediately backed up. "What is this, Skip? Look at his eyes; have you ever seen something like this before?"

"I can't be sure of what it is exactly, but I've heard of similar situations. Was he in that container we just picked up?"

The marshal's eyes got wide as he realized he last left Lucky at the container alone. "This is my fault. I should have made him come up with us."

"This ain't on you, Milton," the captain said as he pulled the marshal out of the mess hall. They were the last two still in there. Everyone else bailed when the shooting started. "I should have listened to my gut. Something was telling me to leave that container alone."

Before they got out of the hallway, another crew member's eyes went black and started to bleed. "We've got a serious problem, Skip!" the marshal declared with a lot of fear in his voice.

The infected crew member started screaming and suddenly fell to the floor of the ship. He was dead. "I think this is the virus called The Reaper's Death. It is a mysterious contagion that is unpredictable and it either kills the infected individual or it drives them mad. It has a one hundred percent mortality rate. Come on, Marshal, there's nothing we can do now but run."

And run they did. The captain led the way down the hall, stopping only to equip himself and the marshal with emergency gas masks and setting off the red alert alarm. The two friends and coworkers decided to get to the escape barrels. They were basically little pods that had a small amount of provisions to help the riders try to survive until help hopefully arrived. Before they could get to them, though, the infected crew members that didn't die instantly came for them. They hated that they had to kill fellow shipmates like that, but they had no choice. The brave marshal and the wise captain mowed them down with their six-shooters like fish in a barrel as they made their way to the actual escape barrels.

Caroline held her arms out as she couldn't stay quiet any longer. "So, by the way your characters talk, they're obviously just plain old cowboys in space. That's a huge enough hurdle to get by with any sort of believability, but shooting guns on the spaceship as well? That's just ridiculous! That's why any other space story uses laser or phaser guns!"

Tommy spoke up as well. "I love your story so far, Walt. I really do, but she's right. If the bullets punctured the spacecraft's hull, it would cause pressure loss and eventually, everyone and everything would get sucked out. If by some miracle that didn't happen, then the stray bullets would ricochet all around landing who knows where. It would be a very dangerous situation either way."

Walter gave the two a brief stare before saying, "They use different bullets while they are on board the spaceships. Their guns can use normal bullets, of course, but while in space they use a special cartridge called cabin plugs. They have the same shape as normal bullets, but they have stored energy in them that shoots out a powerful charge that's deadly to organic life-form. If it hits something that isn't alive, the energy just goes away instead of bouncing around, causing problems."

Tommy smiled. "You just came up with that, didn't ya?"

Walter winked. "It makes sense, don't it?"

"It's perfect. With quick thinking like that, you can overcome any plot hole. I do have a question, though. How was the virus able to close the container when Lucky was in it?"

"You'll see," Walter answered with a devious smile. "Do you really like it so far?"

"Heck yeah! I love your story, bro. You should definitely make it a book. Are you close to finishing this part up, though, because I really need to find a bathroom?"

"Yeah, the shocking conclusion is coming in a minute or so."

With noticeable relief in her voice, Caroline said, "Good, I need a trip to the bathroom as well."

So the captain and the marshal had made it to the bay that housed the escape barrels, but unfortunately, the virus had already spread to that part of the ship. And standing in their way were four of the marshal's best people: Sure Shot Johnny Black, Kate the Outlaw Killer, Blazing Bill Star, and Bad Bobby Stillwater.

"Wonder why they ain't trying to attack us, Skip?" the marshal asked as he gazed at the scary sight of his infected posse staring them down without moving an inch.

"Maybe it's affecting them differently. I sure don't like the looks of this, though. It looks like they want to have a showdown."

"It breaks my heart to no end to have to do this, but we're running out of time. I guess we'll have to oblige 'em," the marshal stated before reloading his two six-shooters.

The captain nodded and followed suit with his single pistol. "I'm wishing I had a duel setup like you, Marshal."

"You and me both skip." He said as both men holstered their weapons and spread out a few feet from each other while staring their opponents down.

The four members of the posse stared back. Their eyes oozed blood, and they looked like they had been sent to collect the two men from Satan himself. The captain's gas mask started fogging up and he quickly pulled it off so he wouldn't have an obstructed view. The marshal noticed and did the same.

"You ready to show 'em why they call you the Neptune Kid, Marshal?" The captain said as his fingers were nervously fluttering just above his pistol, ready to draw at any second.

"Make sure you get Kate, Skip. I can't get her and Sure Shot. They're just too fast."

"I'll do what I can. They're all faster than me, Marshal."

"Just get Kate. I'll handle the rest."

The six stood as still as statues, except for a few trembling hands as they all waited to draw. After a moment of agonizing silence, Bad Bobby Stillwater was the first to make a move as he grabbed for his tomahawk.

CHAPTER TWENTY-NINE

Bathroom Break

*T*he showdown was now underway as Stillwater's grab for his trusty tomahawk had signaled the beginning. Before he could even throw his authentically made Native American weapon, the marshal had drawn both of his pistols and made short work of Sure Shot Johnny and Blazing Bill. Unfortunately for the captain, he was distracted by the intimidating tomahawk and shot Stillwater first instead of Kate the Outlaw Killer. This allowed her to fire two rounds into the captain before the marshal could get her.

"Dang it, Skip!" the marshal mumbled as he looked at the revolting sight of his best people laying dead, and his friend, the captain, wasn't far behind the posse. He bent down to console his coworker and held him by the shoulders.

"I tried my best, Marshal."

"I know you did, Skip. It's a fine line between winning and losing these things. If one of my guns had jammed, I'd be laying right here with ya."

"Listen, Mayberry," the captain mumbled between dying breaths, "get in the escape barrel and make sure nobody boards this ship!"

"I'm taking you wit—" Before the marshal could finish his sentence, he saw a transparent-looking worm about six inches or so in length, crawling on the captain. Before he could do anything, the worm lunged at the captain's face and began boring into his eye socket. In a flash, the worm had buried itself into the captain's head. The marshal jumped to his feet and watched in horror as the captain's eyes started to bleed and he had a furious look overtake him. The marshal turned and began running for the escape barrel. As he did, he saw more of the disgusting worm-like creatures coming out of the eye sockets of his posse members. "It's not a virus, it's a parasitic creature!"

As he closed in on the barrel, he looked back to see the captain and several of the worms coming after him. He got inside the escape pod and closed the door just as the terrible creatures got to him. The captain let out several bone-chilling screams and pounded on the barrel with great ferocity.

"I'm sorry, my ol' friend. You deserved a far better fate than this," the marshal said as he watched the gruesome sight from the porthole of the escape barrel. Unable to watch his friend act like the monster he had become any longer, he pressed the launch button and regrettably went flying into space, leaving the Thunderbird and all his fellow crew members and friends behind forever.

Sometime later, the marshal finally fell asleep from the exhaustion of the whole nightmare scenario he just lived through. He woke up to the sight of the captain standing next to him in the mess hall. He had a bowl of his favorite chili sitting in front of him and several of his posse members were standing around; all of which were either helping prepare for the Halloween party or eating some real food before the festivities started.

"What's a matter, Marshal, not been getting enough beauty sleep?" the captain asked with a big grin.

Before the marshal could answer, a voice came across his radio saying, "Sorry to bother you, Captain, but we've spotted an empty cargo container floating up ahead. Should we bring it on board?"

Without any warning, the marshal jumped to his feet and screamed, "No!"

With great pride Walter stood up from Jamar's chair and said, "The End."

Tommy clapped and hollered, "Bravo, bravo!"

Walter performed several exaggerated bows before his audience of two.

"Not bad, kiddo. Not bad at all." Caroline stood up and stretched.

"Who's next?" Walter asked with ample enthusiasm.

"The bathroom!" Caroline headed for the door.

"Agreed!" Tommy stood up as well. "Would you be so kind to tell a feller where they are, Miss?"

"Gladly!"

A short time later, Caroline walked up to Walter and Tommy as they stared out the window at the breathtaking storm. "Wow, it's crazy how strong the wind is." Caroline rubbed the hand sanitizer on her fingers and palms. "I'd say it's a miracle that anything could survive this. I couldn't imagine being out there right now."

Tommy looked at her and smiled. The alcohol from her sanitizer filled the area. "Thanks for that. I was just considering going out to check on Josh."

"No, Tommy!" Caroline barked, being protective. She looked down and took a step back. "I just, uh, I just think he's fine and you shouldn't risk getting hurt just to see that he's okay."

Tommy appreciated her concern. "Yeah, you're probably right. I sure am glad he got to park the ambulance in the shed. There's no way he could have worked on it out in this mess."

The three watched the trees dancing around wildly and at times they appeared to almost lay over flat from the strong and scary winds.

"I guess it was a good thing Jamar stopped by then," Caroline noted. "He got Josh out of the storm and opened the safe for us."

Tommy nodded in agreement. "Yeah, it was definitely a good thing he stopped by." He took off his hat and rubbed his head.

Walter watched Tommy and noticed that his hat had formed his hair into a perfect square. "Whoa, dude, your bad case of hat hair has you looking just like Frankenstein!"

Tommy threw him a nasty look, then glanced at Caroline. She stared back at him with a serious look on her face before bursting into laughter. "It looks that good, does it?" He now had a disingenuous smile.

"It's that spray color you put in it!" Caroline said before starting another round of laughter.

"The only thing missing is two steel bolts in his neck and some stitches in his forehead!" Walter added between chuckles.

Tommy felt embarrassed and slipped his cap back on. Just as he did, a large tree branch crashed onto the deck, making an extra loud thud.

"I think it's time we get back to the office!" Caroline proclaimed, and the boys agreed as they all bolted down the hallway.

Everyone was snuggled comfortably back into their spots in Jamar's office when Walter asked, "Who's next? Whose turn is it to tell their story? Or do you guys just want to go ahead and forfeit after hearing mine? You might as well go ahead and hand me over the last Cheerwine."

"I don't think so, fart face! Tommy's next. You always save the best for last."

Tommy seemed a bit uncomfortable. "Go ahead. My story doesn't compare to what Walter just told."

"But it's real isn't it?" Walter asked as he placed his feet on the coffee table and leaned back in the desk chair.

"Yeah, but it's super boring compared to your frontier space story."

Caroline spoke up. "Go ahead, Tommy. You said yourself that we got nothing but time to kill and we might as well have some fun."

"Yeah, I want to hear it! Please, Tommy! I'll take back the Frankenstein remark," Walter pleaded with clasped, begging hands.

Tommy sat up and shrugged his shoulders. "Okay, here goes nothing!"

CHAPTER THIRTY

Tommy's True and Terrifying Tale

In the late eighties, a very strange creature was spotted in a small town's swampy regions just under a couple of hours from here. Reports of crazy sightings, unknown animals, and weird lights have always come and gone around here, but this account was different. It actually made the national news. The area's sheriff even made a public announcement and took the situation very seriously after pictures emerged showing some destruction to two different cars that were possibly caused by this unknown creature.

With wide eyes and a curious tone, Walter belted out, "What was it? Was it a bigfoot or something?"

Tommy smiled and shook his head. "It definitely wasn't a bigfoot."

With even more excitement built up in him, he continued asking questions. "What was it then? Did you see it? What did it do to the cars?"

"Cheese and rice, Walter! Calm down and let him tell the story!"

Tommy snickered as he looked at Caroline. "Cheese and rice?"

Caroline rolled her eyes as she explained her quirky saying. "I got in big-time trouble as a kid saying swear words I heard our mom say, so she came up with a slew of substitutes she used instead. Cheese and rice has always been a popular one for us."

Tommy chuckled. "That's funny. I'll have to remember that one."

"Enough with the chit-chat on that stupid saying. Let's get back to the real story!" Walter exclaimed with flailing arms.

"You're the idiot that keeps asking questions. I'm sure Tommy will tell us everything in due time. If you will let him, that is!"

"It's okay, I'm not the best storyteller, but I will do my best."

So roughly twenty years later, Uncle Floyd was dating a nice lady over in Lee County, which just happened to be the area where this mysterious being was spotted those same twenty years earlier. He drove over to be with his lady friend a couple of times a week during this time frame. One Friday night as he was leaving her place, they heard a terrifying scream come out from the woods behind her trailer. Uncle Floyd grabbed a mag light from his truck and went to check it out, but the noises coming from there got louder and more intense. So she made Uncle Floyd come back inside and she called the cops. Uncle Floyd didn't really want her to, but he'd never heard such horrendous noises in his life and he didn't want to leave her alone.

With noticeable concern in his voice, Walter asked, "What did the noises sound like?"

"Uncle Floyd said it was like the door to hell and been opened and the worst beast in there was taking its frustrations out on the woods. He said it was otherworldly sounding for sure, and he'd never heard anything come close to sounding like that. It had a low beast-like sound that you could feel in your chest and yet it was terribly loud."

Several minutes later, two deputies showed up to investigate and Uncle Floyd went out back with them. All three men had their flashlights and scanned the area the best they could, but the trees were too dense to see through. One deputy asked the other if that area wasn't far from where the incident happened twenty years earlier and, to his displeasure, he confirmed that thought. After a few more minutes, the deputies, with undeniable fear on their faces, said it was two animals fighting and there was nothing they could do. Uncle Floyd was pissed and couldn't believe they had said that. It was clear to him that it was just one thing making the noise, and he confronted the officers about the ridiculous statement. They just shrugged it off though and said that there was no law being broken and no one was actively in danger, so there was nothing they could really do, so they left.

Uncle Floyd was furious, but there was nothing he could do either, so he took his lady friend with him to Granny's place. Granny was his sister, and he had lived with her ever since Paw died. She didn't like being alone, and he didn't mind helping out around the place. Plus, it gave him a free place to store all the equipment and other things he needed for the business. He knew she wouldn't mind if his lady friend stayed over a night or two, especially considering the circumstances. So after getting her an overnight bag packed, they hit the road. The noise was still coming from behind the trailer as they drove off. His lady friend had a long, dark, dirt road for a driveway. Just as they were finally getting to the end of it, a small greenish-looking flash ran out in front of his ol' Ranger. Even though he wasn't driving very fast, he couldn't get stopped in time and he ran whatever it was over. He carefully opened his door to check and nothing was there. A little further up the road they heard a thud from the bed of the truck but when they both looked, they couldn't see anything because it was just too dark on the lonely back road.

Well, a little while later they stopped at a Bojangles drive-thru to grab a couple of chicken biscuits and some sweet tea. They were caught off guard by a strange comment by the worker at the window. They made a comment to them about how brave they must be to go gator hunting. At the time, it didn't make any sense at all so they just shook it off and went on home and made the best of the situation.

The next morning, Uncle Floyd went out to get a can of tobacco out of his truck and the driver's side mirror was all messed up. The glass was broken out of it and laying in a pile on the driveway and the chrome mirror itself was all bent up. It looked as if something had literally chewed it up. There were all kinds of puncture marks in it. Whatever had done it had very sharp and pointed teeth. Uncle Floyd called the cops, but this was a different county and besides, he knew most of the squad real good here, unlike the two cowards—his words, not mine—he dealt with over in Lee County the night before. Once the deputy came out, he was insistent that it was a black bear responsible for the damage until they saw the footprints that the creature left behind. It certainly wasn't a bear because the tracks had a three-pointed toe shape about them. The deputy's face went pale when he realized where he saw them before. It was the same type of footprint that was found twenty years earlier over in Lee County when the mysterious creature was spotted back then. The deputy told Uncle Floyd he was just a kid then, but his stepdad was working there as a surveyor when the incident happened and he saw the creature himself with his own two eyes. Uncle Floyd said the deputy was legit concerned and got kinda jerky and started acting real nervous. What exactly was the creature? That's what Uncle Floyd had asked. He didn't pay much attention to the news and couldn't remember the account from the eighties. The deputy recounted one of the first sightings. So the deputy went on to tell Uncle Floyd how the first reported sighting of the Lizard Man was by a young man that had to stop one night and fix a flat tire. The young feller said that when he finished changing the tire and closed his trunk, he heard a rustling sound just several feet from the car. When he shined his light in that direction, there it stood, all seven feet of the pale green reptiloid creature with its blaring red eyes staring a hole through him. The young guy was frozen in fear until the giant nightmare of a being started coming at him.

"Wait a minute!" Walter leaned forward in the desk chair. "So, this thing wasn't a Sasquatch?"

Tommy shook his head with a small laugh. "Nope. Those that saw it said that it was some sort of lizard man."

"A lizard man?" Walter looked beyond puzzled. "That's kind of ridiculous."

Tommy shot him a look. "More ridiculous than a bigfoot?"

Walter sat back in his seat. "Yeah, yeah. Bigfoot just seems more believable, is all. A lizard person seems like pure science fiction."

"That's what everyone else that didn't see the Lizard Man thought, too. But those that did see him were terrified and very adamant about what they saw."

So the deputy went on to tell Uncle Floyd how his encounter with the Lizard Man went. He explained with great detail how he was playing around with some sticks while his stepdad worked and off in the distance, he saw a giant green man with red, glowing eyes walk out between two trees. He ran to his stepdad, who thankfully had a shotgun strapped to his back because of all the hoopla about the man-like reptile up to that point. It was fortunate that he did because the green ogre was coming after them now. His father figure got the shotgun in position and unloaded a few shells into the swamp beast. He hit and injured it and fortunately for them, it ran off. Now scared out of their minds, they got back to their truck and called the police. Strangely enough though, after finding actual blood from the creature at the location where it was injured, the deputy's stepdad was arrested for illegal possession of a firearm.

Caroline sat on the edge of her seat. "Wasn't the gun properly registered or something?"

Tommy took a sip of water. "To the best of my knowledge, South Carolina doesn't have any restrictions or requirements when it comes to shotguns. Back then, it might have been different, but I highly doubt it."

"Sounds like a cover-up," Walter added. "If the gun was illegal, why wasn't he arrested when they came out to investigate? Why wait two days later?"

Tommy pointed at his new juvenile friend. "Exactly! Some folks think the DNA test showed evidence of an unknown creature that the powers that be didn't want getting out, so the deputy's stepdad was silenced."

The deputy went on to tell Uncle Floyd that his stepdad told the court that he made up the story for attention. He ended up losing his job, and they wound up moving over to our county. The deputy also went on to say that one of the biggest reasons he got into law enforcement was because of this incident. He was disgusted at the lack of justice and he wanted to make a difference. Oddly enough, just a few short months later, the very same deputy went missing after going out hunting. To this day, he was never seen again and the legend of the Lizard Man lives on.

CHAPTER THIRTY-ONE

Caroline's Creepy Chronicle

Walter sat in amazement at Tommy's story. "So you're telling us there's a giant green man-lizard thingy running around these parts?"

"Some people believe so." Tommy gave a half grin. "It's no crazier than you seeing the Gray Man, is it?"

"It's not crazier, but it is concerning. At least the Gray Man isn't bad, supposedly. This thing sounds terrifying."

Caroline pointed at Walter. "You wanted to hear some scary stories, twerp, so you better not freak out!"

"I'm not freaking out! I'm just trying to understand. There're all kinds of stories about people seeing things, but it's never fully explained or researched. Sometimes it feels like there's a whole world out there being hidden from us."

Caroline gave her brother a blunt response. "People make crap up, Walter. They do it for attention, as a prank that they think is funny, or just off of a dare or bet from their friends. You can't take this stuff too serious."

Tommy added, "That's true. People do sometimes make stuff up, but I do feel like that if there is any truth to these types of stories, then the powers that be are definitely keeping the truth from us."

"Why though?" Caroline asked. "What do they have to gain from keeping this from the public?"

"I'm not sure, but too many things just don't add up."

"I think Tommy's right," Walter said with conviction. "The way the cops didn't arrest that guy until two days later, that makes no sense. Something is most certainly wrong there."

Caroline shrugged. "We may never know. Either way, I'm ready to tell my story. It's not true, but I imagine if your theory on us being kept in the dark when it comes to certain things, then it very well could be on some level."

Tommy gave Walter an excited look, then turned back to Caroline. "Let's hear it!"

It was Halloween night in an unknown town in the middle of nowhere.

Walter lunged forward in his chair. "Wait just a dang minute!"

Caroline shot him a confused look. "What's the matter with you, barf breath?"

"You gave me all kinds of grief about my story taking place on Halloween, but yours can?"

"Well, yeah, it's pertinent to my story. It wasn't for yours. They could have picked up those space worms at any time."

Instead of continuing the debate, Walter flung his arms at her. "Whatever." He slumped back in his chair.

The year was 1979 and Karen Morrison was new in town. She lived there basically alone; it was only her and her daughter, Beth. Her husband had a special job with the military and they were constantly moving around and he was rarely home. This was, yet again, the case as Karen prepared to take her precious six-year-old daughter out trick or treating.

"How much candy can I have tonight, Mommy?" Beth asked as she adjusted her black hat that sat atop her green-painted face.

"We'll see, dear. It's really not wise to fill up on sugar right before bed."

"Why?" she asked in a whiny tone of voice.

"*Because it's just not good for you. Now run along and get your bag while Mommy checks her makeup.*"

Sometime later, Karen was beyond ready to go home. They had hit up all the businesses and easily accessible houses in the small community but Beth wasn't done collecting candy. On the long, dark, and winding road home, she spotted what appeared to be a dimly lit Jack-o'-lantern between the trees.

"*Turn here, Mommy! I saw a house with a pumpkin!*"

"*Are you sure, sweetheart? Don't you wanna get back home and sort through your candy?*" *Karen asked in a condescending manner. She was through with the kid stuff and wanted to get back home and read her new stack of magazines she picked up at the drugstore.*

"*No, Mommy, just one more house, please!*" *Beth pleaded from the back seat of the old green station wagon.*

"*Fine, Beth, but this is it! We are going home after this!*" *Karen turned onto the driveway that led to the house Beth saw from the road.*

The driveway was in terrible shape and looked like it hadn't been driven on in years. Against her better judgment, Karen took her overzealous offspring to the dilapidated shack. Upon arrival, Karen immediately noticed the absence of the Jack-o'-lantern that Beth supposedly saw. She was also unsettled by the Halloween decorations. They were certainly not store-bought and the ones not made out of sticks and tree branches looked like they could have been several decades old.

Karen turned around to Beth and said, "Are you sure we should go here, dear? This place looks a little too scary for you."

Beth let out a hardy little chuckle. "Oh, Mommy, you're not really scared, are you?"

Truthfully, she was petrified but after that brash comment, she couldn't let Beth know. "Of course not, dear. Grab your bag."

A short moment later, the pair stood in front of a well-worn-out wooden door with strange markings scribbled on it. A dim bluish-colored light gently escaped a single-pane window next to the entrance.

"Can I knock now, Mommy"? Beth asked with her big blue puppy dog eyes.

Against her better judgment, once again, she reluctantly said, "Yes, go ahead."

Beth put her little hand up to the door and knocked. After seeing that the normal way of knocking wasn't making enough noise to alert the shack's inhabitants, she balled up her fist and began banging wildly.

"Beth! What are you doing?" her mother asked with a concerned look. "That's very rude, dear!"

"Well, how was I supposed to know? I want them to be able to hear me."

Before Karen could say anything else, the door burst open, scaring the two. "Who dares disturb me?" said a frail yet disturbing voice from behind an old brown nightgown.

Karen went pale and finally found the courage to utter, "Sorry to disturb you, Miss. We thought you were giving out candy for trick-or-treaters."

"Why should I hand out something for free?" she asked in a menacing tone. "How about a treat for a trick? Or a trick for a treat?" Then she gazed over the two unexpected and unwelcomed guests as if she were sizing them up.

Karen just stared at the nasty hag, not really knowing how to answer her cryptic-sounding questions. Her cold, black, beady eyes felt as if they could suck out her soul, and she was repulsed by the dark brown stains around her mouth. She felt threatened and didn't like it at all. With bass in her voice, she firmly said, "Listen, we just thought you were handing out candy. Now if you don't have anything we'll be on our way."

"I love your costume!" Little Beth said with so much enthusiasm as she gazed up at the unhappy figure now standing before her.

Karen sighed and began apologizing. "I'm so sorry. She's only six."

Without the slightest signal, the old lady screamed something incoherent very loudly and started waving her arms around and then began repeating some sort of chant.

"Come on, Beth!" Karen yelled as she grabbed her daughter's arm and they ran to the car.

As Caroline had gotten lost in telling her story, she hadn't noticed how bad the wind had gotten. Tommy had given Walter a few concerned looks as it whistled around the building with great ferocity. He was hesitant as he said, "Sorry to interrupt your story but I might oughta check out the radio to see what they are saying about this hurricane."

Caroline gave him a stern look of annoyance as she exclaimed, "This is an outrage!"

CHAPTER THIRTY-TWO

Weather Update

Tommy's face had gone blank as he tried to process Caroline's sudden and uncharacteristic act of rudeness. I'm sorr—"

Before Tommy could apologize, Caroline laughed out and smacked her hands together in an unorganized clap a few times. "Gotcha!"

Walter cracked a smile, then Tommy finally loosened up and, with a red face of embarrassment. "Yeah, you got me all right!"

"Of course, we can check the radio. I was just wanting to mess with you." She chuckled. "You should have seen your face!"

Tommy dug through his bag. "I'm glad I could be a source of entertainment for you."

"Well, messing with you has to be more entertaining than my crappy story."

Tommy gave her a perplexed look. "What are you talking about? Your story is pretty awesome so far."

Then Walter chimed in. "Yeah it is! Was the old lady a witch or something?"

Caroline's face went blank. "No. She's just a crazy lady that lives in the woods. She's really not important to the overall story. I only mentioned her because she helps move the trick-or-treating part of the story forward."

Tommy found his portable radio and started cranking a black plastic handle on it. This caught Water's attention.

"Whoa, that's so cool! Do you crank it to make it work?"

"Yep." Tommy continued to spin the handle, building up enough electricity to power the compact unit. "This one doesn't take batteries. You have to use some elbow grease to listen to this one."

"Why do they say that? Our elbows don't have any grease in them," Walter said with his arms out to his sides, expressing his confusion about the old saying.

Tommy laughed out loud. "I honestly don't know where that saying comes from, either. I just know Uncle Floyd said it all the time. I'd imagine it has something to do with working your arm so much that you would supposedly need to add grease to it to keep it working, but I honestly don't have a clue."

Caroline sat forward on the sofa to stretch her back. "Can you find the Ed dude on that thing?"

Tommy raised a brow. "Ed dude? Do you mean Ed Piotrowski?"

"That's him!" It was an obvious eureka type of moment for her. "Susan is always going on about him. She is always saying Ed says this or Ed says that, but I do have to give it to her because he's usually right. He's a very accurate meteorologist."

Tommy nodded. "He's definitely the best weatherman in the entire Grand Strand area. He's got a sweet Camaro, too!"

"Oh really, that's cool. Susan loves him so much that she even has a bobblehead of him in her locker."

Just then, Tommy tuned in to a relatively clear station. A male robotic-sounding voice boomed out through the whiny speakers. Walter gave his sister a look. "Is that him?"

"Be quiet, Walter!" Caroline demanded as Tommy pulled out the antenna to try to strengthen the signal.

"It's not Ed, but at least it's something," Tommy remarked with a shrug.

The robotic voice said, "Hurricane Faye is still currently a category three hurricane at this time with average wind speeds of one hundred and fifteen miles per hour with recorded gusts at times reaching past one hundred and twenty-five miles per hour."

"Holy crap! The wind is blowing that fast right now?" Walter exclaimed before being hushed by Caroline.

"Can you please keep your mouth shut for at least thirty seconds?" She pleaded with flailing arms.

The radio broadcast said, "The storm surge is currently at nine to twelve feet. Hurricane conditions are expected to last in the coastal Carolina regions for the next few hours as the trajectory for Faye heads North West towards the Appalachian Mountain range areas where it is expected to break apart and dissipate quickly. For now, be sure to stay indoors and away from windows." Then the annoying beep-like sound played, and the recording started over with the same message.

Tommy turned the crank radio off. "Looks like we'll definitely be stuck in here for at least a few more hours."

Caroline nodded. "Yeah, it sounds insane out there! Fortunately, it seems to be moving through pretty quick, though."

The wind continued to howl in an unsettling fashion and the window in Jamar's office was making some disturbing popping and cracking sounds. Walter shot the noisy area a concerned look before grabbing the last Cheerwine and stirring it through the almost completely melted ice. "Looks like we'd better finish our challenge before the Cheerwine gets too warm."

Caroline was spooked by the noisy window as well. "It'd take our minds off that crazy wind if nothing else." Tommy nodded in agreement.

So the rest of the holidays were pretty much seamless for Karen and Beth. Daddy was home through Christmas and New Year's, which was most enjoyable for the mother and daughter. Unfortunately, though, little Beth got sick in late spring. Before summer had settled in, the little angel unexpectedly died of her mysterious illness.

Walter, now with his eyes full of concern, said "Wait, Beth, the little six-year-old got sick and died?"

Caroline gazed at her sibling with a serious face. "Sadly yes, but that's not the bad part of this story, not even close. It's just the beginning."

It had been two weeks after Beth's burial and Karen's husband had to go back to work. So now she was stuck in a miserable town, all alone and grieving for her only child. The only relief she could even begin to feel was visiting Beth's grave every day. So one evening, just as the sun started to set, Karen found herself waking up from an unexpected nap. She looked out and could tell nightfall was coming fast, but she felt as if she couldn't face the bleakness of another lonely night without visiting Beth's grave site. She was now faced with the decision of braving the darkness in the community's oldest and biggest cemetery or suffering the heartache of longing for companionship. She decided that at least ten minutes of being at Beth's grave site would give her the best chance of tolerating the lifeless night.

"I better get going," she mumbled as she hopped off the sofa.

Without warning, Walter let out a wisecrack. "If her sofa looks anything like the old ones at Grandma and Grandpa's, that's terrifying enough without adding anything else!"

Caroline and Walter chuckled as Tommy asked, "What's with the couches there?"

Walter let out a despairing moan. "Dude, these things are so ugly!"

Caroline added, "He's not lying. They're these old poofy pink things that are super uncomfortable and beyond hideous!"

Tommy had a look of intrigue. "Oh, I see."

"And to make them even worse, they have this brownness that has like settled on them. It's not stained or anything because Walter and I both have tried scrubbing them clean, but it doesn't help."

"It's probably something in the material. It's aged or something and has changed colors," Tommy suggested.

Caroline then added, "Yeah, that makes sense. Mom won't let us get rid of them."

Just then Walter had a realization and subtly stated, "Hey, I guess if the hurricane destroys the house, at least those awful sofas will finally be gone."

Caroline rolled her eyes. "Seriously, Walter. That's a pretty stupid statement."

Walter snapped back, "Hey, I'm just trying to look at the bright side."

"You're always saying that, Walter! The bright side! Look outside. Do you see anything bright about this?"

Trying to lighten the tense mood that the squabbling siblings had created, Tommy said, "Hey, there's your pen name if you ever do decide to write your story you told us earlier. Walter Bright!"

Walter sat and processed the idea. "Walter Bright. I kinda like it. It's definitely better than Walter Burger. Everybody's always saying 'Like a cheeseburger?' when they hear our last name."

"It does have a neat ring to it, even if I did come up with it." Tommy chuckled. Then he looked at Caroline. "So Karen did go to the graveyard?"

Karen got to the cemetery as the sun was dropping below the horizon. Fortunately, she grabbed a flashlight on her way out. As she closed in on little Beth's grave site, she noticed something out of place. There was a mass of something laying around the area. As she walked up it, she realized it was piles of dirt strewn about. Her heart sank as she shined the flashlight into a freshly dug hole, only to see Beth's casket. It had been opened and her body was gone!

CHAPTER THIRTY-THREE

Winner Takes All

K aren dropped to her knees in horror. She just couldn't comprehend what she was seeing. In a wild panic, she shined the flashlight all around. She didn't really know what she was looking for other than any possible clues as to what happened and where Beth's body was. Suddenly, off in the distance, she saw the silhouette of a man. With caution, she approached and called out to him.

"Hey! You there? What's going on here?" she yelled out.

A short, older man dressed in coveralls slowly answered back, "What's the problem, ma'am?"

She quickly explained what she had walked upon and demanded to know who he was. He told her his name was Joe and that he was the caretaker of the cemetery. He hadn't seen the disturbed grave yet. Karen took him over to show him the scene and he immediately had a realization come to him and it was easily visible on his face.

"I'm sorry to tell you this, ma'am, but this is the work of a ghoul."

She immediately lashed out, "A ghoul? Don't drop some bull crap line on me about that! What do you take me for, a fool?"

"No, ma'am, I'm not taking you for a fool at all. You don't understand. The place has had ghoul problems off and on for years. It's been a good bit since we've had one, but here we are."

"Stop messing with me! What did you do with my daughter's body?"

Seeing that she wasn't going to believe him without evidence, he unzipped his coveralls and showed her a massive scar across his chest. "You see that?" He shined his flashlight on the previously damaged area. "That was from my first encounter with a ghoul. I've worked the same place for thirty years and I can assure you ghouls are very real. This just recently happened so if you follow the loose dirt, you might be able to stop it before it—" He paused for a second as he didn't want to say what was going to happen but he knew he must so he finally mumbled out, "It will eat your daughter's remains."

Karen let out an unnerving scream, then she began to cry. "That's, that's absolutely horrible! Can you help me, please? Can you help me get her back?"

"No, I'm sorry, ma'am. I'm in poor health, but I can give you my machete." Then he reached around to his side and pulled out the large-bladed weapon. "Be sure to shine your flashlight in its eyes. This won't kill it, but it should stun it good. That should give you enough time to get your daughter back. Unfortunately, ghouls have to be decapitated in order to be killed. Go now, there's still time."

"Please, isn't there someone we can call to help? I can't do this. I don't know what I'm doing."

"If you don't go now, all is lost! Just follow the loose dirt and drag marks. It can't be far at all!"

Karen looked up at the dark sky and cried out. After grabbing her face and telling herself that she had to do this, she started following the unintentional trail left behind by the ghoul. After ten minutes or so she had found herself deep in the woods that sat beside the cemetery. She began to feel panic coming on as if the terror or tracking a ghoul wasn't enough. She had become lost and wasn't sure which way would lead her back out. As she stood trying to figure out her next move, especially since the trail had gone cold, she heard a rustling of leaves a few feet away. She shined the light in the direction of the noise and caught a glimpse of a white flash. To Karen's horror, something had ducked in behind a tree.

"Hey, I see you, asshole! Give me back my daughter!" she yelled out as she readied the machete.

Off in the distance behind her, she heard Joe call out, "Ma'am, did you find it?"

"I think so! It's behind a tree over here!"

With a snail's pace Joe came walking up beside her, trying to catch his breath. "I'm slow, but I can still go when I need to."

"Thank God you're here!" she said with a sigh of relief. "There's no way I can do this, but I can help." Then she handed him his well-worn tool as she said, "I'll shine the light so you can take this thing out."

Joe took the machete and crept toward the tree, where Karen saw the white flash. She walked beside him, holding the flashlight. After what felt like an eternity, they got to the area and, as they rounded the tree, Karen let out an ungodly scream. There on the cold, dark ground was her precious daughter.

"Was the ghoul eating her?" Walter asked from the edge of his seat. "It was, wasn't it?"

Caroline gave her brother a wicked smile as she shook her head and said, "No!"

To Karen's ultimate horror, she just laid eyes on her only daughter. The recently lost light of her life was still wearing the white dress she had her buried in, but she was the one bent over a freshly dug-up corpse. It appeared to be an older man, and she was franticly chewing on his face. She slowly looked up and stared into the flashlight with her glossy animal-looking eyes as the formaldehyde and decayed flesh mixture dripped off her chin in a disturbing fashion.

"Is that your daughter, ma'am?" Joe asked with a terrified look of his own.

She nodded as tears streamed down her face.

He went on to say, "I didn't want to say anything earlier but I had just saw another dug-up grave before I ran into you. I'm sorry, ma'am, but it appears your daughter is actually the ghoul."

"No, no! This can't be!" Karen shouted as she sobbed uncontrollably. Between her cries, she started hearing laughter. After finally getting

her crying under control, she realized it was Joe, the cemetery caretaker that was the one laughing. Her anguish turned to confusion as she asked, "What are you doing? What's so funny?"

Right before her very eyes, Joe turned into the old lady from the creepy house at which Beth insisted on trick or treating.

"Wait a minute!" Walter demanded. "Joe was actually the old lady, which was actually a witch?"

"Yep!" Caroline confirmed with a conniving grin.

Then Walter bellowed out in anger, "But earlier you said the witch didn't have anything else to do with the story!"

"It's called misdirection, booger brain. How good would the story be if you always knew what was going to happen next?"

Walter gave his older sister a look of displeasure. "But why? Why is the witch doing this?"

Karen fell to her knees, overcame with complete shock. "What, uh, why? What is this? What's going on here?"

"I'll tell you what's going on here, fancy pants," the witch said with her frail but still powerful voice. "You're getting your just rewards for mocking the Queen of the Night!"

Still confused, Karen asked, "What are you talking about?"

On All Hallows Eve, you and your brat came knocking on my door on one of my most religious days. As if that wasn't bad enough, you had the nerve to parade your offspring around in what everyone thinks witches wear. You had the nerve to mock me straight to my face. So I sent you on your way with a nice little spell that eventually turned your daughter into a corpse eater."

Karen's face went from a look of terror to completely blank. She eventually said, "Why? We weren't mocking you, we weren't making fun of you, and we meant you no harm or ill will whatsoever. It was an innocent trick-or-treating act with an innocent child. How could you? How could you commit such a horrific act?"

"I'll tell you how I could!" the witch snapped back at Karen. "When I saw your vain carcass prancing on my porch, I felt your bad energy.

You had no love for your only child. You wanted me to make her happy so you could be done. You didn't want her taking up any more of your time. You held no true love for that child at all until she was dead. And even then, you couldn't show an act of love by rescuing her when you thought her remains were in danger. Instead, you wanted somebody else to do the dirty work. Now here's your last chance at showing love. Take this blade and cut the head off of the monster that your daughter has become. Give her peace!"

Karen stood up and took an aggressive stance. "That's insane; what gives you the right? Who are you to judge me? What gives you any authority to do this? Tell me now!"

"I'll tell you what gives me the authority; I'm the Queen of the Night! I'm the legend all the tales about witches came from. I'm as old as time itself and my job is to consume extreme vanity as to keep the Earth from falling into total darkness."

"So vanity is the only evil?"

"No!" the witch shouted. She was growing tired of Karen's arguing. "My sisters take care of other energies, but that's nothing for you to worry about. Your only concern now is if you're going to put your daughter down. You must decapitate her. Show her an act of love. She wouldn't want to be the monster she has become."

Karen got up in the witch's face and said, "No! This still doesn't make sense! All we were doing was trick or treating! Why did this really happen?"

To her surprise the witch got an even meaner look on her face as she said, "I appear where the vanity energy is currently strongest. After my arrival, you have a short amount of time to show an act of love. Even as your daughter lay dying, you still couldn't pass the test with the simplest of gestures."

Appalled by that sentence, Karen yelled, "An act of love? All I did was care for her constantly. Before and after her illness! I stayed in a dead relationship with her father for her sake! Don't tell me I don't show love!"

"That's not love, my dear. That's obligation. There's a big difference. Everything you did was just because that's what you thought was expected of you. Not a single one of those actions was out of actual love. Now take the blade and pass the test this time."

Karen stood in dead silence, staring at the heartless hag. She began to slowly shake her head.. "No! No, I won't do that! And you can't make me!"

The witch raised the blade high in the air and screamed out, "So be it then!" She brought the machete down at an angle with great force removing Karen's head from her body. After the lifeless stump fell to the ground, her now fully transformed ghoul daughter ran over and started chewing on her very own mother's remains.

CHAPTER THIRTY-FOUR

Winner Gives All

"Wow, that was pretty dang freaky, Caroline! One heck of a scary story!" Tommy declared with noticeable excitement.

Before Caroline could respond to Tommy's favorable compliment for her story, Walter blurted out, "I don't get it."

Caroline shot him a sour look. "What's not to get?"

"The witch. I don't understand what she actually did, or why."

"She was put in charge of removing a type of bad energy from the planet, which is ultimately about keeping balance."

"Yeah, but who put her in charge of that? And aren't witches usually more selfish? I don't understand why she wants to protect the Earth but then kill a kid in order to do it."

"Because her priorities are different from ours. She's got to take care of things according to how she sees fit."

"I still don't get it, but whatever."

"It's just a story, Walter. You don't have to take it so serious."

Tommy spoke up and interrupted the siblings. "Okay, how are we going to determine the winner? Just by voting?"

Caroline nodded in agreement. "I think that's the best way. No voting for ourselves, though, of course."

Tommy looked at Walter. "Okay, kid, who are you voting for? Who had the scariest story?"

Walter looked down and mumbled, "I did, but since I can't vote for myself, I pick you."

Tommy smiled. "Well, thanks. I didn't think I had a snowball's chance of even getting a single vote."

Caroline was giving Walter a look of dissatisfaction. "He's only voting for you, so I don't win." After hearing what she had just said, she realized it sounded rude. "Sorry, no offense."

Tommy let out a small laugh. "Don't worry about it. Okay, my vote goes to Caroline."

Walter slumped back in the office chair. "Seriously? You really liked her story better than mine?"

Tommy gave Walter a side glance. "I didn't like her story better than yours. We're voting on who told the scariest story. Caroline did that with perfection."

Caroline smiled at Tommy. "Thank you. My vote goes to Tommy."

"Oh, come on! Now he's going to win just because you don't want me to have the last Cheerwine!"

"And you don't want me to have it either, so we both lose." Then Caroline grabbed the cold glass bottle from the mostly melted ice bucket and handed it to Tommy.

Tommy sat up straight on the sofa. "I don't like winning by default. I know my story was the weakest, so in order to do what I feel is right, I gladly hand over my prize to the rightful winner." Then he opened the glass bottle and handed the Cheerwine to Caroline.

"This is bull crap!" Walter cried out.

"Don't be like that, man. You lost fair and square, so just accept it like a champ. You don't want to be marked as a sore loser."

"It just sucks. I'd think I'd might really like to be an author, but I can't even win a silly contest against two other people."

"You're right. This was just a silly contest. Winning or losing, this isn't a sign that you wouldn't be a great author. This was just for fun. There's no need to dwell on this. Now be a good sport and tell your sister congratulations because that's what I feel like the Neptune Kid would do."

Tommy really hit home with that comment and as much as it infuriated him, Walter pulled himself together and looked directly at Caroline. "Congratulations. Your story was the scariest. I hope you enjoy your Cheerwine."

Caroline smiled at her brother. "Thank you, Walter. You can have some. I really don't mind sharing." Then she extended the bottle toward her little brother.

"No, thank you. I'm going to take a nap if that's okay." He placed his backpack on the floor just to the right of the couch and lay down next to it, covering himself with his jacket.

"Here, take the couch. Tommy and I will go hang out in one of the dining room booths."

Walter shot his sister a look of concern from the office floor. "Are you sure it's safe? I don't want to put you guys in harm's way."

Caroline waved off her brother's concern. "We'll be fine. The wind has died down some and it's mostly raining right now. If it gets really bad again, we'll come straight back."

"All right." Walter threw his backpack on the table, unknowingly knocking a Cheerwine bottle cap to the floor and it rolled up under the couch as he laid down on it.

A few minutes later, Tommy and Caroline had nestled into a booth in the middle of the dining area. Now sitting across the table from each other, Caroline said, "Thanks."

Tommy gave her a look of slight confusion. "What do ya mean?"

"The Cheerwine. Thanks for giving it to me." Then she took a big gulp of the cherry-flavored soda and then held it out for Tommy to grab.

Still giving her the confused look, Tommy asked, "What's this about?"

"I'm trying to share. I wouldn't have it if it wasn't for you. I figured the least I could do is give you some. If you don't mind sharing, that is."

Tommy smiled and took the bottle. He held it close to his lips. "You don't have cooties, do ya?"

Caroline laughed. "I have the worst case of cooties you could ever imagine!"

Tommy let out a laugh, then took a big swig of the drink.

As he held the bottle up and the liquid poured freely into his mouth, Caroline said, "Oh, and mono. I have mono."

Tommy instantly stopped drinking and almost spat out what was in his mouth. After a few coughs and a few chuckles from Caroline, he mumbled, "I thought I could taste it!"

With a big smile, Caroline said, "I'm sorry. I have a horrible sense of humor."

"Nah, it's a good one. I can really appreciate that chop-busting humor." Tommy handed the drink back to her.

"Man, I wish we had some steamed blue crabs. Do you like crabs?"

"Sure, I'm not sure I've had steamed ones, though. One of Uncle Floyd's favorite places always carried deviled crabs. I used to get them with the fried flounder plate. Good stuff."

"Those are okay, but nothing beats a bushel of fresh steamed crabs covered in Old Bay."

"What's Old Bay?"

"It's a spice that was created in Baltimore. It's the perfect seasoning for steamed crabs."

"Does any place around here steam crabs the way you like?"

"The 45th Ave Deli in North Myrtle Beach has the real deal. Just like back home."

Tommy wanted to ask her if she'd like to go sometime with him, but the way she said home made him think twice. "You miss home, I take it?"

Caroline stared off into the distance, pondering Tommy's question as the rain fell with tremendous fury now. It was hitting the building so hard that it was becoming difficult to hear each other talk, even in such close quarters. "I mean, I do miss it, but mostly I just miss a lot of things from there. I don't miss the cold weather and traffic jams, that's for sure."

"Well, if you ever get real homesick and want to be in bumper-to-bumper traffic to make you feel at home, just hop on 501 in Conway during tourist season."

"Oh gosh, don't get me started on that! I nicknamed it Highway Hell."

They both shared a laugh for a few seconds.

"That's a fitting title for it, for sure!" After the laughter died down, he asked, "So are you going back up north once things shake out?"

"I'm not really sure. I think I'd rather be down here, but I don't even know what I want to do with my life. I turn twenty-one in the spring and kinda feel lost. I just feel like I'm floating through life with no purpose."

"Well, if it's any consolation, I could offer you a secretary job. I'm sure I could use some help after Josh leaves."

Caroline instantly developed a surprised look. "What do you mean? Where's Josh going?"

They continued to pass the Cheerwine between them as Tommy explained how Josh had planned to run off to Las Vegas. Then he told her how he would be the sole owner of the wastewater removal business once they got the money back home and sorted. The rain continued to pound the golf course clubhouse as the friends chatted away.

CHAPTER THIRTY-FIVE

Closing In

Caroline and Tommy spent the next couple of hours telling stories and jokes in the cozy booth of the eating area, and they occasionally snacked on the cake after Tommy quietly grabbed it from Jamar's office while Walter napped. It was now 4:37; the storm had quieted down tremendously, and the sky was significantly lighter.

Walter was now stumbling up to their table after leaving Jamar's sofa, and rubbing his eyes. "Is it over already?"

Tommy slowly shook his head. "No, I don't think so. I'm pretty sure it's just the eye of the storm."

"So it's like halftime then?" Walter smirked as he scooped a finger full of cake icing.

"That's a good way to put it. I should probably check on Josh." Tommy hopped up and walked toward the door. Just as he exited the entrance of the golf course's clubhouse, Josh was climbing the steps, getting ready to enter.

"Come on, let's get the cash loaded while the storm's eye is here!" Josh was ready to barge right on in.

Tommy prevented him from doing so. "So you got the ambulance fixed?"

"Yeah. We're good to go now."

"What was wrong with it?"

"Clogged fuel filter." Before Tommy could respond or ask any further questions, Josh immediately added, "Tell your friends to get packed up, too. We can't leave them here."

Tommy gave Josh a sideways look. "Uh, that's up to them. I'd love to take them home to finish riding the storm out, but they'd probably be safer here. They don't need to be on the road during this storm."

Josh let out a displeased snicker and then barked, "It's not an option. They are going!"

They were now staring each other down with intimidating looks.

"You might be in charge of this mission, but you are not in charge of them!"

"I told you, man, no loose ends. Besides, they won't be the first ones I've taken care of."

Tommy's face paled, and he felt like he could vomit. He had suddenly realized what Josh meant. His mind flashed back to how strange Josh acted the morning after he brought the ambulance home. Then he thought about all the bleach Josh had used cleaning it up and how he claimed that the previous owner had been hauling meat with the decommissioned medical hauler. "Wait just a second, the missing man on the radio; they were talking about Old Man Hardee, weren't they? You, you did it, didn't you? You actually killed someone." Tommy stared down his cousin, waiting for a response. After Josh failed to give him one, he shouted, "Didn't you? I thought it was odd that you couldn't change the station fast enough when they mentioned a missing man."

Josh remained silent. His face easily gave away the fact that he was indeed guilty. "I did what I had to. I'm getting ready to do it again."

"The hell you are!" Tommy took a few steps toward Josh and gave him a threatening look.

To his immediate surprise, Josh wasted no time pulling out a Glock pistol from the inside of his fake EMT jacket pocket and cocked it. The sight of Josh's pistol infuriated Tommy. He suddenly bolted inside to warn Caroline and Walter to flee the site, but Josh was hot on his heels and the siblings were standing just inside the door and about to find themselves in immediate danger.

Caroline had a surprised look. "What's wrong? What's going on?"

"This asshole has finally snapped!" Tommy outstretched his arms as he backed up to his friends while keeping a close eye on his cousin.

Josh's face wrinkled up. "Snapped? I'm your family. I'm the only family you got and you dare to stand there calling me the asshole?"

"That's hilarious coming from the guy pointing a gun at *his* only family." Tommy placed heavy emphasis on *his*.

"Come on, man. Don't blow this over some strangers you just met. We've got the money packed, the ambulance is fixed, it's calm enough to drive for the moment, and it will be dark in a few hours. Everything is going our way now except for them. Help me get them in the vehicle and let's get this over with."

Caroline watched Tommy real close to get a true sense of his reactions. She felt he would protect them, but she had to be sure. "What are we going to do, Tommy?" she whispered.

Before he could answer her, Josh screamed, "We are getting in the ambulance, now!"

Tommy stood tall and pointed at Josh. "They are doing what they want! If they want to come home with us or stay here; it's their choice!"

"I'm in charge here and they'll do what I say!"

"You are in charge of the heist, that's it!"

"And since I'm in charge of the heist, that means I have to protect it. That's exactly what I'm going to do!"

Everyone stood in silence for a moment and as they did so the sun became unusually bright. It was as if someone had turned a dial up causing it to become far more intense. This caused an odd sensation to fill the room. The fact that the constant wind was completely gone and not a single drop of rain was falling only added to the uncanny vibe that had now consumed the building. Tommy finally broke the surreal quietness. "You're going to have to do it! You're going to have to kill me!"

"What? Are you serious?" Josh was visibly shocked. He couldn't believe his cousin was standing up to him in this manner.

"If you think I'm going to go along with such disgusting measures just to rob a crook, then you ain't my family and never was!"

Josh gave Tommy a look of bemusement.

"Before you give me one of your bleeding heart speeches, cuz, just know that if you cared for anything other than yourself in this life, then you'd know there's no way I'd ever go along with such an atrocity. What would Granny say about this?"

Josh was visibly distressed and growing angry at being called out. "Granny's dead. Why would her opinion matter for anything now?"

Tommy let out a laugh in disbelief that Josh could make such a disrespectful comment. He slowly shook his head. "You just never did get it, did ya? Granny took us in and raised us when no one else would have even given us the time of day!"

"So what? Where did that get her? She's dead now, and it doesn't matter."

"The hell it don't! That's what you don't get. That's how you honor someone you loved. You do what they would do, you apply the lessons in life they taught you! That woman did everything for us and now you're going to shoot me with the very gun she bought you for Christmas? She didn't really want to get it, but

I talked her into it. I told her how you were actually responsible with guns when we'd go hunting or to the shooting range. I guess I was way off."

"I'm not going to shoot you, Tommy. We are getting in the ambulance and we will deal with them at the draining fields."

"No. They stay or leave. The choice is theirs, but not one of us is getting in the ambulance with you unless you give me that gun."

Josh closed his eyes and took a deep breath. "You're seriously gonna make me do this?"

"I ain't making you do anything! If you shoot me, it's because you're a killer and that's on you, not me!"

Slow and deliberate, Josh raised the gun and had it pointed straight at Tommy's head. Before he could pull the trigger, Caroline suddenly shouted, "Please, don't! We'll go."

Everyone else looked at Caroline with wide eyes before Tommy cried out, "No!"

"He's going to kill us anyway, Tommy. You might as well live."

"What kind of life do you think that would be for me? I finally meet the girl of my dreams and I'm just supposed to let you die? That's not happening!"

Caroline clutched her chest and her face flushed, but the moment of silence was disrupted by Walter's sobs as the two of them stared at each other. This situation was more than he could handle.

Tommy gave him a sympathetic look. "It's okay, pal. I'm going to fix this." He gave Walter a quick wink.

As Tommy was about to go after Josh to disarm him, before he could move, they heard a loud, disconcerting thud from the side deck of the clubhouse, which caught Tommy off guard. So he held off on his gun-grab attempt for the moment. His first thought was that it was another tree branch landing on the deck like before when the trio had their bathroom break, but the wind was not blowing strong enough for that to have happened. He also noticed the noise sounded different. It wasn't the same thud.

Josh kept the pistol on Tommy as he looked over toward the closest window from where the noise came. "Who's there?"

Suddenly, a sound of a footstep on the wood deck broke the silence. All of them exchanged looks of utter bewilderment as another footstep echoed.

"Who's there, damn it!" Josh shouted with more than obvious fear.

Another footstep echoed, followed by another and then another.

Dread overtook the room, and the tension was undeniable. It was terrifyingly quiet and the four occupants couldn't hear anything but their own heartbeats as they waited for another footstep. As it hit, Josh cried out, "I've got a gun here and I'm not afraid to use it!"

Walter had noticed that the outside light had become a very bright shade of gray and seemed to get brighter with every footstep. He got closer to Tommy and grabbed his hand, which surprised him, but went along with him. Then, he grabbed Caroline's hand, and they started backing up slowly.

"Show yourself now!" Josh screamed at the top of his lungs, but there was no answer and the footsteps stopped. The four stood in agonizing silence. "I ain't got time for this! I'll take care of whoever that is after I take care of you three! I'm sorry, Tommy. My whole life has felt like I've been trapped in a prison and there's no way I can stand to go to a real one, not for anyone, not even for you. You give me no choice!" He zeroed in on Tommy and aimed. The three clung to each other in fear, waiting for the inevitable.

CHAPTER THIRTY-SIX

The Arrival

1822

A young prim and proper man of perceptible high class took his last step off of a mighty wooden ship. It had just docked at one of the few available jetties of the very busy port town of Charleston, South Carolina. The unrelenting sun and time spent on the ocean left their mark on his Caucasian face and dark brown hair. Seagull calls were abundant as the warm salty air blew all about without ceasing. Up ahead in the distance, he locked eyes with a familiar face. "Well, I'll be, Smiley? Is that you?"

"Yes, sir, Cap'n! It's me. How are ya, Little John?" Smiley's well-worn black hat, with a wide rim that drooped down, kept the heat off of his medium-brown colored skin. "Boy, are you a sight for sore eyes? Look at you in that big new gray suit!" Then the two embraced in a long, friendly handshake with several pats on each other's backs and shoulders. "Big John…and your mother wanted to meet you here, but they just weren't up for it. I begged them to send me instead. I hope you don't mind, Cap'n."

"Of course not, Smiley! I'm very glad to see you. Besides, you know how Mother hates the heat. As bad as I want to see her, I'm very happy they sent you instead. She would have complained the entire trip home."

Smiley let out a low chuckle. "Where's your belongings, Cap? I brought an extra steed just for your luggage." He pointed at the travel-ready livestock. "I got them ready as soon as I seen the ship coming in on the horizon."

Little John used his left hand to block the sun from his eyes as he looked at the horses. "Is that my Maybelle?"

"Sure is! Your parents got you a new saddle for her as a welcome home present." The two rushed over to them. "Your father has had several offers from folks wanting to buy her while you were away, but he always turned them down."

"It's a good thing. I'd never forgive him if he would have. Maybelle's the mightiest horse this side of the Mississippi." He gave the larger-than-normal beast several strokes. "Boy, look at that saddle. It's a beauty!" The black leather contrasted the horse's bright white hair, which was peppered with varying shades of gray spots that were scattered heavily in some areas and fairly light in others.

"Yes, sir! I thought it was the perfect complement to her rare coat."

"That damned grand tour that Father insisted I traveled after school took me all over Europe and of all the things I've seen, I didn't see a single animal that compared to Maybelle. Several were amazing in their own right. Outstanding Hackneys, Dartmoors, real big Bretons, and even several stunning breeds of Arabians, but none of them could compare to my Maybelle."

"I tried to take real good care of her for you, Cap'n. I did my best to groom her on a regular basis and I rode her every time Big John would allow it."

She let out a subtle neigh and shook her head, causing her well-manicured mane to flop around wildly.

"You did a fine job, Smiley."

"Thank you, sir."

"I must say, Smiley, you're a brave individual to come here by yourself to get me. And I see that you even brought my rifle. Did some of the laws change while I was away?"

"I don't think so, Cap'n. Big John wrote me a pass, and he said he put in it that I wasn't to be harassed for any reason, even for carrying a rifle. He said he wasn't going to have his son traveling home without decent protection."

"That sounds like something he'd do." He grinned with a subtle head shake. "Did anyone give you trouble?"

"A couple of fellows accused me of stealing the horses. I told them I wasn't crazy enough to steal anything, much less three animals like this, then just parade them around out in the open. After I showed them my pass, they never said another word and practically vanished on up the road."

"Ha, Father's name still carries weight, I see."

"That's for sure, Cap'n!"

"We'd better get going. We got about three days of hard traveling to do and times a wasting."

"Yes, sir! I'm sure you're more than ready to see Emma."

Little John's face grew serious. "You couldn't even begin to understand how bad I've missed her, Smiley. There has barely been a moment where she wasn't on my mind, much less a whole day since I kissed her goodbye on that sandy shore next to her parents' house."

"She sure is ready to see you, too, Cap'n. I rode over to her place with Big John right before coming down here to meet ya. He wanted to remind her that you'd be home in a week or so. There was no need it that, though. Emma had been keeping up with the days since you left, and she knew it was getting close to your return. You should see how she's got that place looking; it's like a small slice of heaven over there."

His interest now piqued; Little John smiled. "Is that right?"

"Absolutely!" Smiley said with great enthusiasm. He raised his arms to help portray the grandness that awaited his master. "There's all kinds of greenery placed all about, a galore of food supplies gathered up, and even a fresh layer of paint on the house!"

Little John's excitement was now nearly impossible to contain. The look that was now on his face troubled Smiley a bit. He looked like a man possessed. "Forget my suitcases. Let's get going!"

"Are you sure, Cap'n? It won't take me long to get them packed."

"There's nothing of any real value in them. Anything of true importance is on me." He patted the pockets on his coat.

"Sir, ar—"

"Don't question me. That's an order!"

"Cap'n, I would absolutely never question your authority. Especially since that time when we was knee-high to a grasshopper, and you caught me playing in the creek. You jumped in and joined me when you heard your father coming and said it was your idea for us to be in there. A body don't forget something like that. Your father would have whooped me something fierce if he had known I ran off to play instead of doing my work. Please don't ever think I'd disrespect you, sir. I was just figuring you probably have some gifts packed for your family and I'm sure they'd be disappointed to not get them and you'd eventually regret not bringing them home."

Little John took a hard, long look at the ship. "I suppose you're right. I did purchase Mother an elegant jewelry box in France that she will surely adore. That's why you're one of my most trusted friends, Smiley. You always say what I need to hear."

"I just try to return the courtesy you've always given me, Cap'n."

Little John gave his servant a solid head nod. "Let's get the items packed; it'll be much faster if I help."

✻ ✻ ✻

Before Smiley knew it, it was the final day of their journey. Time had passed by quickly for him, but unfortunately for Little John, the trip had been agonizingly slow. His beloved Emma was all his mind could see, and he desperately longed to be in her arms and taste her kiss on his lips. The early morning mist was quickly fading as Smiley got the horses ready for the last leg of the journey. Meanwhile, Little John freshened up and shaved the stubble off his face from the past few days with his expensive German razor made from Damascus steel he had picked up on his European trip.

"You're looking good, Little John. Ms. Emma's not going to know what to do when she sees you." Smiley finished buckling the saddle on Maybelle.

"That's all right because I'll know what to do." He flashed a conniving grin. "I can't wait to run my fingers through that sandy blond hair of hers and get lost in those deep green eyes."

"Sounds like you've got it all figured out, Cap'n. We're ready to ride when you're done."

Little John gave his face a quick feel to make sure he hadn't missed any spots then he hopped to his feet. "Say no more, Smiley, let's ride!"

CHAPTER THIRTY-SEVEN

Consumed

1822

A few hours later, the traveling duo was closing in on Little John's beloved Emma's house when the surrounding skies grew exceedingly dark without any warning. "That sure is one nasty storm rolling in," Smiley noted with a worried look.

"Indeed," Little John said to his servant as he studied the fast-moving clouds.

Smiley took off his big black hat and wiped his face with the sleeve of his shirt. "Do you think we should go back to that farm we rode by a little bit ago? They probably wouldn't mind if we took shelter in their stables while the storm passes."

"No. We're almost there. Emma is waiting for me and my insides feel as if they could just burst wide open if I don't get to her soon."

"I understand that feeling, but this storm seems to be moving quick, sir. I just don't think we're going to be able to beat it."

Little John looked at the bleak skies once more. "I think you're right. We won't make it, but I will."

"Cap'n? I'm sorry, but I don't follow what you mean."

"Exactly. Don't follow. You get yourself and the pack horse back to those stables and I'll ride like hell to beat this storm. We're far too slow to beat it riding together. You can meet me at Emma's once it's clear." Before Smiley could respond, an enormous thunderclap rang out, startling both men and the animals. Maybelle let out a tremendous neigh and turned to the left in a panicked fashion. "Easy, girl! Whoa!"

Smiley still had a well-planted look of concern on his face as he pleaded with his master. "Sir, I don't doubt your ability, or Maybelle's for that matter, but I think we'd better get ourselves back to that farm. From the looks of the sky, this storm's gonna be a monster. There just ain't enough time left for us to beat it."

"Nonsense, Smiley. I can just make a shortcut there through the marshes and save half an hour, at least!" Little John pointed to the swamp-like area that was now parallel to the trail they were traveling.

"The marshes? Sir, that's straight foolish talk. Nobody can get through that mess."

"Nobody has a Maybelle either, though, do they?"

"Cap'n, I'm not sure having ten Maybelles could get you through the marshlands. Let's hurry and get back to those stables."

Little John shook his head no, got his bedroll and rifle off of Maybelle's saddle, and extended them to Smiley. "Here, get this on the packhorse. I need to lighten Maybelle's load."

Smiley's face now grew grim. He couldn't believe his master was actually going to attempt such a foolish endeavor. "Please reconsider, Cap'n. Not for me or even yourself, but please think of Emma and your folks. I just don't see this ending well."

"Come now, Smiley! You act as if I'm a foolish greenhorn of a boy that's never been off the homestead. I figured you'd have more faith in me than that."

"It's not you that I don't have faith in, sir. It's the marshes. They say that even the Indians won't dare tread in there."

Little John looked back down the trail and to the skies once more. For a moment, Smiley thought he was coming to his senses, but right as his stress began easing, without warning, Little

John yelled, "Yah, Maybelle!" He took off into the dangerous marshlands.

"No, Cap'n, please don't!" Smiley screamed out to his superior, but it was in vain as he splashed ahead through the waterlogged vegetation. To his surprise, Little John was making it through and seemingly easy as well, until several yards in. The grasses of the marshlands had become even more unstable. Unfortunately, Maybelle made a misstep in a less dense area, causing her front legs to sink up to the tops of her front shoulders.

"Easy, girl!" Little John yelled to his frightened prized animal as he dismounted her. To his dismay, he sank up past his knees despite landing in a slightly denser patch of the mire. He was now full of fury but he remained quiet and kept his anger in check to help keep Maybelle calm.

"Just stay put, Cap'n! I'm gonna try and get a line to ya!" Smiley was in a great hurry as he untied all the luggage from the packhorse to free up the rope it was tied up with. The sturdy cases fell all about and the clunking noise they made hitting the ground spooked the horse. Smiley calmed the scared animal down after a few seconds, just as a large lightning bolt lit up the sky, followed by an ear-shattering clap of thunder. All three horses let out fear-filled neighs and the two with Smiley tried to run off while Maybelle squirmed in the muck, causing herself to sink further in. The mud rose up over her back legs and Little John tried to calm her down, becoming stuck up to his armpits.

"Smiley! Help! I'm in trouble here!"

"Just a moment, Cap! I gotta get these two tied up and I'll be right there!" Smiley worked franticly to restrain the frightened animals.

Seconds later, another ear-piercing crash of thunder filled the air. Fortunately, the servant had already secured the horses to a tree branch, but unfortunately, Little John and Maybelle were still struggling in the cold, thick mud. She was all but covered now, as her head and neck barely protruded out of the muck.

"Smiley! Get a loop around her head before she goes all the way under!"

"I'm working on it, Cap'n!" Smiley readied the rope for a rescue attempt. In a flash, he had a lasso made and threw it toward the mighty mare, but it narrowly missed.

"You almost had it, Smiley! Try again!" Little John yelled in encouragement from his dire position.

Smiley pulled the rope back to him as fast as possible, but before he got it back, the rain started falling. With the lasso now back in hand, he gave it a few twirls over his head and chucked it with all his might. He yelled "Get on there!" to the rope and to his pleasure it went around Maybelle's neck in a perfect fashion.

"Excellent job, Smiley!" Little John exclaimed with great excitement. The rain was now falling at a tremendous rate and he had to hold his hands just out from his chin to keep the splashing out of his face from where the precipitation was hitting the mire in the marshes with great force.

Maybelle panicked even more now that the lasso was choking her, but it was helping to motivate her to move. "I think I'm killing her, Cap'n!"

"Just pull. She's going to be dead for sure if she stays in here. The water's already starting to rise!"

"Yes, sir!" Smiley pulled with all his might, but it was useless. He dropped the rope and ran over to the horse he was riding, and after untying it, he brought it over to the edge of the marsh. He grabbed the rope attached to Maybelle and wrapped it around the front of the saddle. *I'm sure glad Big John got these new saddles with this horn on 'em!* he thought as he grabbed the reins and started pulling. "Yah, horse! Yah!"

Maybelle thrashed wildly, but with the assistance of the other horse, she was freeing herself.

"It's working, Smiley! Keep pulling!" Little John pushed on his prized horse, trying to help all he could while keeping his head above the deadly mud.

"Yah!" Smiley continued to yell while pulling the reins. The rain was falling so hard that the brim of his big black hat was sagging down on his face, making it difficult to see. Also, the saddle was sliding to the back of the rescue horse, but fortunately, Maybelle was inching closer to solid land and she was now positioned to where Little John could push her from behind.

"Come on, girl. Please don't perish here because of my foolishness." He was applying pressure to her hindquarters. Just then, another lightning strike of biblical proportions lit up the sky. It was so bright that it literally hurt both men's eyes. Before the blinding light had dissipated, another deafening explosion of thunder rocked the entire area. The heart-stopping sound caused Maybelle to leap completely out of the glue-like gunk for a split second. As she made a huge lunge forward, one of her back hooves struck Little John's temple with a glancing blow.

The strike to Little John went unnoticed by Smiley as he pulled even harder on the horse's reins when he saw the progress Maybelle was making. After a few more struggling leaps by the edge of the unforgiving sludge, the unique equine miraculously got a secure foothold and escaped certain doom.

Smiley raised his arms for a brief celebration. "We got her, Little John. Now we just gotta get you!" Upon removing the rope from Maybelle, he moved to the edge to fling it to his master, yet to his terror, Little John was motionless as the unyielding rain pummeled his face. "Captain!" He shouted as loud as he could. He couldn't understand what had happened. *Surely, he didn't get struck by lightning. I would have noticed that,* he thought as he threw the rope at John. It landed right beside his face, but he didn't budge.

Little John was still conscious after being hit in the head by his beloved horse, but he couldn't move at all. The dread of certain death rushed through him and this was far more terrifying than the sticky mud that clung to his now limp body. His eyes fixed on the sky as he went deeper and deeper into the unholy water and earth. Regret now filled him, along with fear, and the murky, gray sky above was the last thing he saw before the rain beat him without mercy into his watery grave.

Smiley continued to throw and retrieve the rope, hoping to either snag a part of his master or snap him out of his mysterious daze. As he worked the now filthy and saturated material, he continued to shout, "Captain! Please grab the rope!" After several more futile attempts, he brazenly took two giant steps into the marsh to retrieve Little John with his own two hands. He soon realized that simply would not work as he instantly sank up to his hips in the atrocious mush. After a brief struggle, he got back to the safety of solid land just in time to see his master's head tragically sink below the soul-sucking marsh. The rain was falling at an even harder rate now and Smiley felt completely defeated and beyond mortified at what he just witnessed. He lay lifeless on the trail from where he had just exited the mire as he wept for his friend. "Damn it to hell, Little John! Why couldn't you just listen?"

CHAPTER THIRTY-EIGHT

Thunderstruck

Back at the Loggerhead Dunes golf course clubhouse, Walter, Tommy, and Caroline clung to each other in fear as they awaited their gruesome fate at Josh's demented hands. Tommy was furious at himself because he didn't follow through with his plan of disarming his disturbed cousin, but for some reason, that odd and unexpected sound that came from outside the building had stopped him in his tracks. Regrettably, there was nothing he could do about it now, though, so he just clenched down a little harder on his new friends and whispered out to them, "I'm so sorry. This is all my fault."

Josh took one last deep breath and held it while he aimed at the trio. As he was about to pull the trigger, with no warning, a giant bright gray flash of blinding light suddenly shot straight through the window. An ear-shattering explosion rang out, along with the sound of glass shards flying about as the bolt of lightning struck Josh squarely in the back, knocking him directly to the floor. The force from the unexpected blow knocked the other three down as well, and it took several seconds for them to gather their wits.

"What? What just happened?" Caroline was completely dumbfounded. Her eyes were glazed over as she began to scan the area and eventually got back up to her knees.

Walter looked up at the charred and now glassless window and performed a double take. For the very smallest fraction of a second, he could have sworn that he saw a smoky gray face looking at him, so he hopped up and ran in that direction.

With some effort, Tommy got back to his feet, and he went to check on Josh. Light vapors of smoke radiated off his body and he was severely burned. Tommy turned him over. Josh was gone. There were no signs of life coming from his cousin's damaged body. "I guess you didn't plan on that, did ya, pal?" Tommy whispered with a subtle yet justifiable smirk into his cousin's ear.

"Guys, come look at this!" Walter called out from the front door.

Tommy rushed over to help Caroline off the floor, and they hurried over to him. They were completely stunned to see a perfect fresh set of wet bootprints on the damp wooden porch. Oddly enough, they started in the area where the loud thud originally came from and stopped as well as faced the window where the lightning hit. The three stood in amazement at the peculiar sight.

"I'm freaked out! Caroline squawked, grabbed Walter by his shoulder, and latched onto Tommy's arm.

Walter was in awe. "They just suddenly stop right there at the window. "

Tommy chimed in. "It doesn't make any sense for them to just stop right there."

Caroline then added, "Who was it? Where could they have gone? There's no way they could have just jumped off the deck, especially from that position! It doesn't make any sense at all!"

"It had to be the Gray Man!" Walter shouted. "I just knew Amos was telling me the truth! He said it was a good thing to see the Gray Man, and it was! He saved us! He just saved our lives!"

The hair on the back of Tommy's neck was standing on end as the ominous storm clouds that were quickly returning grabbed his attention. "Come on, we gotta get going. Whether it was the Gray Man or not the eye of the storm has almost passed over and the walls are closing back in on us. We got to get our asses out of here and dispose of the ambulance while we still can."

"What are we going to do about Josh?" Caroline's tone was insincere. Realizing her offense, she quickly said, "I'm so sorry, Tommy."

Tommy stood in silence for a few seconds as he watched the wind pick up. "I guess we'll put him in the second body bag we had packed."

Caroline got directly in front of Tommy and grabbed his face with both her hands. "Are you sure you're okay?"

Tommy grabbed her hands and slowly lowered them. "I knew he had issues. I knew he was a loose cannon, but I swear I never thought he'd ever be capable of that. Turns out he was just a complete manipulator. He'd say and do anything to make you think he cared about you so much, but it was all a lie just to get what he wanted. This sure has taught me a lesson, though. I'll never let anybody try to boss me around again, ever!"

Minutes later, Tommy had the ambulance backed up to the front door, ready to load. As he placed Josh's remains in the second body bag, Caroline came from the back with the last of the trio's belongings. "That's it. That's all of our stuff."

Walter grabbed what he could and took it to the ambulance. Tommy asked, "So you think we're good? All the damage looks like it was just from the hurricane?"

"I think so. The cameras have been off since before we entered the building and I really don't think that there's any reason to believe someone was here."

"Except for that big safe being empty," Tommy muttered with a worried look.

"Well yeah, but like you pointed out earlier, who's he going to tell?"

Tommy gave her a slight nod, then he switched the safety on Josh's pistol back on, laid it on his chest, and zipped the bag up.

Caroline helped place him on the stretcher, along with the body bag full of money, and they strapped everything down. Tommy asked, "So that's it? Are we good to go?"

"Yeah, I'll lock the door on our way out."

Minutes later, the stretcher was now secured in place, causing the small back area of the ambulance to be even more cramped as it was already full of the gear and tools that were brought along for the heist. Nonetheless, the trio was ready to hit the road as soon as the back doors to the getaway vehicle were closed. Then, they heard a strange voice approaching from the side.

"I figured you already had this place burned down by now, at least already on fire. And why the hell haven't you been answering my calls?" She came around the corner with a bold look that vanished the instant that she found herself face to face with the three new friends. Her face became pale as the sheet that was on the stretcher.

"Ms. Hoilman?" Tommy was now completely consumed with confusion. "Is that you?" She was dressed in the same type of fake ambulance uniform as Josh and Tommy were wearing; she was even outfitted with the same cap and had her blonde hair protruding out the back in a ponytail. She, too, looked like a legit medical transport specialist.

Her shock turned to anger. "Where's Josh? You're not suppose—" Then she trailed off and eventually stopped talking.

"Not supposed to still be alive?" Tommy shot her a look of contempt. "So I was going to be killed regardless of their presence and you two were going to burn the building down? How did I not see that coming?" He thought about all the supposed extra gas Josh had brought along with them.

She was now growing even more flustered by the unexpected turn of events. "Where is Josh?"

"He's dead!" Tommy yelled.

A look of panic engulfed her face. "You killed him?"

To everyone's surprise, Walter suddenly belted out, "We didn't kill him, the Gray Man did!"

Her face now expressed great confusion. "Where is he? Can I see him, please? What do you mean the Gray Man killed him? Who else is here?"

"Look, I know it sounds insane, but Josh literally got struck by lightning right before he was going to plug us. We don't know if the ghost of the Gray Man had a hand in it or not, but either way, he's dead now instead of me." He paused. "You were supposed to be on your way to Vegas with him right about now, I take it?"

"Argentina. I have our passports and everything ready to go."

"Ah, so Vegas was just a misdirection. Makes sense." Tommy nodded his understanding. "Josh was the master at that. He never mentioned you being involved with this, not at all. Knowing how he operated, though, he was probably going to kill you, too!"

"Can I see him, please?" She crawled up into the medical transporter.

With coldness in his voice, Tommy responded, "What's the point of that at the moment? I've been hoodwinked and the plan has gone entirely off the rails. How are we going to straighten all this out?"

"Please, just let me see him. I don't care about any of that now!"

With obvious hesitation, Tommy moved the money to the side and unzipped the bag, barely exposing Josh's head. Then he looked back at Ms. Hoilman, who was pointing a pistol directly at his face.

CHAPTER THIRTY-NINE

Taking Care of Business, Again

"That was supposed to be you lying there dead!" Ms. Hoilman shouted in anger.

Tommy stared the crazed lady down. "Sorry to ruin your plans."

"I can't believe this! We've had this planned for months! Jamar was going to pay for treating me like trash! Josh was going to help me take his money and then we were going to turn his precious building into ashes!"

Tommy shook his head in disgust. "Figures."

After taking a deep breath, Ms. Hoilman said, "Fortunately, I guess they are only slightly altered. Taking Jamar's money will be a big enough blow to that egomaniac, and I guess you'll be the one driving us to the draining fields to get rid of the evidence instead."

Tommy let out a hardy laugh. "Uh no. I ain't driving you anywhere. I've already had to stare down the barrel of a gun once today and I came out on top. I'm feeling pretty lucky. If you want to go to the draining fields, you can drive yourself there."

"I don't think you understand. I had a deal worked out."

"You had a deal worked out with Josh, as did I. Albeit a different plan that fell apart six ways to Sunday, but it was indeed a plan." Tommy was feeling as if he was negotiating a contract proposal for his business and, for once, he was in the catbird seat.

After a moment of silence, Ms. Hoilman finally said, "Fine. We'll split it fifty-fifty. Let's make a new deal. We'd better get going, though. This wind is really picking back up."

Tommy ignored her urgency to leave and replied in an overly relaxed manner. "No, I don't think that's an acceptable offer. Ya see, that deal is cutting out my two new friends here."

Ms. Hoilman shot them a dirty look. "Wait a minute. You work here, don't you?"

Caroline's heart rate rose, and she didn't want to respond to her but did so anyway in a low tone. "Uh, yeah."

"What are you even doing here right now?"

Before Caroline could answer, Tommy stated, "They were just here riding the storm out because they didn't have anywhere else to go. They only ended up in this mess by complete happenstance."

"Well, isn't that nice? So we split it three ways then? You, me, and them?"

Tommy stood tall in the back of the now-crowded ambulance. He crossed his arms as he thought about the current offer. After a few moments, he uncrossed his arms and as he held them to his sides displaying great arrogance, he said, "Three ways sounds about right to me except it'd be among us, the three of us. I don't see any need for us to cut you in."

Flabbergasted by the implied and open disrespect, Ms. Hoilman yelled, "You arrogant ass-hat! You listen here and you listen good! You wouldn't even have got the money out of the safe if it hadn't been for me!"

Tommy shot his new friends an insincere surprised look. "Hold up! That's where you're wrong. Apparently, Jamar was already onto your thieving ass and, at some point, he changed the combination on the safe."

"What are you talking about?"

"We didn't get the safe open because of you. Josh worked the dial like a madman, but it was a tremendous failure. He didn't even come close to getting it open. My new pal, Walt, was the one that discovered that your boss had accidentally left it open when he made an unexpected stop here this morning. It's nothing short of a miracle that we even ended up getting the cash out."

Overwhelmed by that information, Ms. Hoilman stood silent for several seconds. "Okay, well, you still wouldn't have even known about the money if it wasn't for me!"

"That's a true statement but only when it comes to your original partner." Tommy looked down at Josh's body. "But ya see, I had no idea you were involved. You can try to justify your supposed right to this money, but I just ain't seeing how you connect to any of this anymore."

"I connect in the fact that if you don't start driving to the draining fields, I will shoot you in the face! So I heavily suggest that you start driving!"

"Okay, just hold on. Just for argument's sake, let's say you do shoot me, shoot us all for that matter, then what? Do you know where the draining fields are?"

Ms. Hoilman stood in complete silence.

Tommy smirked. "That's just what I thought. You can't get to the draining fields, can you? You also can't go to the police because then you will end up exposing yourself in Jamar's illegal activities. Then to top it all off you can't even go to Jamar because he will know you were the one that originally plotted against him and tried to rip him off yourself before it all fell apart."

Walter and Caroline gave each other a quick grin as it seemed Tommy had put the unexpected guest in her place.

Ms. Hoilman's face wrinkled up. "You think you're so smart, don't ya? Well, you're not! You're nothing but a reject son to a father that was a complete imbecile. My boy used to come home telling me about his poor little pathetic friend that had to live with his grandma because his dad kicked him to the curb for his hussy new wife. I used to fall asleep laughing about it because I had already thrown that sorry chump to the side myself."

"Wait, what?" Tommy had a blank look on his face. "Did you just say you were with my dad?"

"Regrettably. You were still in diapers when I finally saw what a dead end he was, so I up and left."

Tommy's face now grew pale, and he was looking like he could vomit. "No, this can't be. Are you my—"

"No, don't worry about that, sonny. I'm not your mother, thank God, despite the fact that I could have been. I didn't get pregnant with Greg until just about a year after I left your supposed father," Ms. Hoilman declared in a snobby manner. "They say your mother left the state and never looked back. I wish that's what I'd done as well." After an awkward moment of silence, she finally said, "Well, that's enough of memory lane and I guess you're right, any claim I have to that cash is invalid. But since I have a gun and you don't, I'll just take the cash now and you can worry about everything else."

"Hold on a second! I've got to know. How did you even get Josh involved in this crazy mess to start with?" Tommy displayed tremendous anxiety as he waited for the answer.

"After some time and research, I had finally formulated my plans to get back at Jamar for being the pompous ass he is and for putting up with his bull shit for the past couple of years. So I decided to go to a pool hall, looking for a jackass to help me carry out said plans. Your cousin was there, and I always had heard that he had a big reputation for doing illegal things, lots of illegal things. Once I looked into who he was and realized your father was the brother to his mother, I knew I had my sucker. As easily as I had manipulated your father in the past, I knew controlling Josh would be a walk in the park."

"You obviously didn't know him as well as you thought. He was a master manipulator in his own right. If he was willing to kill me, then he was for sure going to kill you."

She wasted no time replying in a snarky tone, "Not if I had killed him first."

Tommy shrugged with a head nod. "So you're just going to kill us and leave us right here? And you actually think you'll get off completely scot-free, don't ya? They'll be a massive manhunt for you when you don't show back up to work. You're beat. Why don't you just give up and go home?"

"No! I'm in trouble with Jamar either way now. When he comes back to an empty safe, he'll know I was involved in some manner, so I'm not leaving without the money!"

Tommy thought he was on a roll until she said that. He now realized she did, indeed, have the upper hand with that fact, but he still tried to reason with her. "Should we just put it back then?"

Caroline gave Tommy a look of shock. "Put it back? Why on Earth would we put it back now?"

Tommy looked at Caroline. "Because Jamar will be after her now and it will only be a matter of time before he catches up to her. Once that happens, she'll out us to him as well and you guys will be in serious danger. I won't let anything happen to you. So I think it's best that we just put the money back. This whole thing was a huge mistake from the very beginning and I should have never let myself get talked into it in the first place."

"No!" Ms. Hoilman shouted. "I'm taking the money! Thanks for your concern, but Jamar will never be able to find me!"

Tommy rolled his eyes to the side. "Yeah right! You don't cross people like that. I'm sure he's got tons of connections. Trust me, this won't end well for you!"

"No, the money comes with me!" She extended her arm to appear more threatening with the pistol that she was waving around.

Tommy held his arms out to his sides as he began pleading with her. "Don't do this! Think about your only child, Greg. I just saw him the other day. He said he's got a kid on the way. You're going to be a grandmother! Think about that before you do this! We can put the money back and forget it all." Tommy looked down at his now-deceased cousin, Josh. "Most of it, anyway."

"No, that little brat, Greg, and his floozy girlfriend can rot in hell! Now, unstrap that bag from the stretcher and give it here!"

"No! If you don't care about Greg, then that's on you, but I'm not letting his mother do something that will get her killed! I think more of Greg than to let that happen! It's a damn shame that you don't!"

Without warning, Ms. Hoilman fired the pistol in Tommy's direction. It narrowly missed his arm and exited through the cab, breaking the windshield and causing several cracks.

"Okay! Fine! You win, you damn crazy bitch! Take the money!" Tommy unstrapped the body bag that housed the treasure that she so violently demanded to have.

Caroline bit her bottom lip to help keep her composure. She was livid that they were going to lose the money—to Ms. Hoilman, of all people—especially after considering all that they had been through in the past several hours. *I can't let this happen! Tommy deserves to have his father's car. I won't let the remnants of his psychopathic cousin's plans ruin this for him!*

As Tommy freed the tied-down bag, he immediately threw it at Ms. Hoilman, hoping to catch her off guard. "Heads up!"

His plan worked perfectly, as it caused Ms. Hoilman to lose her footing and she had to lower her pistol to help regain her balance, and Caroline saw an opportunity to take her out. With haste she grabbed one of Josh's toolbox kits from the back of the ambulance, took aim at Ms. Hoilman's face, and swung for the fences.

CHAPTER FORTY

Hauling Cash

Caroline's aim from her deadly swing was slightly off, but she still connected with enough of Josh's old dirty toolbox to send Ms. Hoilman flying backward. Now, off-balance and scared that she'd fall out of the ambulance, she went ahead and jumped out, losing her footing upon landing. She fell to the pavement, landing hard on her side. She looked up to see the money bag laying on the back of the medical hauler as she had dropped it before jumping out. She did, however, hold on to the pistol and once she saw Caroline pull the moneybag back in and start closing the back doors to the ambulance, she opened fire.

"Drive, Tommy!" Caroline shouted as the wild bullets narrowly missed her as they passed through the back doors. "This bitch is crazy! Get us out of here!"

Tommy bolted past the walk-through of the ambulance that joined the back of the cab and plopped down in the driver's seat. In a flash, he put the machine in gear and took off.

Ms. Hoilman was furious as she watched the money drive away. She slowly got up off the pavement, rubbed her hip where she landed, and started chasing after the ambulance. "Stop! Come back here with my money, you assholes!" She fired several more shots at the fleeing vehicle. One bullet hit the left side-view mirror, causing it to shatter.

Tommy flinched as the shards flew about. "Are you guys okay?" He drove down the winding road that led back to the highway.

"Yes, keep driving!" Caroline instructed from the back as she watched Ms. Hoilman struggling to keep up. She was trying to run as fast as she could, but her injured hip was slowing her down significantly.

Several seconds later, Tommy had come up to the entrance. At least two inches of standing water was sitting on the blacktop. "Do you guys see her anywhere?"

"No. Looks like we finally got away from her!" Caroline climbed into the passenger seat. "Get right here, Walter." She pointed to the walk-through. Walter squatted down in the area.

Tommy looked at his companions. "Here goes nothing." He carefully pulled out onto the currently abandoned and waterlogged highway. The skies had grown extremely fierce once more and yet again the rain began falling.

"I can't believe this!" Tommy slapped the steering wheel. "That piece of crap played me like a damn fiddle, and he was going to kill me!"

Caroline stared through the windshield. "Yeah, it's nuts thinking we almost died back there."

Tommy quickly looked at Caroline. "Yeah, that, too! I was actually meaning how Josh had literally planned to kill me after the heist. I'm so sorry you guys got dragged into this, but the fact you were there changed things enough that you two pretty much saved me. Had you not been there, I'd probably be dead right now. It'd be me on that stretcher instead of Josh."

Walter chimed in from his squatting position. "The Gray Man saved us all!"

"I don't know what all happened back there, but it appears that way, pal. I wish he could have saved me from making this bad decision in the first place." Tommy turned right onto a different road to avoid the barricade that was in place when they came in. It was a wide four-lane highway with a turning lane in the middle.

After several seconds, he broke the silence. "I just can't get over the fact that Josh thought so little of me. I was the closest family member he still had and the closest thing to a brother. Hell, I was even the closest thing to a true friend that psycho had, and that's how he repays me! That double-crossing piece of—"

"I know this was bad," Caroline said, cutting off his tirade. He gave her a short, dissatisfied look. "Is bad. I know this whole situation is bad, but now you can save your dad's car and we can properly invest the rest of the money and all three of us will be set for life!"

Tommy matched her upbeat enthusiasm with a lifeless response. "That's a great idea, but let's not put the cart before the horse. We still got a long way to go and now there's a dangerous, money-crazed cougar that's gonna have it out for us!"

"Well, like you said earlier, she can't turn us in."

"No, but she can make our lives a living hell. We'll have to watch over our shoulders with her. This is a bad spot to be in with a person like that."

Walter looked puzzled. "Why?"

"Because she already hired Josh to rob and burn down her place of business and they were gonna toss me to the side like the pawn I was for them. There's no telling what she'll do to get the money from us. She basically hired Josh to be a hit man for her. I'm sure she'd do it again in a heartbeat to get rid of us."

With complete concern plastered on her face, Caroline asked, "What should we do then? How do we fix this?"

After a long pause, Tommy regretfully said, "Give it to her."

Walter clamored out, "Give what to her?"

"The money! I don't want you guys getting hurt or even possibly killed for this!"

After a moment or so, Caroline suggested, "Let's at least keep enough for your dad's car. I don't think she will know any of it is missing. She should still feel as if she's won and I imagine she will leave us alone due to that fact."

Tommy bluntly replied, "Or she will still try to have us killed for being witnesses."

Caroline, with more than noticeable frustration, snapped back, "I don't know what to do then!"

"I don't either! This whole thing was a massive mistake!"

"Uh, guys, are those blue lights up ahead?" Walter pointed ahead through the cracked windshield that was now allowing droplets of water to seep in from the driving rain.

"Dang it!" Tommy reached for his mask out of his fake EMT medical jacket. Unfortunately, it was still damp from all the alcohol that Jamar had caused to spill on it earlier. He pulled out a backup mask for Caroline as well. "Here, put this on! And Walter, you hunker down and sit on the steps that lead to the side entrance there. Don't say a word!"

"Geez, this thing smells of booze real bad!" Caroline declared with a disgusted yet worried look.

"I know, this whole thing is beyond bad! Just put it on and look upset!" Tommy slowed the big ambulance to a crawl as he approached the police officer's car. The public servant hopped out of his patrol car and started walking to the trio.

The ambulance let out an ear-piercing screech as it finally came to a complete stop. The mighty diesel engine hummed with perfect precision as the police officer approached Tommy's door. Hail suddenly started coming down as Tommy lowered his window.

"Bridge is out up ahead." The slightly older and very intimidating officer gave the windshield a strange look. He was holding his arms above his head to block the marble-sized ice from pummeling his head.

"That's just great," Tommy declared, just before noticing how much hail was falling. After a significant-sized piece hit the officer on the cheek and caused him to wince, Tommy said, "You might want to get back in your car, sir."

The officer gave Tommy a menacing stare. "Where are you headed?"

Tommy didn't want to tell him the truth, but he wanted to get the best detour directions possible to the immediate area. "Tabor City."

The officer looked puzzled. "Tabor City? What's there? Why are you going all the way out there in weather like this?"

Tommy's heart was in his throat now. He didn't know what to say, but fortunately, Caroline chimed in. "Funeral home. My, uh, uncle was struck by lightning. He didn't make it."

The officer's eyes widened, and his puzzled look increased. "Where did he get struck by lightning?"

Without hesitation Caroline blurted, "Murrell's Inlet."

The police officer now had an unsettling grin on his face. "That's odd. I haven't heard anything come across the radio about a lightning victim."

Tommy shrugged. "Yeah, that is odd. We got the call about an hour ago or so."

The officer nodded toward the front of the ambulance. "What happened to your windshield?"

"Oh, that? We're not exactly sure what did that. Some sort of debris from the storm hit it a few miles back."

The officer stood staring at the hole, seeming to not hear Tommy. "That looks just like a nine-millimeter passed through that. Are you sure somebody wasn't shooting at y'all?"

Tommy shook his head. "I don't think so."

"Tell ya what, why don't you go ahead and show me your report."

Tommy was trying his best not to panic. He didn't know what to do or say. "We uh, we don't have it with us."

The officer's face became serious in an instant. "I'm gonna need you to go ahead and shut it down for me."

Tommy was now on the verge of hyperventilating. He went on the offensive, hoping he'd send them on their way. "Is this really necessary? I'm just trying to get this fellow to the funeral home."

"Well, considering we've got a missing man, now along with a possible missing ambulance that belonged to him, and considering what you're telling me doesn't add up, yes, this is necessary. Not to mention the really strong smell of alcohol coming out of the cab. Now please turn the vehicle off and exit slowly for me."

CHAPTER FIFTY-ONE

Out of Nowhere

Tommy was almost in tears as he reached forward to turn off the ambulance, but stopped short. Tommy thought to himself, "*a 200 year old ghost just saved my hopeless life, only for me to end up arrested soon after.*" Just before shutting the engine down, he gave the police officer one more despairing look, who immediately reciprocated with a very blunt response. "Turn it off, now!"

As he grabbed the black plastic that covered the bow of the key, a sickening thud sounded and a blue flash zoomed straight past Tommy's door. Before they could even process what was happening, a blue sedan crashed into the barricade just past the officer's car.

"Oh, my God, Tommy!" Caroline shrieked out in terror.

"What's going on, guys? What the heck was that noise?" Walter slowly and carefully crept toward the front and looked through the windshield.

Tommy was speechless as he gazed at the blue sedan. He was just seconds from getting arrested and now, to his horror, the officer was now lifeless and stuck between the mysterious car and the now overturned barricade. The sedan driver was trying to reverse it, but it was stuck on the sandbags blocking the road and couldn't get free. After several seconds of the engine revving high and tires screeching out, the driver gave up and hopped out. To the trio's surprise, it was Ms. Hoilman, with her pistol in hand.

"Drive, Tommy, drive!" Caroline shouted out in a complete panic.

Tommy had already put the big machine in reverse and he stomped down extremely hard on the gas pedal as soon as Caroline started screaming.

"She's lost her damn mind, piloting the ambulance backward, trying to flee from Ms. Hoilman. He quickly pulled off his mask and Caroline immediately mimicked that move.

"Get back here with my money!" Ms. Hoilman demanded as she trotted toward the ambulance. After a few long strides, she gave up chasing them on foot as the hail had left a treacherous layer over the ground.

Tommy had swung the ambulance to the side to get turned around, but he paused and was watching Ms. Hoilman through the driver's side window. They were thirty yards from his cousin's mentally unstable mistress as they awaited her next move.

Caroline looked at Tommy in sheer shock. "What do we do now?" She was completely terrified. "She may have just killed a police officer. I'm not so sure she would let us live even if we did give her the money."

Tommy shook his head and uttered, "No, I don't think she planned on letting us live either way. This is batshit crazy."

The three of them gazed in fear as Ms. Hoilman moved towards the policeman she had completely run over and aimed her handgun at him. After a few agonizing seconds, they watched her pull the trigger and a sickening shot rang out.

"No! You bitch!" Tommy screamed out, then slapped the steering wheel in anger.

Walter held the sides of his head in despair. "What do we do? What do we do?"

Ms. Hoilman put her pistol in her coat and walked over to the officer's patrol car. She stopped at the door and ominously pointed toward the ambulance. Tommy pulled the gearshift lever down into drive and responded to Walter's question. "It looks like we run!"

The big and heavy ambulance made a few tire screeches from where it momentarily lost traction in the standing water, and Tommy's hard acceleration didn't make things better. Ms. Hoilman saw the trio was going to run from her again, so she jumped into the patrol car. After several seconds of flipping switches and pushing buttons, she cycled through all the sirens and flashing lights options and finally got them all turned off. She put the car in drive, and—like the manic she was—took out after them.

Caroline watched her in the rear-view mirror like a predatory hawk. "Oh no, Tommy! Here she comes!" Unfortunately, though, they were the prey in this case.

"Ugh!" Tommy clamored. "Why did the police car have to be a Charger? This big turbo diesel ain't no joke, but we'll never outrun her!"

"Yeah, but we're a lot bigger!" Walter proclaimed. "Couldn't we use our size to our advantage and run her off the road?"

"That's a great idea, Walt!" Tommy stopped applying the accelerator.

Caroline immediately noticed the decreased speed and engine noise. "What are you doing? Why are we slowing down?"

"Because I'm going to knock this bitch into next week!"

Ms. Hoilman was coming up quickly on the trio and smiled when she pulled up beside the ambulance. "I got you now!" She lowered the passenger side window and pulled out her pistol. After a few seconds of trying to zero in on her aim, she pulled the trigger, hoping to shoot out the front left tire.

Fortunately, the bullet missed the tire just as Tommy was instructing Walter. "Sit down now, here in the walkway, and brace yourself. It's about to get bumpy!" After he saw that his newfound friend did as he asked, he jerked the steering wheel hard to the left, crashing into the right side of the patrol car. After the initial shock of the unexpected hit and getting over the disturbing crunching metal sound, Ms. Hoilman fought the steering wheel with all her might to stay in control. With a few swift hand movements, she regained control of the patrol car, albeit it was short-lived. Tommy smashed into her once more, driving her fully into the turning lane of the highway they were currently on.

"Whoa! How's it going up there? Sounds like you smashed her good!" Walter was bubbling with enthusiasm.

"Shut up, Walter!" Caroline demanded as Tommy plowed into her yet again. This time, their unexpected foe spun out and the back of the patrol car crashed into a section of guardrail on the opposite side of the road. "Take that, you bitch!" Caroline shouted as Tommy pumped his fist in celebration.

"You got her? Is it over?" Walter waited in agony for an answer.

Tommy shot him a quick look. "She spun out and backed the police car into a guardrail. I'm not entirely certain that she's out of commission, but it was a very hard hit. I'd be very surprised if the car can drive after that."

"Yeah, she's not going anywhere," Caroline added. "Besides, when the cops get her information from her car that she hit the officer with, it'll be over for her for sure!"

Tommy agreed "Yeah, that wasn't very smart of her at all. I guess after she found out this scheme wasn't going to work out in her favor, she lost it."

Caroline nodded. "She definitely lost it all right." Then she mumbled, "That poor officer. She just straight up murdered him."

A despairing expression crossed Tommy's face as he drove on. He looked at Caroline. "Didn't you say something about investing the rest of the money so that we'd be set up for life?"

Walter glanced at his sister. "How the heck can you manage to do that, sis?"

"With cryptocurrencies."

Walter frowned. "What is that?"

Tommy gave Caroline a confused look. "You mean like Bitcoin or something?"

"Not exactly. Bitcoin will eventually fade away. At least that's what my old coworker believes. He says there are a few other cryptocurrencies that will eventually overtake the market because of their superior technology."

"Do you know which ones that is? Which ones to buy?" Tommy turned yet again onto a different road. The rain was falling in sheets at the moment and visibility was good at best.

"Yeah, I'm pretty sure I can talk to him and get all the details. He really knows his stuff. He was just able to quit his job at the golf course after taking some profits from his investments. Why do you ask? Especially at the moment?"

"That police officer back there. If we can get out of this alive, and you can make the money grow, then I think we should split it four ways. The fourth split should go to that officer's family. That was beyond awful. Josh had it coming to him, but not the policeman. He was just doing his job."

After a short conversation, the trio of friends had all agreed to Tommy's idea, they would soon turn onto the road that led to the draining fields. Beaten and bruised from the clash with Ms. Hoilman, the mighty ambulance weathered the storm and perfectly plowed through the wind and rain.

"The turn should be just up here. My gosh, this rain is something else." Tommy carefully searched for the next road.

Seconds later with noticeable dread in her voice Caroline stated, "It doesn't look like we're going to make it."

CHAPTER FORTY-TWO

In "Hydro-Plain" Sight

The brakes of the big beast screeched out in their familiar squealing sound as Tommy brought their trusty ride to a stop. The current road had been covered in at least a couple of inches of standing water the entire time they were on it, but the newly found obstacle appeared to be too much for them to handle.

"Is there another way to get there?" Caroline asked as she studied the now major flood stream that had just formed only yards from the entrance to the road they needed to take.

"I wish," Tommy responded with a grim look along with a matching tone of voice. "This is the only way to get there."

Now peering out the windshield with his new friend and older sibling, Walter asked, "What should we do then? Just put the ambulance in the floodwater and let it carry away the evidence?"

"I'm not sure the stream is big enough to carry it away," Tommy answered. "They say it only takes about a foot or so of rushing water to carry a car away, but this ol' gal ain't a normal car. She's a lot heavier and has a pretty low center of gravity."

From the passenger seat, Caroline looked at Tommy. "Could we get to your stashed work truck from here if we did have to leave it?"

"Yeah, but it wouldn't be easy. We'd have to walk a long way back to where this stream would be crossable. We really can't leave this thing here in plain sight though. When somebody finds

Josh's body in it, I imagine it'd only be a matter of hours before the police showed up at the house."

What about all that gas in the outside compartment of the ambulance? Couldn't we just burn up the evidence?"

"Walter! You apologize to Tommy for even saying that! That's awful!"

"No, he's right." Tommy nodded. "All that gas Josh was going to use to burn down the clubhouse could be used in here. It won't come close to consuming everything, but it should destroy it enough to where it can't be easily identified."

Caroline placed her hand on Tommy's arm. "Are you sure you want to do that?"

"No. I don't want to do it at all, but if we can't get this thing buried over at the draining fields, then we'll have to do something and for now, that's the best plan we got." After a few seconds of watching the rain and the flooding stream in front of them, Tommy sighed. "I'm gonna start moving the gas cans back there with you, Walt. You open and close the back door as needed for me. Okay?"

"Got it." He gave a thumbs up.

Moments later, as Tommy was putting the last gas can into the back of the ambulance, he caught a glance of a car way off in the distance. "No way! You've got to be freaking kidding me!"

"What's wrong? What is it?" Walter asked as he held the door open.

"She's coming!" Tommy shouted, then he jumped into the ambulance and slammed the door behind him. "I can't believe she's still driving that same police car after wrecking it!"

"What? What do we do now?" Caroline asked as she watched Tommy get back behind the steering wheel.

Walter beamed and he cried out, "Get us across the stream!"

"I'm not sure I can, Walt!"

"Listen, I just had an idea come to me. It wasn't like, oh, let's just do this because it's our only option. I really feel like that's what we're supposed to do. Besides, we either get swept away and still possibly survive, depending on where we end up, make it across and get over to the draining fields, or stay here and get shot by a crazy lady that's almost here!"

Tommy looked at Caroline, hoping for a better suggestion, but she plainly said, "I mean, I guess he's got a point."

Tommy shrugged almost whimsically as he pulled the gear lever into drive. "Here goes nothing!"

Tommy used great caution, inching the ambulance into the floodwaters. He entered slowly but then almost immediately picked up speed, but not so much that he could easily lose traction.

"So much for turn around don't drown!" Caroline clung to the interior door handle and her seatbelt for dear life. The water had all but covered the tires as they steadily chugged along. "I can't believe we're doing this!"

"Come on, baby, we're almost halfway home," Tommy said to the ambulance while he worked the steering wheel and feathered the accelerator.

"Hurry, Tommy, she's almost here!" Walter warned before sitting back down in his walk-through spot.

Tommy responded to Walter's warning by pressing significantly harder on the pedal, which unfortunately caused the back tires to lose traction and the retired medical hauler began slipping sideways in the current.

Caroline looked back to check on Walter, but she saw the police Charger coming directly at them at a very high rate of speed. "Oh no, Tommy, she's going to ram us!"

The trio braced for impact as the stolen patrol car collided hard into the large, diamond-plated bumper mounted on the back causing significant damage. The crash made a tremendous sound with a force that caused Tommy's and Caroline's heads to smack against the headrests. Poor Walter went sliding toward the back door, but fortunately for him the gas cans had piled up and cushioned the blow, keeping him from getting seriously injured. When he regained his balance, he gave the petrol containers a curious look.

Unaffected by the crash, Tommy kept the accelerator pressed down to the floor. It had become obvious that they weren't going to make it across until Ms. Hoilman crashing into the back of them gave just enough of a push to power through, hopefully.

"Come on, baby, we got it now!" Tommy shouted as they began slowly exiting the swift-flowing stream. The powerful diesel engine roared, sounding like it was about to experience a catastrophic engine failure just as it completely exited the water. "Yes. Yes, yes! I can't believe we made it!" Putting the ambulance in park, he laid his head on the steering wheel as the engine now had a gentle purr, causing it to seem as if it were letting out a sigh of relief.

"Thank heavens!" Caroline gleefully shouted as she unbuckled her seatbelt and looked back to check on Walter. "Are you okay, runt? Tell me you're okay!"

"I'm fine." He picked up some items that were strewn about because of the collision.

Tommy got up and went to the back of the ambulance. He was sporting a very serious look as he opened the body bag that housed Josh's body and grabbed his pistol. "You two stay here."

"Where are you going?" Caroline joined him in the back.

"I'm going to finish this! Stay here!" He exited the ambulance and slammed the door behind him.

"Stay here!" Caroline said to Walter, opening the door and quietly closing it behind her. She carefully came up behind Tommy and they both gazed at Ms. Hoilman. It was obvious she was seriously injured as she clung to the beacon bar on top of the police Charger. The patrol car had gotten stuck in the middle of the stream on a downed tree several feet down from where she crashed into the ambulance. Smoke from the damaged engine faintly rose from the back of the hood until the swift-moving floodwaters covered it up, causing it to sink even further.

"How was crashing into the back of us while we're stuck in the middle of a flood stream supposed to benefit you?" Tommy called out just under a dozen or so feet away. "I mean, it helped us out, but that was a bold strategy."

As Ms. Hoilman continued to cling to the car with undeniable fear she shouted, "I couldn't see how deep the water was until it was too late to stop. I still tried to, but it was useless. You'd better give me that money, right now!" Her cap was missing, and her hair was a mess as blood ran down her face from a head injury that had occurred when she ran into them.

Caroline responded in a threatening tone of her own. "You're not in a position to be demanding anything, other than help I guess, but instead you hang on for dear life while still barking out orders. What is wrong with you?"

"Yeah!" Tommy nodded in agreement with Caroline. "And then killing a police officer in cold blood and leaving the scene of the crime with all your information that they could identify you with on your car! They'll hunt you down, even if it takes forever!"

"That wasn't my car, idiot!" Ms. Hoilman clamored back. "That was our getaway car. Josh stole it about a month ago. He didn't want us to be trackable, especially if we had to leave it behind. He thought of everything."

"Almost," Tommy mumbled. "What's it going to take to end this?"

Ms. Hoilman's face wrinkled up. "All of it! All of the money now or I'll hunt you down 'til my dying breath!"

"I'm about to make that a reality! Your last breaths are just seconds away!" Tommy cocked Josh's pistol.

CHAPTER FORTY-THREE

Feeling Gassy

Caroline stood in shock at Tommy's comment. She grabbed his arm. "What are you thinking? You can't do something like that!"

"I've stood by my whole life and let people like her and like Josh bully other people around and I'm not gonna do it anymore. Just keeping quiet, trying to keep the peace, trying to let cooler heads prevail, but I'm done with that garbage! She threatened all of our lives. I'm not letting that slide. I did with Josh and it almost got us killed. I'll never let that happen again!"

"But you're not a killer!" Caroline exclaimed, with her arms outstretched to her sides.

Before Tommy could reply, Ms. Hoilman shouted, "No, he's definitely not a killer. He's too much like his daddy, worse actually. At least he wasn't still a virgin at twenty-five years old." Then she gave Tommy a sneering look.

He was now filled with an abundance of fury and rage, but not at the uncouth comments from the likes of Ms. Hoilman. It was the reminder of how little Josh actually thought of him since he had made fun of him behind his back and especially to the likes of her. With a stone-cold look on his face, he raised the gun and aimed it at her head.

"No, Tommy!" Caroline pleaded once more.

Tommy held the gun on Ms. Hoilman and cocked his head to look at Caroline. "She killed a police officer in cold blood. We are all three witnesses to that. She won't stop killing and anyone that gets in her way is in grave danger. I have to do this not just for the good of us, but for the rest of humanity. She's too dangerous to be left alive!" Then he looked back at the deranged criminal. His face wrinkled up as he began to apply pressure to the trigger.

Just before sending their foe to the hereafter, Walter slung open the backdoor to the ambulance, yelling, "Wait!"

"What are you doing, Walter?" Caroline demanded to know, but he remained quiet as he threw the cash-filled body bag onto the road just short of the raging flood stream.

Without taking his eyes off Ms. Hoilman, Tommy asked, "What are you up to, bud?" He kept the pistol pointed at her just in case she tried something.

"The person that told me about the Gray Man is named Amos." Walter hopped out of the battered ambulance. "So far, he's been exactly right on what he's told me. To add to that, he also told me to always listen to the voice in my head." He continued to talk as he now dragged the body bag along beside him as he slowly walked toward the others. "He said that voice would never steer me wrong, no matter what. Well, that voice is telling me something that my grandpa used to always say." He was now across from where Ms. Hoilman was with Tommy and Caroline. "Gramps used to say that when you're dealing with a person that's being unagreeable, sometimes the best way to deal with them is to just give them what they want."

Ms. Hoilman still clung to the top of the patrol car. "Your grandpa sounds like a smart man. You give me that money and I'll disappear! You guys will never see me again!"

Walter went on to say, "I'm thinking that what Gramps was getting at is that by giving the person what they want, you get them out of your hair. And when you're out of their hair, they can't blame you for being upset anymore. They have to see that they are the ones causing their own misery."

With a loud sigh Ms. Hoilman bluntly stated, "Look, kid, I just want to get that cash and get out of here!"

The flood stream's water level had risen about a foot or so, but the wind and rain had just slacked off considerably for the moment. Walter crossed his arms and tilted his head as he stared back at Ms. Hoilman. "Nah, I don't think you're being honest. Like Tommy just said, you can't leave any witnesses to your crime."

"Plus, you already wrecked the getaway car," Tommy added as he lowered the pistol. He was still watching their foe with great intensity despite that act.

Ms. Hoilman's eyes widened. "I just told y'all that was the getaway car Josh had stashed! I have one of my own close to your granny's house. I swear you all will never see me again! I mean it!"

"Oh! Well, then I think that it is only fair that we give you what you want after hearing that," Walter replied with a nod in a sarcastic manner. "Tommy, will you help me?" Walter bent down to pick up the body bag.

"Wait!" Ms. Hoilman cried out. "Help get me off of here! Then I'll happily get going on my way!"

Walter ignored her pleas and looked at Tommy, waiting for a response to his request. Tommy was now staring back and mumbled, "What are we doing here, Walt?"

"Trust me," he said with a very serious face. "This is exactly what the Neptune Kid would do!" Then he shot him a sneaky smile and immediately went back to looking serious.

Tommy stood as still as a statue processing the strangeness Walter was conveying. Eventually, he slowly bent down and grabbed the other side of the body bag. He finally gave Walter a slight smile with nervous eyes.

"Wait, what are you doing?" Ms. Hoilman nervously asked. "Throw me a rope or something! I'm sure there's one in the ambulance."

Caroline was completely at a loss for words while watching her brother. She was eventually able to mutter out, "What are you up to, bologna brain?"

Once Tommy had picked up the other side of the body bag, he realized what Walter's plan was and he thought it was brilliant. "Don't worry, sis." He winked at Caroline. "Little brother knows what he's doing."

"Ready? On three!" Walter bit his bottom lip, which helped him hold back a smile.

"Wait! Help me get off of here first!" Ms. Hoilman demanded.

Walter and Tommy had started swinging the body bag left to right, getting ready to toss it to their helpless foe.

Caroline responded to her hated work superior's demand by shouting, "Like I said a minute ago, you're not in a position to be ordering people around anymore. This isn't Loggerhead Dunes, so if you want the damn money, you're getting the damn money the way we want to give it to you!"

"One!" Walter called out.

"No! You can't do this! Wait!" Ms. Hoilman pleaded with genuine concern in her voice.

"Three! Walter screamed as he let go of his side prematurely, then stumbled around in a forced comical manner.

Tommy wasn't ready to let go, but quickly did so and went along with Walter's shtick, saying, "What happened to two?"

The body bag fell just short of the patrol car's hood and almost immediately went below the surface of the muddy raging water. "Aw, would you look at that! I'm so sorry, we almost got it to ya." Walter held back the laughter.

Completely furious, Ms. Hoilman screamed, "No! What have you done?"

"You better hurry and grab it!" Tommy added as he pointed. "Wait, there it is! It resurfaced for a second a few feet further down."

Ms. Hoilman was hesitant to let go of the light bar on the half-sunken patrol car but she took a deep breath and released her grip, knowing that her prized bounty would be gone if she didn't do so. As she reached out toward the body bag, the swift-moving current grabbed her and swept her away in a flash.

"What was in that bag?" Caroline asked as the trio watched their unrelenting villain exit their lives in an extremely speedy manner.

"Well, I can tell you this; it's not what she thinks it is," Walter disclosed as Ms. Hoilman franticly reached for the bag in vain. They were both carried off like the rest of the occasional debris that ended up in the water and presumably to their ultimate demise. The trio continued to watch in awe as her body sank below the surface of the swiftly flowing water and they never saw her resurface again.

CHAPTER FORTY-FOUR

Reckoning

"So, where did you put the money, Walt?" Tommy asked with noticeable concern.

"The money is still where you left it. After she crashed into us, an extra body bag flew out of one of the compartments," Walter answered as they now walked back to the ambulance.

"That one was probably supposed to have me in it," Tommy mumbled with an unsettling look.

"So what exactly did you put in that body bag? It looked just like the one that was filled with the money." Caroline questioned.

Tommy answered for Walter, "A couple of the gas cans. I heard them clank together when we picked the body bag up together. That was a clever move, kid!"

Caroline turned and looked at her brother. "What made you think to do that?"

"Like I said before, Amos. The thought of him telling me to always listen to that voice in your head. And you. I thought about you."

"Me? Why do you say that?" Caroline asked as they climbed up into the ambulance.

"Because you're always quoting Gramps. I'm pretty sure that's why I thought of the 'Give 'em what they want' line. Plus, I figured she would take herself out for us if I gave her the right bait."

"Well, I'm glad you did that." Caroline disclosed. "I didn't want Tommy to actually shoot her."

"Yeah, I really didn't want to do that, but I was going to."

Now settled back in the ambulance, Caroline said, "Did we do the right thing?"

"She would have killed us a million times over if given the chance," Tommy stated with an intense stare. "You heard what she said; she had her own getaway car stashed. I'm fairly certain that means she was going to kill Josh. If he didn't kill her first, that is."

"I know," Caroline added in a somber tone. "It just feels bad watching someone get swept away to their death and not really feel anything."

Walter chimed in. "When you watch that same person run over a police officer on purpose and then shoot him in the face, it kinda makes it hard to feel sorry for them."

"That's true," Caroline said in agreement and slightly shook her head with glazed-over eyes. "This whole thing has definitely been insane."

Tommy gave Caroline a long look and noticed that she seemed to be disturbed by all the chaos. He turned the ambulance up the road that led to the draining fields. "I'm really sorry you guys had to see all this. I can't apologize enough for getting you all involved. This money wasn't free. We'll all be paying for it for years to come."

Almost two hours after first leaving the clubhouse at the golf course, the trio had finally arrived at the drain field.

"That's the last of the gear," Tommy said as he set his backpack at Caroline's feet along with everything else that they wanted to keep from the ambulance. Then he got close to the siblings, with a stern look on his face. "Are we good here?"

Caroline and Walter gave each other a look before she eventually answered, "As good as can be expected, I guess."

Tommy took a step back, looked down, and then came up close again. "What I really mean is, are you two really okay with this? I need to know that this all never leaves the three of us. If you want to go to the cops, turn me in, turn in Josh's body, and explain it all to the police, that is okay. I won't argue against any of that. But before I bury this ambulance, that is now about to be my cousin's coffin, in a ton of literal shit, I need to know that this story will never get out. If you can't take this secret to your graves, then tell me now before I commit this horrible act."

Walter looked straight into Tommy's eyes. "I swear to you, I will never say anything. Why would I, especially if you give us some of the money to help save our beach house like you said on the ride here? Even if you don't, we owe you. Big time!"

Tommy shot Walter a look. "Why do you think you owe me anything? You guys were just trying to get through the storm and we interrupted that and drug you into all of this mess."

Walter immediately said, "Yeah, but seeing how Josh was, we're lucky you came with him instead of some other hired thug that wouldn't have thought twice about taking us out."

Caroline spoke up. "I think what Walter is saying is that this thing could have gone a million different ways, but we're glad you were around to help."

"Besides all that, who would even believe it?" Walter asked with outstretched arms.

Caroline chimed in. "He's right, you know. No one would ever believe this story. I don't even know if I do. I don't even really understand what happened. I swear to you as well Tommy; we will take this to our graves. What about you? Are you okay with this?"

Tommy stared into the swampy area where he was getting ready to submerge the ambulance. "No, I'm not okay. This was all Josh's idea. Bury the getaway vehicle where no one would ever suspect. Then cover it with the contents we got from an old lady's septic tank several days ago. It really was ingenious. I sure never thought I'd have to be burying him here, too, though."

Caroline gave Tommy a long and compassionate look. "We don't have to do this, Tommy. We can turn it all into the police and he'll get a proper burial."

Tommy's stare became more intense as he disclosed some disturbing information to his new friends. "Josh never had anything proper his entire life."

The siblings stood in silence, letting their new friend talk. It was obvious he needed to vent his frustrations.

"Do you know the reason he lived with Granny?" Tommy shook his head. "Oh man, that's a humdinger of a story. Get this; his father ended up performing a murder-suicide on his mom."

The siblings regrettably gave each other a sad look before hanging their heads and remaining quiet.

"Did he learn from that, though? No, that piece of crap was going to kill us!" Tommy shouted toward the ambulance as if he were talking directly to Josh. "I was the only person still left on the face of the Earth that gave a single damn about him and he was going to shoot me in my face! But despite that fact, I really hate doing this. This is the worst thing I've ever done. Sadly, it's probably what happened to Old Man Hardy as well."

Tommy went to the driver's side of the ambulance, placed a cinder block on the accelerator, and then pulled the shifter lever into gear. The mighty machine roared out one last time as it drove fast and hard straight into the muck. Next, Tommy hopped up into the vacuum truck Josh had stashed there. He carefully backed it up to the edge and put the trusty workhorse in park. Then, he grabbed the hose and pulled the lever, which caused the contents to fly out with great pressure. Tommy aimed the quickly exiting waste the best he could and filled the back of the ambulance through its open back doors. It was beyond heartbreaking for Tommy to think about his cousin's dead body being covered in human waste in the back of the ambulance, but this was his doing.

It didn't have to be like this, Tommy thought. Several minutes later, the vacuum truck was empty, and the ambulance was submerged and completely covered. Tommy gave the site a hard last look, then the three climbed into the work truck and drove in silence to his grandma's old place to finish riding out the storm.

CHAPTER FORTY-FIVE

Best of Both Worlds

"I ain't gonna lie. I'm super jealous of you, Walter," Tommy said from behind the steering wheel as he was driving along on a busy road.

Walter looked up in the rearview mirror from the back seat and his eyes locked directly with Tommy's. "Why's that?"

"Why's that?" Tommy responded in a mocking tone. "Because of all the candy you're getting ready to get. You lucky dog you!"

"Don't worry, I'll share my bounty."

"That's nice of ya. I wouldn't do you like my uncle Floyd did me one time."

"What did your uncle do to you?" Caroline asked from the passenger seat.

"One year, Dad was out of commission with a hurt back and he couldn't drive me around trick or treating, so he got Uncle Floyd to take me instead."

Walter quickly asked, "How were you dressed up?"

That question caught Tommy off guard. He leaned his head back for a second to help jar his memory. "Uh, I'm not sure. I might have been Indiana Jones that year. It was either that or Captain America."

"Oh, I figured it would have been Frankenstein." Walter slyly grinned with a low chuckle.

Tommy looked at him through the rearview mirror with squinted eyes and a light chuckle of his own. "Don't start that crap again!

Walter laughed. "Sorry, tell your story. I'll be quiet."

"Where was I? I lost my train of thought when I was rudely interrupted." Then he shot Walter a nasty look over his shoulder.

Amused by their boyish banter, Caroline reminded him. "Your uncle Floyd was taking you trick or treating."

"Ah, yes. So, Uncle Floyd was beginning to get up in years at that point and he wasn't overly excited about doing it, but he took me anyway. And let me tell ya, he took me everywhere. I'm not even joking. He was literally taking me to places I hadn't even heard of. We crossed the state line into North Carolina two different times! I was so tired and ready to go home, but he'd just say, 'You ain't that tired are ya, boy?' I was completely exhausted when we finally got home."

With a big grin, Caroline commented, "Nah, it wasn't that bad, was it?" Then she eagerly awaited the answer.

"We didn't get home 'til after eleven! And it was a school night!"

Caroline cracked up at that answer and let out a few hand claps as she laughed. "That's hilarious!"

Amused by the story, Walter looked confused. "I thought you said he wasn't really that excited to take you out?"

"Exactly! That's what makes this story so crazy. I don't know if he was being absent-minded and just driving around without paying attention to the time or if he was trying to teach me a lesson. Now that I think of it, it was kind of like the old story where the crazy dad makes the son smoke a whole pack of cigarettes at once when he finds out he's been smoking."

Walter then asked, "Why would a dad make his son smoke a whole pack of cigarettes if he was mad that he caught him smoking to begin with?"

"Great question, Walt. The theory is that the kid will get foundered or sick on the cigarettes and never want to do it again. I'm not sure how smart or effective that method is."

Caroline smiled. "Did you want to go trick or treating the next year?"

Without hesitation, Tommy answered, "Yes, but I was for damn sure not going with Uncle Floyd!" The three of them shared a laugh for a few seconds. "Wait, there's more!" He raised his index finger.

Caroline gave him a surprised look. "What the heck else happened?"

"Well, being out in the country like this, not everyone has deep pockets and heavy purses. The people are generous enough and are happy to give, but they just usually ain't a bunch of rich folks running around these parts. Plus, there were a lot less houses and people back then, even though it wasn't really that long ago. So I had a pretty good haul at the moment and I'd even offered Uncle Floyd a piece or two, but he didn't want any. Then we went into this trailer park we came across. A lot of the porch lights were off, but Uncle Floyd made me knock anyhow. It was so embarrassing, especially since I knew they didn't want to be bothered if their light was off. I did as he said, though.

"Most everyone was pretty nice, considering I was out of line by knocking and most of them gave me something. But when I got to this one trailer, I knocked and waited a few seconds, but there was no answer. I went to leave, but Uncle Floyd hollered from the truck to try again and wait a minute. Regretfully, I knocked again. After a few more seconds, a light inside turned on. I was getting really nervous now because I thought whoever answered would be furious. I was actually hoping no one was home, but the light had confirmed that they were. After what felt like forever, a little old man finally answered the door. He had been asleep and looked confused. As bad as I hated to, I barely whispered out 'Trick or treat.' He just looked at me, then he turned around and walked off."

"So he was so mad, he didn't even speak?" Walter asked with wide eyes, looking at Tommy's face in the rearview mirror.

"That's what I thought at first, but he left the door cracked and I could see him walk into the kitchen. After what felt like an eternity, he returned. And boy oh, was I excited. He had a full-sized candy bar in his hand!"

With a fist pump, Walter hollered, "Sweet! What kind was it?"

"My all-time favorite, a Chew-Tastic Chunk! I felt like I'd found the Holy Grail!" He looked at them both with excitement. "Wait, that's right. I was Indy that year." He suddenly remembered. "I felt like all that dragging me around Uncle Floyd did was worth it after getting that. I thought that how I felt was how Indy must have felt when he found his lost relics. It was an amazing feeling. You just didn't get full-sized candy bars around here. I know it's not as big of a deal now, but back then it was.

"After we finished up there, I had to switch bags because I had so much. I think we stayed out another fifteen minutes or so then finally we were on our way home. Before I got the Chew-Tastic Chunk, I was just going to go to bed but not now. I was making plans on eating it right before I got into the shower. Then I just had to brush my teeth and lay down. I had it all planned out. Once he dropped me off at home, I ran straight to the kitchen table and dumped out my bags. I scoured over all my hard-earned treats but my grail wasn't anywhere to be seen. At first, my blood pressure rose, and I felt panic come over me. I just couldn't believe it was gone. There wasn't a wrapper or anything. No trace of it whatsoever. It was like I had imagined it. I finally accepted my loss, and I was so disappointed."

Caroline asked, "What happened to it?"

"I found out in another conversation a few days later that Uncle Floyd ate it while I was walking house to house. I had offered him some earlier but no, he had to wait 'til I got the only full-sized candy bar that I ever got trick or treating my entire time of doing it!"

"That sucks. At least he left you with his wastewater removal business." Caroline smirked.

"I mean, yeah, he more than made up for it. He didn't even have to take me out, but boy, he sure did crush my dreams that night. I just wanted to let Walt know that I'd never do that to him. It should be in the bro code or something."

"Thanks, Tommy. If I get any… What did you call it again?"

"Chew-Tastic Chunk. It's an old candy. They are hard to come by these days."

"If I get any, they are definitely yours." Walter slipped on his round sunglasses completing his costume, which was inspired by his favorite professional wrestler, The Priest. "How do I look?"

Tommy looked in the rearview mirror. "You look good, kid!" He brought the antique wood and teal-colored metal automobile that he helped his father restore to a halt just inside a massive housing development. "Welcome to The Farm. I had a customer tell me this is the place for trick or treating. He said that several of the houses hand out full-sized candy bars, a few places actually play Halloween-themed movies outside on projectors, and there's even a house that does marshmallow roasting!"

Walter smiled. "Wow, that's awesome!"

Looking at Tommy, Caroline smiled from the passenger seat as she turned around to tell Walter, "We'll be back here in two hours to get you. Keep your phone on and be careful."

"I will. Hey, don't forget we're going to Salty's afterward. Tommy owes me a round of air hockey and you owe me pizza!"

They both let out a hardy laugh for a few seconds.

"Don't worry, kid, we didn't forget.

"Maybe we can talk more about taking a skiing trip this winter while we eat. I'm determined to prove that Bigfoot exists."

Caroline turned to face her brother once more and asked, "Haven't you had enough of paranormal and scary things for a while?"

"Nah, I'm always wanting more of that! When I prove Sasquatch is real, I'll be famous!"

Oh, by the way, I got you a surprise." Tommy reached under his seat and pulled out an authentic replica of a wrestling belt. "I know the Priest never did win the world title, but we can't have you walking around being a wrestler for Halloween without the Infinity Wrestling League Championship strapped around your waist."

"Holy crap, this is so amazing!" Walter shouted out with immense happiness in his voice. "I can't believe you got this for me! Thank you so much!"

"You're welcome, champ. Now get going. We got a lot of hanging out to do later."

"'Kay, see you in a few hours." He joyfully exited Tommy's Woody without taking his eyes off his new prized possession. After a few steps, he held the championship belt over his head and shouted, "I'm the champ! Give me some candy!"

"God, he's such a nerd," Caroline mumbled as the two chuckled at Walter's excitement.

"So, what do we do now?" Tommy asked Caroline with a wide smile.

"Well, apparently the Legend of the Gray Man is true since Hurricane Faye didn't destroy the beach house like so many other homes, I was wondering if we could go back to the Gay Dolphin to pick up a few things. Now that the insurance is paid up, I think it's time for a minor remodel."

"I think that's a good plan," Tommy said with a small head nod. "Just don't change it too much. I love the retro feel."

"Oh, no! I like it, too. I just mainly want to get rid of those ugly sofas."

"Yeah, those things gotta go for sure!" Both of them nodded in agreement, then Tommy visibly cringed as he thought about the atrocious and severely outdated furniture. "That all sounds good to me. Now that you say it, maybe we should get a few things for Granny's old place, too. It does kinda look like it could have been an old filming set for *Little House on the Prairie*."

Caroline's face lit up. "Hey yeah, beach house and a country cottage, best of both worlds!"

"I love that idea! Oh, I almost forgot." Tommy reached under his seat and pulled out a Carolina Panthers jersey. "I got you something, too." He handed it to Caroline.

"You're like Santa Claus over there, pulling stuff out from your seat." She held up the bright blue sport top and looked it over. "Oh, this is very nice. Don't think I'm getting rid of my Ravens jersey, though."

"I wouldn't dream of it. I figure this way we got an AFC team and a NFC team to pull for. The best of both worlds, again!"

"I love it!" She leaned over and kissed him on the cheek.

In return, he gave her a sly yet charming smile, and put the Woody back in gear. "Away we go!"

EPILOGUE

A light autumn breeze with the slightest chill leisurely stirred back at the dreary, draining fields. It was the very place where Tommy had regretfully submerged the mighty ambulance, which coincidently, was now the tomb for his troubled cousin's corpse. The sun was descending below the horizon on another Hallows' Eve. It projected the most powerful eerie shade of orange imaginable, which contrasted with the dark areas of the gloomy forest where the day's light could no longer penetrate, in an impressive manner. Among the uncanny scene was a mysterious male figure, resting on a large and partially buried rock by the lifeless muck, sitting in total incomprehension of what was occurring as he looked all around. Off in the dark distance, he heard the faintest whisper. He listened with great intent, hoping to figure out where the voice was coming from. After a few moments, he caught sight of the dirt road leading to his current position. After careful consideration, he stumbled over to it and realized that the voice was slowly getting closer. As he stared down the lifeless lane, he caught a glance of a shadowy figure heading his way.

Not knowing what else to do, he started shuffling his feet in that direction. He occasionally looked back at the lifeless mire he had just found himself sitting by. "Hello. Is there someone there? Can you help me, please?"

Although there was no response, the volume of the mysterious voice was increasing louder and the silhouette was getting closer.

The confused man stopped after only walking about six feet. He now stood in complete silence, watching the figure come closer, step by step.

After several agonizing seconds, it sounded like the person headed his way was possibly singing. A short moment later, a powerful male voice echoing out confirmed that thought. While the singing man kept creeping closer, the melody became familiar but some of the lyrics sounded very strange. It was apparent that he was belting out "When the Saints Go Marching In," but there was something peculiar about it. It didn't seem to be a well-known verse.

"Oh, when the stars fall from the sky, oh when the stars fall from the sky, oh Lord, I want to be in that number, when the saints go marching in."

With growing nervousness he called out, "Hello?"

The singing man was close enough to hear, but he didn't give the confused individual the slightest response as he continued "Oh, when the moon turns red with blood. Oh, when the moon turns red with blood. Oh, Lord, I want to be in that number, when the saints go marching in."

The continuous singing with lack of any acknowledgment whatsoever to his cries for help, topped off with the extremely ominous lyrics, now had him in a petrified state. "Sir, please, can you tell me what's happening? I don't understand any of this!" he shouted with outstretched arms. He was now completely terrified.

The singing man ignored his pleas and kept marching toward him. "Oh, when the horsemen begin to ride. Oh, when the horsemen begin to ride. Oh, Lord, I want to be in that number, when the saints go marching in."

Now just within several feet of him, he could see that the singing man was an older Black fellow wearing overalls and a tee shirt. The scared man screamed out, "Who are you? Why is this happening? I don't even know what's going on here!"

The singing man finally quieted down. After a few seconds of looking the scared man over, he said, "Wait, that ain't right."

"What's not right? Can you please help me, sir? I'm so confused and scared; I don't understand what's happening to me. I don't know why I'm here."

The singing man looked straight into his eyes. "I forgot the trumpet verse. How could I have forgotten that one? Silly me."

The scared man looked down as he broke out in tears. "Why won't you help me?"

He scratched his salt-and-pepper goatee. "Ya know, that's the thing. No matter how bad we've messed up, we can always make it right."

"Sir, can you please help me get out of here? I just sorta came to over there on that rock. This place seems oddly familiar, but I don't really know where I'm at."

"Ah, simmer down, son. You'll be alright, just come with me."

"Wait, who are you?"

"Some folks used to call me Smiley. That was a very, very long time ago, though. My birth name is Amos. I'll answer to either."

"Where are you going? Can you please help me make sense of all this?"

"Just calm yourself down; everything will be clear as crystal before you know it."

"What's over there?" The scared man pointed to the stagnant, dark muck. "I'm getting a weird feeling from that spot."

"Ah, don't worry about that. It's just a couple of old, worn out vehicles. Now come on, son, we got work to do. Let's see, where was I?" He patted the scared guy on the back as they walked further into the woods. "Oh yeah, that's right." Then he cleared his throat and resumed his singing. "Oh, brother Josh, you are my friend. Oh, brother Josh you are my friend. Yeah, you're gonna be in that number, when the saints go marching in."

www.ingramcontent.com/pod-product-compliance
Lightning Source LLC
Chambersburg PA
CBHW072109300726
48975CB00003B/767